Chapter One

Welcome to the P...

It took an age to find the fucker, but find him I have.

I discover he has a family, a simple little wifey and two teeny weeny cutie kiddies. Such a delicious additional set of detections.

The planning takes a while, it needs to be meticulous, but who cares? After such a long time waiting, the preparation is almost as satisfying as the act.

So, he is still at work and I am in his meagre house. I tell the smiley, semi-pretty, mousy wifey that I am a distant relative of his and she foolishly and incuriously welcomes me with joyful, open arms. I have chocolates for the tiny tots, laden with a sedative, of course, and my very special props are hiding within my William Morris decorated carry bag.

Little wifey tells me she is preparing dinner for when he arrives home from work and invites me to join them for the meal; an invitation I am all too pleased to accept. I am told he will be delighted that I have come to visit. I am tempted to tell her that he will be the exact opposite but wisely keep my counsel.

I encourage the cutie kiddies to eat some chocolates. Wifey whimperingly objects, some shit about spoiling their meal and very bad for their teeth but, upon my insistence, she relents just enough for the chocolates to serve their sleepy, sleepy purpose.

Some further pointless small talk and hey presto, the tots collapse in a slow stupor and wifey, before I strangle her, is incandescent with worry. 'What's wrong with them? We must call the doctor,' she squeaks and pleads as I surreptitiously produce a rope and, from behind, place it around her scrawny neck and tug with joyous abandon. I almost climax with delight but know I must save myself, for these acts are only the hors d'oeuvre to the overall proceedings.

She chokes with a whimper and slowly, almost comically, topples to the ground. Then, rope in hand and with a minimum of fuss, the Lilliputian Sleeping Beauties follow their mummy to the land of evil, dark oblivion.

Now it's time to set the stage for the fucker!

With a pencil, after the drawing of a dog, I scrawl a cross and a tick on each of their foreheads (Right or wrong, who knows?) and then I fish out the caricature faces, elastic bands attached, from my bag. (Yes, I have been studying them for some time and really do think their rendered images truly do them justice!) I place them one by one on their faces, wifey first, the sickeningly scrawny boy second, and the tiny totty, the sickly sweet, sugary girl last.

So deliciously cute!

Now the heavy work! I lift the tots one by one and sit them in chairs at the table. The first topples from the seat and I find the need to tie them to each chair with rope fished from my bag of delights (Yes, I am well prepared!) and then, with a little sweat and puff, drag little scraggy wifey to another chair and tie her firmly in place.

Time for some culinary action in the kitchen!

Dutiful, tame, squeaky, skinny wifey has been cooking a lamb casserole which smells sickeningly tempting and domestic. I fish out some bowls, cut some freshly baked bread (nothing smells better!), and then ladle out a portion of the delicious stew into the bowls for each member of the happy family. I seek out some cutlery and, broad smile in place, humming a happy tune, set the table and place a bowl in front of each of the eager diners, and, of course, one for the soon-to-arrive and hopefully suitably famished absentee, the guest of honour.

I finish the preparations just in time for as I place the fucker's bowl on the table, I hear the front gate squeak, hopefully signalling his arrival. I shake, almost convulse, with anticipation, place the caricature of his face upon my face, and take a seat at the table facing the dining room door, opposite wifey and with the hungry teeny tots to each of my sides.

Such a sweet and lovely family we make!

'I'm home, love.' His familiar voice stuns and taunts me.

I hear him throw his work bag to the floor and stride towards the dining room door. He enters with a cheesy smile and I chuckle as he sees us, and his face falls faster than a novice skier.

He appears stunned (ha ha), his face the hue of unblemished snow (Exultation!), and he is, with fear, joyously paralysed, as if superglued to the dull and tasteless carpet.

'Welcome to our tea party, Dusty,' I merrily pronounce. 'We have been so, so anxiously waiting for far too long for you to join the fun and games.'

I cackle, guffaw, howl as he flinches but remains immobilised, and I salivate at the prospect of finally, deliciously ending my interminable, overly long wait to get my revenge on the evil fucker.

Chapter Two

The End of the Road for Jonas Brookes 1

'Your name for the records,' DC Rashid, late twenties, kind of pretty, prompts, while looking slyly towards the dusty black boxy recorder sitting ominously opposite me to the left of the desktop. It seems to buzz annoyingly continuously, like an insect or drone, but I am not sure if it is my imagination playing cryptic games with my many phobias. She shifts awkwardly in her seat as she speaks, and I speculate whether it is the chair or the situation that is making her uncomfortable. I suspect it is the latter, or possibly both.

'Joel Taylor,' I comply quietly with a hint of boredom and passive aggression.

'Your address, Mr Taylor,' DS Brookes, middle-aged, well, probably fifties (Okay, the new middle age!), scruffy and overweight, adds in an ill-concealed attempt to arrest the momentum of the interview from his apparently junior colleague.

I give him, DC Rashid, and the buzzy recorder my address, and watch her scribble something (securely screened by her left hand) in a notebook that I had inexplicably previously failed to see her place upon the desk. I silently question what she could possibly find to note down alongside as simple a fact as my name and address, which they are already aware of, but to be honest, who the hell knows, or cares?

'The same address,' I hear DS Brookes' sarcastically loud whisper with a conspiratorial nod to his companion, which she ignores with surprising alacrity.

I ignore the question, if it is one, and watch DC Rashid scribble something else in her ghostly surreptitious notebook.

'You did not want to move away then?' the sergeant annoyingly persists, and then raises his eyebrows just enough for the gesture to indicate that he expects me to reply on this occasion.

He wipes his sweaty forehead with his shirt collar, portraying an aversion to the increasing heat of the small, bleached room as I contemplate whether to answer. I find the enclosed space stifling but valiantly endeavour not to display any discomfort.

I say firmly, 'It is our home. Matilda certainly doesn't need any more upheaval at this time in her life.' And I say nothing else.

There is an uncomfortable pause and then the sergeant finally responds with a smile. Or is it a smirk?

'Of course, that makes perfect sense, Mr Taylor. The kiddie certainly doesn't need any more upset; she's had plenty already with one thing and another.'

His response reeks of mockery and, with a smirk, he shifts his bulk in the chair, eliciting a creak and an echoing move from DC Rashid. I remain still, and consider where this is all leading to.

'Do you not find it uncomfortable, unnerving, or painful?' DC Rashid interpolates with an air of apparent concern.

DS Brookes clears his throat, an action I, and from her scowl, DC Rashid, interpret as an admonishment for the interruption. DC Rashid responds with a further rapid scribble in her notebook, which I interpret as an ill-conceived attempt to hide her embarrassment, or maybe, angst.

I unfold my arms and slightly lean forward, an action that appears to elicit a minor jerk away from the desk by DC Rashid.

I am curious.

I ignore her question.

DC Rashid looks intently at her notebook, sniffs, and blinks rapidly.

'What is your job?' Sergeant Brookes asks me. I am finding it difficult to avoid looking at his colleague. 'What do you do for a living? How do you make your money?' he persists, with what I perceive as a touch of accusation of wrongdoing. This is accompanied by a further clearing of his throat. I speculate that this is his indication that I should reply.

I smile. Even smirk.

'You do not approve of my profession?' I probe, for I know he knows the answer to his question.

He is very aware of what I do, or maybe, he is truly not.

It is six months since the incident, my wife's death, suicide, but it seems as if it was a lifetime ago.

'Did your wife have death insurance, was she insured?' he enquires pointlessly persisting.

The question comes out of the blue. I am knocked back for a fleeting moment.

I compose myself, recline and refold my arms. I take in a deep breath. I consider leaving. I contemplate asking for a solicitor. I wonder if, guess that, this is an accusation of wrongdoing.

'You know she was!' I finally retort with annoyance and a little louder and more aggressively than intended.

He bobs his head and I glimpse DC Rashid inventing a supplementary entry in her notebook; her crutch, I deduct.

'You correspondingly know that I am a rich man and have no need for the insurance money,' I continue, 'and you are extremely likely to have been informed that I have placed the insurance money in my daughter's trust fund. I have not, and never intend to touch a penny of it.'

There is an uncomfortable silence which is finally broken by a loud tap, tap, tap on the door.

'Come in,' DS Brookes responds loudly and with a touch of irritation.

I turn around to look at the opening door, and I see a young man in uniform enter with a tray of three steaming, plastic cups and a plate of biscuits. He looks nervous, and keeps a noticeable distance from me as he positions his commodities on the desk. He avoids eye contact with all but DC Rashid. I discern a knowing smile between them and wonder if they might be in a relationship.

Coffee and biscuits in place, the young policeman silently shuffles out of the room with no response from DS Brookes. DC Rashid keeps her head down, and then accepts a roughly offered plastic cup from her companion.

DS Brookes offers me a cup, but I shake my head. 'I only drink water,' I tell him.

DS Brookes ignores me, smiles, and places the cup in front of me.

He sips from his cup, winces, sniffs loudly and then, eyes wide open, looks directly at me.

'Disgusting! How do you make money gambling, Mr Taylor?' he asks. 'Most of the clients we deal with come to this bastion of correction because they waste all their money on horses, dogs, and fixed odds betting terminals, or whatever they are called in your wide and wondrous world of vice.'

I glance at him with incomprehension. I notice some scum from the coffee on his top lip. I notice him lick it away self-consciously with a fat, purple-hued tongue and I just manage to stifle a gag.

'Am I a client?' I ask out of devilment, as I had noticed his reluctance to use the word. I guess he would have been happier using the good old-fashioned term 'criminal'.

I detect a slight sign of annoyance, which the DS endeavours to hide by taking a further taste of his coffee, which is followed by a broad, but clearly false, smile.

'Please answer the question, Mr Taylor,' he says as he hastily composes himself. 'It's my job to ask them, after all.'

He grins widely and wipes his mouth with his not-too-clean right hand.

'And I guess my job, to answer them,' I say. 'I am well informed and very intuitive. I am very selective, a maths genius and I am extremely intelligent,' I then tell him.

DS Brookes cracks a genuine smile, as does DC Rashid.

I smile back (not genuine). 'My supposition is that this is not always the case with most of your so-called clients.'

DS Brookes does not respond verbally, but chokes back a laugh, sips his drink, winces, and scowls.

'Bloody terrible, cheap coffee, too much fake milk and no bloody sugar,' he says with a Cheshire cat grin. 'Did you get on well with your wife?' he probes, seamlessly changing the subject and carefully placing the coffee cup back on the desk, and annoyingly too close to me.

I notice a slight nervous intake of breath from DC Rashid. She looks down shyly, or is it with a hint of fear, as I slyly glance up at her.

I do not respond and instead, with the fingertips of my right hand, I slightly push away the coffee cup that was placed in front of me.

DS Brookes sniffs loudly, and as I give him a momentary glance, he opens his eyes capaciously.

I remain taciturn and move my glance above his head.

'Why would your wife kill herself?' It is a natural and predictable progression.

I drum my fingers on the desk and contemplate how I should respond to a question I have been asked too many times already.

DS Brookes and DC Rashid both glare at my moving fingers and then quickly look up.

I take a deep intake of breath.

'Sergeant Brookes, I have been asked this question so many times that it is becoming somewhat tedious!' I carefully and calmly respond. 'And my answer has not changed and will not ever change.'

I stop drumming my fingers and cross my arms in what could only be interpreted as an indication of defiance, although I am not sure it really is.

'For the recorder please, Mr Taylor.' It is DC Rashid with a surprising air of calm and an encouraging nod of her head.

I take another breath, shallow this time, and swallow hard.

'My wife suffered from depression, on and off,' I elucidate. 'It is possible she killed herself, as it is also just as conceivable that it was a tragic accident. She could easily have by mischance fallen from the balcony.'

I uncross my arms and look up at the ceiling, noticing for the first time a water stain almost directly above me; it is oddly the shape of a carillon bell.

'I do not know, Sergeant Brookes; your guess is as good as mine, I'm afraid. I only wish I did. I only wish I could have prevented it.'

There is a pause as DC Rashid leans over and surreptitiously whispers into DS Brookes' left ear.

I strain to hear but fail miserably.

'Was she the type of person to have left a note if it was suicide?' DS Brookes asks after listening to his colleague and then thinking deeply for a moment.

I do not answer but instead ask, 'Why am I here?' I am annoyed but mask my anger with a demure cough.

'Then you think it was an accident?' DC Rashid prompts with what I can only interpret as a smile of encouragement, but who knows?

I do not respond but look squarely into DS Brookes' sad eyes. 'What exactly are the inconsistencies that you told me you wanted to discuss, sergeant?' I then look back at DC Rashid and say, 'I do not know.'

They glance at each other and seemingly conspiratorially nod in unison.

'You knew her better than us. Surely you must have an idea,' DC Rashid persists.

I shake my head in frustration and do not reply.

DS Brookes adjusts his not insubstantial behind in his chair, and clears his throat. There is a worrying rattle from deep in his chest.

He smiles at me and changes the subject. 'If it is not too painful, could you please tell us about the day your wife died, Mr Taylor.'

The sarcastic fuck!

DC Rashid shyly looks away as my cheeks redden with a slowly building anger.

DS Brookes does not break a seemingly kindly stare.

I take a deep breath to calm my nerves and prepare to instigate a well-trodden path of historical recollection.

It is a day I have not forgotten and, to be honest, am never likely to consign to oblivion.

'I got up at half past five, intending to catch the 6:29 train to London,' I slowly and reluctantly begin.

DS Brookes fails to disrupt his laser attention while DC Rashid annoyingly and too loudly fiddles with the lid of her pen.

'It was a normal procedure and one we had carried out on a weekly basis for some time. My wife gave me a lift to the station in our car at quarter past six, with my daughter in the back accompanying us since we were reluctant to leave her in the house alone, although it was a very short journey.'

I take a deep breath and, with a gulp, swallow hard.

'I need some water,' I declare while turning my head to look at DC Rashid.

DC Rashid glances at DS Brookes, who nods an approval.

'DC Rashid is leaving the room to fetch a glass of water for Mr Taylor to quaff,' DS Brookes whimsically explicates to the recorder.

DC Rashid stands up, scraping the chair noisily as she shoves it away behind her. I squirm at the noise and grit my teeth to control any possible adverse vocal reaction.

She leaves the room with a fleeting glance towards me and her colleague, but without a word.

I am left looking at an empty chair. I am unwilling to look at my lone companion. Time seems to stand still as we wait. We both remain silent. We both shun eye contact. Finally, there is a knock on the door.

DC Rashid enters and places a plastic cup of water beside me on the desk. I wonder why she bothered to knock.

'Thank you,' I say, and she nods an acknowledgement.

I pick up the none too clean cup and sip the disgustingly tepid water as DC Rashid sits back in her designated chair. I place the cup on the desk and cannot help wincing from the warm metallic taste.

'Please continue,' DS Brookes quietly prompts.

I try to recall where my narration had paused, take a deep inhalation of air and hold onto the desk tightly.

'My wife parked outside the station. We kissed. I kissed my daughter also. I checked that the train was running. It was. I waved goodbye. I went to buy a ticket. You know all this already DS Brookes.'

I pause. I do not look at my interrogators. My focus is blurred by the memory and quasi tears. 'It was the last time I saw my wife alive,' I stutter, mildly choke and whisper.

There is now a long hiatus as I develop a grief or temporary guilt-induced amnesia. I sense my questioners but do not glimpse them through my tear-filled optical privation. I am unsure of the length of delay but find myself being woken by the shrill and possibly concerned voice of DC Rashid.

'Mr Taylor! Are you okay?' she says.

I look up and spy my interrogators looking at me intensely.

DS Brookes looks disconcerted, although I detect a suggestion of disbelief at the extent of my upset.

I shake my head, clear my throat and continue.

'I watched the car move into the distance and then went to buy a ticket. I remember glancing at the newspaper stand and scoffing at the latest absurdly semi-racist headline on the anterior of the *Daily Mail*. I recall being pushed aside by a plump guy and quietly laughing as he picked up a copy of the said newspaper. As I often do, I mused at such a choice of reading material.'

I pause and spot DS Brookes looking towards the ceiling of our bleached cell. I suspect betraying his disagreement with my sentiments, or maybe not.

'Do you read the *Daily Mail*?' I ask, almost mockingly, accompanied with a smile.

He smirks. 'Load of pompous tosh, it's *The Sun* for me or the *Daily Star* on a good day,' he says.

He breaks out a wide grin.

I do not believe him for a second.

'Please continue, Mr Taylor.' It is DC Rashid attempting to wrest the conversation back to a semblance of relevance.

I hesitate.

I cannot continue at this stage.

'Mr Taylor.' It is DS Brookes. 'Are you sure you are alright?'

I find it difficult to understand his expression; it could be concern.

It is a problem I frequently confront.

I take a few deep intakes of breath. 'I find it, life, everything, excessively problematic,' I tell them.

My interrogators glance at each other.

I read some puzzlement but cannot be confident of my judgment.

I grit my teeth. 'I often struggle to recount things verbally over an extensive period of time,' I say.

I have broken out into a cold sweat and my skin feels prickly. I grab the glass of water and sip it in an anxious attempt to stabilise my interaction. It is lukewarm and now tastes of bitter calcium, and I almost gag in response.

'You have a written statement,' I whisper, 'I do not need to tell you this anymore.'

There appears to be an extensive recess, but my perception is not always the same as others.

'I understand, Mr Taylor,' DS Brookes interjects. 'I am aware of your problem.'

DC Rashid clears her throat with the minimum of noise.

I believe she is embarrassed at the use of such a phrase.

'It is not a problem,' I pronounce sharply, 'it is a gift.'

DS Brookes bobs his head in response. 'Not the most appropriate word, Mr Taylor. I apologise profusely for any perceived insensitivity on my part.'

I deduce he appears discomforted and that the apology is probably not at all sincere or meant.

'Let me ask you some questions to smooth the way forward,' he continues while enigmatically smiling at me copiously.

'If you wish,' I respond disinterestedly.

I glimpse DC Rashid; I meet her eyes and she promptly rests her gaze on the table.

The whitewashed walls suddenly lack their lustre and seem to be closer to me than before.

'You travelled on the train without any hindrance,' DS Brookes prompts.

'Yes, the train was on time for once,' I say with a fake grin.

I recall one of my episodes on the journey. I heard an exceedingly quiet squeaking noise. I could not fathom its origin and gradually became convinced it was my mobile phone. The mobile rested in the top pocket of my jacket. The squeak continued at regular intervals. After a while it became clear that the noise was being transmitted from my stomach and was likely to be the result of an imminent heart attack. I sat for an indeterminate age wondering what to do. I progressively became more alarmed and agitated.

'Mr Taylor!'

I jump and leave the train at the sight and sound of DS Brookes sitting before me.

'Once again, did anybody see you on the train on that day?' he asks with a hint of displeasure.

It was a stupid question.

I adapt my deliberations and reply in a way I have learned to do.

'Many, many, people saw me but nobody I knew,' I tell him.

'You were on the train, weren't you?' he says with an equal air of accusation and humility. I am unsure whether it is a question or a statement of fact.

I am suddenly struck by the use of the phrase 'way forward'. I hate it and I retrospectively squirm at its use.

'Do not say that,' I involuntarily say out loud.

DS Brookes, I perceive, looks confused, and glances at his colleague who slowly and almost unperceptively shrugs her shoulders and silently mouths something to him.

He holds his hands up in mock surrender and confusion.

'The "way forward",' I mumble, 'I do not like it being used, it really offends me. I cannot help it.'

DS Brookes continues to look confused, thinks for a moment and then acknowledges my comment with his customary nod and a ready display of blemished teeth. 'I apologise, Mr Taylor; I will determine to permanently delete such word usage from my moderately limited vocabulary.'

He glances at his cohort conspiratorially. DC Rashid smiles back and lightly shakes her head.

'You were on the train,' DS Brookes recaps and repeats with a hint of amusement in his voice.

I pause and cross my ankles under the table. I have a slight tingle in my toes. It comes and goes; I am told there is no medical reason for it. It could be my imagination, but I am sure it is not.

I clear my throat of a trickle of slime. 'You know I was on the train, DS Brookes; you no doubt have video evidence to prove it, and I am sure somebody would have recognised me.'

He blinks. 'Yes, we do as a matter of fact,' he retorts with a hint of exasperation and I wonder why he asked the question in the first place.

There is a pause and we all simultaneously take a sip of our drinks. It is as if comically or tragically rehearsed and coordinated.

'Did you go straight to your meeting when you arrived in London?' It is DC Rashid.

I respond with a slight bow of my head. 'Yes, I was there until the initial worrying call came from the school.'

'Over six hours,' DS Brookes appears incredulous. 'Five minutes for a meeting is long enough for me, any longer and my notorious lack of patience kicks in.'

I glimpse at DC Rashid who seems to express a smile of encouragement in my direction. I wonder why, as I also wonder if I could have misinterpreted her response.

I smile back, I think it is appropriate but may be mistaken. 'We were discussing a book deal,' I elucidate and lie. 'It was a terribly long-drawn-out and tedious matter and not particularly satisfactory in the end, I'm afraid.'

'Why was that?' DC Rashid appears genuinely interested while DS Brookes just elicits an annoying Boris Johnson smirk.

I am not sure whether any of this is pertinent but play along with the game.

'It was a money issue,' I dishonestly respond.

'You did not leave the building for six hours?' DS Brookes annoyingly persists.

'You know I did not,' I snap. I know they have taken statements from the individuals involved (well, who were supposed to be involved) and will, once again, have video evidence of my movements in London.

DS Brookes once again smirks for just an instant. 'It has been known for witnesses to be lying, mistaken or deceived you know, Mr Taylor. Happens all the time in my world.'

I cough in an attempt to hold back amusement. 'I am sure you are right, but it is unlikely in this case, I would suggest. I'm sure Agatha Christie would think up a ludicrous explanation to suit your biases, but in the real world I was in a boring, overlong and unproductive meeting.'

I hear a noise from outside the door to our whitewashed cell. It sounds like a dropped tray. I ponder when I will get the opportunity to eat. I check the time. It is half past eleven.

I muse on the telephone call I received from Matilda's school.

'You may well be right,' DS Brookes retorts with a chuckle. 'If only Dame Agatha were here to assist me and DC Rashid, all would be cleared up in an entertaining instant, and, no doubt with an unforeseen large twist in the tail.'

He glances at his colleague and she pushes her chair back from the table and then pulls it forward. I discern an increase in her rate of blinking. She appears to be in preparation for something, she looks embarrassed or suffering from a mild dose of stage fright.

She demurely elicits an almost inaudible cough and glances down at her notebook. 'The school called you at 3:31 pm to tell you that your daughter had not been collected by your wife at the appointed time.'

It is a statement of fact that I deem not necessary to respond to.

She looks at me. 'How did you feel when this happened, Mr Taylor?'

I feel a pang of fear as I re-live the moment. 'I believe that I suggested to Mrs Steele, the school receptionist, that my wife had probably been held up in the traffic. I asked if she had tried calling my wife's mobile phone and that I was sure that she would be there very soon.'

I pause, knowing that two sentences are usually my upper limit when it comes to oral communication and a sense of panic is likely to ensue if any further vocalisation is delivered or required.

I take a deep breath.

DC Rashid seems to take a while to recognise that I have stopped and studiously stares down at her notebook.

She finally looks up and smiles. 'She had already tried your wife's mobile and had no rely.' Once again, a statement of fact. 'You agreed to call your after-school child carer, Mrs Keene. Is that right?'

I nod. 'Yes, that's right.'

There is a pause.

'Matilda believes her mother is a soft toy,' I pronounce, 'a pink poodle.'

My interrogators are silent. DC Rashid kind of grins; it is almost the look of a concerned teacher. DS Brookes appears to feign a smile, but it oozes a sneer of impatience and contempt.

'We were in a shop a week or so after Rachel died,' I resume, and then immediately pause. I grasp my plastic cup of water and take an almost pointless gulp of air. The cup is empty but for a shallow film of liquid attempting to cover its foundation.

DS Brookes glances at the cup as I place it back on the table. He appears to acknowledge the lack of water in the cup and, although he has the tumbler next to him, he defers offering a top-up. I detect his slender smirk at my discomfort and feel a tinge of anger.

'We were queuing up to pay for a painting set I had promised her after the funeral.' I stop to take a breath and hold back a tear. 'She suddenly ran away from me. I panicked for an instant and then saw her leap towards the pink toy poodle.'

I lean across the table. DC Rashid once again slightly cowers away. She looks at me with embarrassment as I lift the water tumbler and refill my cup with some more disgustingly tepid and not very clear water.

'I remember her shouting across the shop, "Daddy, it's Mummy, it's Mummy. Mummy has come back to live with us. To look after us again."'

I take a sip of water to mask a touch of distress and a sniffle.

'She was hugging the poodle and kissing it gently on the lips, just as she did when with Rachel.'

I listen to the silence in the room. I perceive the faint mumbling from the bowels of the police station. I make out the rumbling of the constant traffic passing by outside. Matilda's voice echoes in my ears. 'Mummy is much, mucher happier now; I knows she smiles lots, lots more now she is in heaven with the angels. God tolded me.'

There is an inaudible mumble from DS Brookes and a petite cough from DC Rashid.

'Yes, let's continue,' DC Rashid finally articulates, displaying a fair degree of embarrassment.

I bow my head in charitable submission. 'I called Mrs Keene and she agreed to collect Matilda from school,' I say.

'When did you get the call from your neighbour, Mrs Maxwell?' DS Brookes enquires. He looks me fixedly in the eyes as I glance at him in response to his question.

I pause for an instant. I need to gather my thoughts. I need to get what happened clear in my mind.

DC Rashid taps her pen against her notebook, but I do not sense any sign of irritation.

'I was at the railway station,' I reply. 'She said she had been calling me for a while. I had been on the underground train, the Jubilee line. There had been no reception, as often happens on our world-leading metro system.'

DS Brookes acknowledges this with an incline of his head and a grin.

'What did she say?' DC Rashid asks with a possible look of pity.

She knows the answer.

I shuffle my chair back in an abrupt loss of congeniality. 'Is this really necessary?' I enunciate, and the room and its occupants disappear.

It is a perplexingly out-of-body experience. I sense the atmosphere and noise of Waterloo station. I hear my mobile phone ring. I notice the caller is Joan Maxwell. I break out in a sweat and almost lose my footing as the blood gushes from my head. Rachel is dead.

'Why did you call Mr Stevens about the dog?' I am back in the stifling hot white room. It is the gruff loudish voice of DS Brookes.

I blink rapidly and sense a slight dizziness.

I glare at DS Brookes incomprehensively; he seems surrounded by a haze for a fleeting second.

'Mr Taylor, why did you make a call about the dog?' he persists with a hint of irritation.

'I don't know what you mean,' I say. 'You were asking me about Joan Maxwell's call.'

DS Brookes clears his throat with a smoker's cough and sits up straighter in his chair.

'You called Mr Stevens five minutes after you received the call from Mrs Maxwell.'

DC Rashid coughs blithely and glances at me expectantly.

'It seems a rather irrational and inconsiderate reaction to hearing that your wife has fallen from your terrace and died,' he persists.

I shake my head slowly and try to gather my thoughts. 'Joan said that what happened, "the suicide", as she put it, occurred a while before she contacted me,' I stutter. 'The dog would have been in the house alone for some time. He is quite delicate.'

I hesitate and notice DS Brookes prompt DC Rashid to write something in her notebook.

It seems pointless; the conversation is being recorded.

'The dog would have been upset with all the activity. He is very sensitive,' I say, a little unconvincingly.

I stop.

'I have problems with emotions. I do not always know what to do,' I forlornly attempt to explain. 'I am not like you.'

DC Rashid lightly coughs again, and as I glance at her she smiles and nods her head with a hint of understanding and encouragement.

DS Brookes slumps a little in his chair. 'Then why did you not tell us about the call to Mr Stevens in your original statement? And to be perfectly clear, Mrs Maxwell heard your wife fall and denies saying anything of the sort to you.'

He sits up straight and places his hands together on the table. I notice a drop of sweat trickle down the right-hand side of his face and nestle in his bushy sideburns. He blinks at the irritation but does not wipe it away.

I look into his eyes. They appear cloudy and a little sad.

'In the circumstances, it did not seem important. It still doesn't,' I reply to the first question after a short pause.

He smiles. 'You were asked to give a full statement, Mr Taylor,' he perseveres with a hint of annoyance and then sarcasm. 'The rest of your statement was apparently meticulously accurate, was it not?'

'It did not seem important under the circumstances,' I repeat, louder this time and with a clenching of my hands.

DC Rashid shuffles her chair back very slightly. 'Did you consciously leave it out of your statement, Mr Taylor?' she asks.

I shake my head. 'No, of course not.'

'Mrs Maxwell claims she never mentioned suicide.' DS Brookes again. He sweats arrogance.

I grab my water cup and sip the warm liquid, and wince.

'It was a muddled and stressful conversation for both of us,' I reply with an admirable calmness.

DS Brookes smugly smiles. 'She asserts that the presumption was yours alone, Mr Taylor.'

I notice a fly trapped in a spider's web in the right-hand corner of the ceiling. I wonder why I had not noticed it before. A spider does not appear to be in residence.

'Let me read out the relevant part of her statement,' DS Brookes continues while stretching for a scruffy sheet of paper placed on the floor beside him. 'She was asked to repeat your conversation as accurately as she remembers it. I will read part of her reply.'

I am intrigued by why I had not noticed some paperwork on the floor before, but I maintain my focus on the freshly observed empty spider's web.

'Joel, Mr Taylor, was silent for some time after I told him his wife was dead. I could hear nothing but the background noise of the station, the chatter of the crowds around him and the continuous announcements over the Tannoy. I attempted to elicit a reply from him. To be honest, I was really concerned for him since I knew they were such a close and loving couple. I finally spoke to him louder than was possibly polite and he responded with a mumble that I failed to hear over the background noise. I prompted him to repeat what he had said and he asked how she had died. I was, as you would probably understand, a little hesitant to give him the dreadful details and tried to put it off. He said that he needed to know, he was very insistent and quite forceful. I can remember taking a deep breath and telling him that she had fallen from the terrace of their house. To tell the truth, I felt awful even saying it and would have preferred to not say anything, but he was very upset and very insistent. He was silent for a moment and I distinctly heard a sharp intake of breath. He then asked me if she had killed herself. I really did not know what to say since I had presumed from the first moment of discovering that she was dead that it had been an awful accident. The possibility of suicide had never crossed my mind. I, too, took a deep breath and gathered my thoughts before telling him I had no idea and didn't think it was the case. I told him I thought it had been a tragic accident.'

DS Brookes places the crumpled piece of paper, the so-called statement, on the table and exhibits a smug smirk.

DC Rashid intently stares at the floor with a hint of embarrassment.

'Your statement does not mention that you brought up the possibility of suicide,' he persists.

I stay silent as it strikes me that it is a comment and not something to be answered.

A silent impasse ensues, which I finally feel that I am obliged to breach. 'Like I said, we were both in a muddled, distressed state, it is possible one of us was wrong. I do maintain, however, that it is Joan that is mistaken. I am exact in memory; it is something I excel at, as you no doubt know.'

DS Brookes takes hold of the statement and kneads it with his right hand. I sense that he is struggling for a suitable response.

DC Rashid comes to his rescue with a petite clearing of her throat. 'Joan Maxwell was very insistent on the point when she was spoken to very recently.'

It is almost delivered with embarrassment and prompts a look of admonishment from her senior colleague. I sense that the existence of the recent conversation with Joan Maxwell was not for my ears.

It is two days after Rachel's death and Joan Maxwell is sitting opposite me at the kitchen table. She is cradling my attempt at the making of a cup of tea and sniffling with an appropriate sadness.

Joan is my semi-detached neighbour. 'Our balcony friend', Rachel had called her.

'I told the fat policeman that I was baking some scones when I heard a loud bang,' she tells me, 'and another less loud, as if an echo, a few moments later.'

It all seems a little insensitive, but I grit my teeth and nod an acknowledgement to her comment.

'I ran out of the front door and…' she stops. 'Thankfully, Hugo turned up at that point. He looked flustered, red in the face while rapidly manoeuvring his motorised wheelchair towards me.'

I say nothing.

'He was such a help; I don't know what I would have done if he hadn't…'

She stops and sniffles, looks to the floor and then looks up and tries to smile.

'She was such a lovely young woman and such a loving mother,' she continues a little hesitantly.' It is almost as if she is plucking from her mind the right things to say, 'So very, very sad for you and that lovely little daughter of yours.'

I begin to cry, push back the chair, stand up and quickly leave the room.

I startle and hold back a tear in the present and shift my numb bottom in the uncomfortable plastic chair.

'Joan Maxwell's father, Hugo Coles, is 103 years old, well, that's what he told us,' I say.

DC Rashid nods her head and smiles while DS Brookes just slowly shakes his head.

'He once told Matilda that she would be very famous,' I continue. 'He told her he knew, since he was there to see it. He smirked as he told her the fairy tale and there was a tear in his right eye as he told it.'

I pause and DC Rashid looks concerned. She clearly suspects the old man has dementia, as do I.

'You do know that Joan Maxwell's daughter committed suicide?' I tell or ask them.

DS Brookes shuffles the paperwork in front of him and clears his throat with a little more drama than needed. 'It almost seems as if you are in denial, Mr Taylor. I fail to understand why you should not admit to asking Mrs Maxwell whether your wife had killed herself. It really doesn't make sense nor matter a jot in the end.'

He pauses and looks me in the eyes, almost in a gesture of challenge. 'It is a perfectly understandable reaction, considering you wife's medical history.'

'Because Mrs Maxwell's daughter killed herself,' I bark louder than intended.

DC Rashid starts demurely.

DS Brookes once again shuffles the paperwork and then appears to study the statement, or whatever, on top.

I notice a red inscription halfway down the page. I am unable to read it.

It is intriguing.

There is an extended intermission as I focus intently on it. The silence is intermittently fragmented by the heavy smoker's breathing of DS Brookes and the delicate but obtrusive inhalation of DC Rashid who ultimately breaks the impasse with a similarly delicate but barely noticeable cough.

'I did not mention suicide in the telephone conversation with Joan for obvious reasons,' I stress. 'It would have been insensitive.'

I notice that the spider has appeared in the web and is vigorously cocooning a small insect; I think it is a fly of some description and imagine it could it be me.

DS Brookes nods his head slowly. 'I guess we will never know. Memory is such an unpredictable organ, as is the truth.'

'Mr Stevens said that you sounded very concerned and that you were extremely insistent that he checked up on the dog.' It is DC Rashid.

She flushes a touch and glances down at her notepad as I angrily looked at her.

I hear my stomach rumble and begin to feel slightly light-headed.

'I have a blood sugar problem,' I explain as a dizzying fog sleeves the room. 'I really need to eat something urgently.'

DS Brookes glances at the biscuits on the table.

I glimpse an inflection of his head towards them. 'I am gluten intolerant and sugar is by far the worst antidote to my problem,' I elucidate quietly and with a minor involuntary slur.

He smirks and pushes his chair away with a surprising agility for such a large man.

'Let's take a break. I could do with a smoke,' he pronounces and walks rapidly from the room.

I am left staring in his wake, as is a seemingly perplexed DC Rashid.

It is once again two days after the incident and Joan Maxwell comes through to the kitchen. I have finished crying and stare out of the window at our small but pretty cottage garden.

'Carrie is still missing,' she tells me.

Carrie is her ginger cat.

'I have no idea how she got out,' she continues.

Carrie went missing on the day Rachel died.

'I definitely closed the front door when I went out to investigate the, er, noise…'

She seems embarrassed.

'The back door was closed and locked and the balcony door was closed, it's a mystery.'

A tear creeps down from her left eye.

'I'm sure she will show up,' I tell her, less than convincingly.

She shakes her head. 'I am so sorry, Joel; my missing cat must be the least of your worries at this time.'

She attempts a smile and I fake a smile back.

I glance at my watch and I notice that ten minutes have elapsed.

I am sitting in what I detect is a police canteen.

There is a plate of pale green limp salad sitting uninvitingly in front of me.

DC Rashid is also sitting, somewhat more invitingly and smiling, opposite me.

She appears to have an identical bland lunch placed in front of her.

I blink and shake my head, trying unsuccessfully to recall the events of the missed ten minutes.

The canteen is swarming with uniformed and non-uniformed officers intermittently speckled with civilians. How do I know? They are surprisingly simple to distinguish.

'You mentioned Hugo Coles,' DC Rashid says.

She has a Caucasian-toothed broad smile on her face. She really is very pretty. I do not trust her though.

'*The* Hugo Coles, the climate activist?' she continues.

I wonder why we are sitting here and why she is asking about Hugo.

'How long do I need to stay here?' I ask her.

I scan the table and pick up a silverish metallic fork.

DC Rashid flinches.

The fork is greasy and holds the deposit of a former meal between one of its tines.

I shudder.

I carefully place it back on the table and push it away.

'I need a clean fork,' I tell her. 'This one is disgusting.'

She smiles unconvincingly and pushes her chair away from the table.

I watch as she walks across the room towards an array of trays holding what is likely to be dirt and germ-infested cutlery. I do not hold out much hope of receiving a clean enough utensil.

I continue to watch DC Rashid with intense awareness.

It strikes me suddenly. She does not belong. She is not acknowledged by anyone.

I suddenly recall her paying for the meals. I am waiting at the table, and the obese woman serving her treats her as a guest, not a regular, I am sure.

How do I deduce this? It is something I can do. Maybe!

I suspect DC Rashid is as much a stranger to this environment as I am.

I am intrigued but could be wrong.

I study the array of humanity and only notice the return of DC Rashid as I hear a range of forks on the not-so-clean tablecloth placed in front of me. The clatter is not loud but betrays a minor sign of irritation from my companion, or is it adversary?

DC Rashid beams a smile and sits down opposite me. I scan the forks and find none that come anywhere near meeting my strict hygiene requirements.

'They are not clean,' I comment. 'None of them are fit to be used.'

DC Rashid nods her head. 'I know, the place is a tip. "Plague Central" DS Brookes calls it. He has a theory that Covid developed here.'

I nod, smile and doubt that DS Brookes would be bothered by a little bit of grease and grime. Or could I be wrong?

'Why are you sitting here with me?' I enquire.

She shuffles in her seat, clearly betraying a surprising discomfort at my question.

However, she beams a white-toothed smile which I do not believe is genuine for a nanosecond and then forks a mass of pastel green limp undressed salad into her mouth.

I squirm inside just thinking of the potential health risk of the filthy utensil and the decaying vegetation that she has just placed in her mouth.

It is difficult not to retch and I breathe deeply through my nose to ward off the compulsion.

'It is part of the job description,' she feigns with a shrug of her small shoulders and a not very genuine smirk, 'Junior's act as minders in the force.'

I grimace as I pick up a piece of the dressing-free lettuce with my right hand, and notice that her smirk halts abruptly.

'You do not work here,' I pronounce at a barely audible level.

She hears me and I sense her desperately attempting to assess my declaration.

There is a distinct pause while she forks a further contaminated morsel of bland greenery into her mouth. I know it is an attempt to find time to gather her thoughts. I suspect she knows that I know this.

'Why do you say that?' she probes while seemingly faking amazement.

I notice that she has not denied it.

'Who are you, DC Rashid?' I ask.

The canteen is a hive of activity all around us, but it suddenly seems as if we are back cocooned in the white room with our roles reversed.

'You do not work here,' I needlessly persist.

She glances around as if searching out an excuse to leave and then beams her wintry smile.

'It is only my second year here. I guess you have noticed that I am a bit awkward,' she lies.

Her bottom lip betrays a miniscule shake and her face a barely noticeable blush.

'You do not work here,' I continue to persist.

She shakes her head and scoffs. 'Tell me about your relationship with Hugo Coles, Mr Taylor.'

'You do not work here, so who are you?' I repeat.

I start as a loud crash emanates from the centre of the canteen.

DC Rashid reacts by reaching, for a split second, for her pocket and then halting the action just as rapidly.

She knows I noticed and looks a touch sheepish.

'A dropped tray,' she quietly pronounces with a smile.

'Are you carrying a gun?' I enquire.

She scoffs at my suggestion. I suspect she has in the past.

'I am on detached duty. I am helping out DS Brookes. This is not my usual station,' she quietly stutters unconvincingly.

I purse a smile and slowly shake my head. 'You are no more a police officer than I am, Detective Constable Rashid.'

The invasive background noise of the canteen, which had quietened as a result of the dropped tray, has now annoyingly resumed.

DC Rashid leans forward in her seat and places her shoulders on the table. She breathes in heavily and fixes her eyes straight onto mine.

I blink rapidly, and instinctively move back in response. I do not like people getting close to me. It makes me panic or lash out.

She appears to acknowledge this and promptly leans back into her chair. I suspect she knows more about me than she has so far divulged.

'I am partly here to watch out for people like you,' she suddenly explains in barely a whisper. 'We, in a roundabout way, work for the same people. I, we, need to make sure you are safe to continue your work for us.'

Her smile has disappeared and she pauses, I presume, to wait for a reaction from me.

I have learned over time how I am expected to behave in specific situations. This is to mask the way I am. It does not always work.

I look over her shoulder and wonder why I had not noticed DS Brookes sitting in the outer reaches of the canteen before. I am not surprised to see him sitting alone with a plate of fish and chips and a book in front of him.

He acknowledges me with a negligible incline of his head and a broad mocking smile, followed by the cramming of his mouth with a large forkful of ketchup-smothered chips.

His cheeks bulge and fragments of food aerosol in all directions as he munches into the greasy potatoes.

'Mr Taylor,' DC Rashid breaks my reverie.

I reluctantly look away from DS Brookes.

'We need to make sure that you do not get into trouble,' she continues, before, with a look of disgust, pushing her plate of anaemic flaccid salad away from her.

'I take it DS Brookes thinks you *are* a Detective Constable,' I say.

I glance once again at the fat detective sergeant, notice his smile of acknowledgement and realise that I know the answer; nothing is likely to get past DS Brookes.

'That's what he has been told and he seems to accept it,' DC Rashid replies with apparent confidence and a lack of perception.

'He doesn't believe it,' I reply.

She just smiles and slowly nods her head. 'You may well be right, but who cares in the end?'

There is a pause.

'I do not understand why you are here.' I eventually break the silence.

She shuffles in her seat. 'I told you we need to be certain that you are not in any trouble,' she whispers irritably.

She glances behind at DS Brookes. 'DS Brookes thinks you killed your wife,' she continues. 'And to be honest, I don't care if he is right. My job is to protect a national asset, whether or not you are a criminal.'

I close my eyes for a moment and then I look at her incredulously and fleetingly look over to discover that DS Brookes is no longer sitting at his table.

I muse over how I missed his departure.

'I didn't,' I reply, 'and if you are working for who you say you are, you know that I was in London at the office when my wife died in that terrible tragic accident.'

She smiles and then looks at her watch. 'We have ten minutes before we need to get back to the interview room. Let's take a walk outside, it will be easier to talk,' she suggests while pushing her chair back to stand up. 'You never know who might be listening in here.'

She walks towards the exit and it appears that I have no option but to agree to her suggestion.

'I need to know what contact you have had with Hugo Coles,' she continues as she walks away.

I am compelled to reluctantly follow her.

'My daughter told me that we do not have wars anymore. "They were in the olden times", she said,' I tell her.

I am standing in a miserably bleak concrete car park. DC Rashid is standing next to me holding a half-smoked cigarette in her left hand. I step back instinctively and cough.

I do not like cigarette smoke. It offends me.

The woman who calls herself DC Rashid takes a long intake of nicotine, pollutes the air with an exhalation and then throws the cancer stick to the floor.

It remains smouldering in a shallow puddle and continues to pollute the local environment.

'She sounds sweet,' she replies with a hint of a cough. 'You are so lucky to have her.'

I perceive the reply to indicate that I should continue, although I know our time together is limited.

'I told her that wars are still taking place all over the world and likely will always do so.'

I pause and want so much to be with Matilda.

'She asked me why,' I say.

As I continue to think of Matilda, DC Rashid smiles knowingly. 'What did you tell her?' she asks.

I glance down at the smouldering cigarette, which seems to be refusing to die, and instinctively step further away as I notice its refusal to stop its steady fouling of the local airspace.

'I told her the truth: for land, for power and for resources,' I say with a hint of resignation.

DC Rashid nods, I suspect not in total agreement, and then stamps her foot onto the offending cigarette. It is clear that she has finally noticed my discomfort or at least decided to acknowledge it.

'They call DS Brookes "Columbo" at this station,' she tells me. 'He is notorious for getting an idea and flogging it to death. I understand that he is more often right than wrong as well.'

She pauses and glances at her watch.

'He thinks you murdered your wife,' she continues. 'He told me that he instinctively knows this to be true and he will make sure you are prosecuted for it.'

I am momentarily distracted by the boom of a military plane flying overhead and fail to respond.

DC Rashid looks at her watch again. I am not sure if she requires an answer since she knows that I was in London on the day of my wife's death. She was, in all likelihood, in the same building recently.

'We have three minutes. What do you know about Hugo Coles?' she states and asks.

She glares at me expectantly.

I am sitting in our kitchen with Matilda and Hugo. Matilda is sniffling and Hugo looks unduly concerned.

'Mummy shouted much, much at me,' Matilda blubbers quietly and sadly.

I stay silent, as does Hugo.

'I told her I wanted to look after the planet and all the animals when I leave school and she saids I should forget about all that Green rubbish and get a real job when I grows up.'

She begins to cry again. 'It is not rubbish, it is not, it's not,' she sobs.

'I'm sure she doesn't mean it,' I untruthfully reply.

Hugo gives Matilda and me an understanding nod and smile.

I wake from my reverie and I once again look at the sky; the clouds are threatening rain but the temperature remains high. 'Climate change', I am sure Matilda will tell me later.

'He is Joan Maxwell's father. He lives in an old people's home. He comes to visit every so often. He sometimes wanders over to my house to bring Matilda a small present. He appears to like children. He is a very old man who appears to be intelligent and kind,' I reply.

I gasp for breath. It has been a great effort to say so much in one go.

DC Rashid inclines her head. 'He buys your daughter presents?'

I am unsure whether it is a question or a statement and remain mute.

She stares at me and then finally speaks. 'What has he bought her?'

I deep mine my memory and look away from her as I recall the necessary details.

'Cuddly toys when she was younger. A polar bear, a panda, a tiger. All very cuddly and, of course, in danger of extinction.'

I stop and await a response. This seems so unnecessary. I fail to understand why we are discussing an elderly neighbour but cannot find it in myself to ask why. It is a symptom of my condition or privilege, as I call it. Reasons for discussing trivial matters barely task me.

'What did he last buy her?' DC Rashid persists.

I pause for a moment although I know the answer instantly. I notice DC Rashid fiddling with the pocket where she keeps her cigarettes. I construe that she is desperate for another nicotine fix.

'He bought her a copy of *This Changes Everything* by Naomi Klein,' I begin to explain. 'A little old for her. It had the inscription:

> As long as the general population is passive, apathetic, diverted to consumerism or hatred of the vulnerable, then the powerful can do as they please and destroy our precious earth. Matilda, I hope you will not let them do it.

I stop and glance at DC Rashid. She doesn't appear to recognise the modified quote.

'Chomsky. Well, sort of,' I almost whisper while distastefully looking at the ugly mud-smeared cemented path that we are standing on.

She inclines her head, convincing me that she is unfamiliar with the author of the quote and therefore the adaptation. 'The book doesn't surprise me,' she finally almost mumbles. 'Doesn't surprise me in the least.'

My curiosity, which has been mounting, finally forces me to ask, 'Why such an interest in Hugo? Do you know him? Are we interested in him for some reason?'

She ignores me. 'Let's go back to our pointless chat with Columbo,' she says. And with a flick of her hair, she heads off for the entrance to the police station.

Chapter Three

A Chance Encounter on a Train

The train, no surprise, is stationary and will be arriving very late at my destination. Due to signalling problems, an announcement, all of thirty minutes ago, had screeched almost unintelligibly. There has been silence from the train company mouthpiece since, and I wonder if we (the passengers) are doomed to live the rest of our pointless existences stuck in the middle of nowhere in this filthy carriage.

I sigh loudly and resume reading *Curtain,* Agatha's final gift to an undeserving world; this one anyway!

I hear a sniff and then a sneeze. I look up. It is an annoying oily boy, possibly eleven or twelve years old, kitted out in the uniform of some posh, overpriced, elite public school for the indulged and the entitled, sitting opposite me pretending to read a book; *Animal Farm,* if I am not mistaken. I imagine he is really fantasising about removing my dress, and likely more.

I catch him staring at my legs and picture him wanking in his posh boy dormitory while thinking of me. I cross my legs to give him a flash of underwear, smile at him and he blushes as he rapidly looks down at his book.

'You are staring at me, silly little boy,' I say quietly, with a modicum of sexy menace and a flutter of my eyelashes.

He squirms, his face flushing the colour of beetroot.

He reminds me of a young Jacob Rees-Mogg, side-parting, round eyeglasses and a long sad face, which I smilingly fantasise about smashing into a bloody pulp.

I shake my head to dispel the daydream and, instead, devise a much better, quite delicious, plan for the fucking annoying stuck-up, spotty-faced little shit.

'My name is Olivia,' I tell him with an alluring smile, 'What's your name, you smart handsome young man?'

Chapter Four

The End of the Road for Jonas Brookes 2

I am once again seated in the white room, my room, 101. DS Brookes and DC Rashid are sitting in their familiar places, as am I.

DS Brookes, failing to cover his mouth, barks a rattling cough.

He exhales the stink of cigarette smoke.

I stifle a gag but wince anyway.

I glance around the room and notice that the spider's web has disappeared and I wonder whether or why the room has been cleaned while we were eating lunch.

DC Rashid continues to play her part as DC Brookes' faithful assistant with terrific aplomb.

'When did you meet Diya Dianey?' DS Brookes finally speaks. His voice betrays a smoker's rattle and his vein-lined cheeks shine scarlet from his gasping coughing fit.

DC Rashid remains impassive in her now revealed real role as my apparent protector.

'Six weeks and four days after my wife died,' I instinctively reply. I am good with remembering such facts.

DS Brookes looks down at the paperwork in front of him. It appears to be made up of scruffy handwritten scrawl and has inexplicably multiplied since our adjournment.

I suspect the DS is not good with computers.

He shuffles the top paper and feigns reading from it.

I deduce this is for effect rather than having any practical purpose.

'Wasn't it a bit soon after such a tragic loss?' he asks disapprovingly and with a barely hidden smirk.

He remains looking at the paperwork and speaks so quietly that his question is almost inaudible.

'These things happen.' It is DC Rashid coming to my rescue.

DS Brookes glares at her and then displays his yellow teeth with a broad smile.

'I guess they do, detective constable,' he mumbles with a chuckle. 'Mr Taylor, I have been told that you were seen with the fragrant Miss Dianey before your wife died.'

His voice is raised to almost a shout and he turns his glare my way.

His fake anger is almost laughable, but I stifle a response.

DC Rashid glances at me and, with a slight nod of her head, only just perceptively encourages me to reply.

I notice a small dot of ketchup on the lower lip of DS Brookes and a grease stain on his shirt collar.

It has the potential to annoy me in ever-increasing graduations.

I am not sure what to do.

'It is not true,' I reply, whilst looking fixedly at the red drying speck on his lip.

DS Brookes grins and I quietly will him to wipe away his irritating mark of lunchtime gorging.

'You were seen at the Odeon cinema with her on the 23rd of June last year, Mr Taylor,' his tone now once again controlled and conciliatory. 'The girl or woman at the counter is quite clear that it was you with an Asian lady.'

He pauses as if this pronouncement was an exhausting effort and unblinkingly stares straight into my eyes. He knows that this troubles me.

I remain silent.

'You were there, Mr Taylor.' It is DC Rashid. 'We know, because you paid for the two tickets by credit card.'

She looks fleetingly at DS Brookes who persists in his staring. He appears to be terrifically self-satisfied, but I am stunned that he does not know the correct circumstances of my visit to the cinema.

I shake my head violently to break the glare from DS Brookes and dig my nails into my left hand to control my briefly inflamed temper.

'I do not like people looking into my eyes intensely, at all really,' I enunciate softly but with a hint of anger.

DS Brookes ignores me. 'You were there, Mr Taylor, so do not try to deny it,' he states with a blind but unjustified confidence.

I am tempted to deny it just to annoy him but relent after a short pause.

'If you had checked your facts, you would know that I was there with a friend of my wife who happens to be Bangladeshi and Muslim and looks nothing like Diya, and, unlike my wife, was keen to see the film and, kind of against my wishes, was invited by my wife on my behalf.'

There is a silence which is finally broken by a demure cough, or is it a stifled laugh, from DC Rashid.

I believe that she already knew this.

I also begin to wonder whether DS Brookes did too, since he appears to continue to have a self-satisfied look on his face.

I look up and the spider has miraculously appeared once again and has something trapped in an equally magically revealed web of great intricacy.

I suddenly feel as if I am captured in the web.

DS Brookes once again shuffles his paperwork and he oozes smugness.

I watch as he slowly glances up and I witness a sly grin.

'Sorry, Mr Taylor, you are quite right.' He continues to talk quietly, 'It was a different day altogether, the 23rd of July at seven o'clock that I meant to talk about. Silly me, hey ho, these things happen. Do forgive me for such an error.'

He glances conspiratorially at his imagined, or not, colleague.

I perceive a look of concern from DC Rashid which could very easily be interpreted as a mistake on her behalf.

DS Brookes, I am sure, is capable of detecting the tiniest facial inference.

He looks away from her and for a moment betrays a sign of puzzlement followed by a nod of his head as if confirming something he has suspected from the beginning.

He glances once again at his notes, an obvious attempt at temporary diversion.

'You were seen at the same cinema in the evening with a different Asian woman. The description I have is miraculously close to that of Miss Diarney.' He enunciates this without looking at me but instead as if reading from his scrawl.

I conclude that he does not need the notes but does not wish to look at me.

I observe, stare at, DS Brookes for longer than I expect is normal before replying.

'Whoever told you this is very much mistaken,' I utter.

'The same woman who served you on the 23rd of June thinks differently,' DS Brookes says to the desk, continuing to feign reading.

There is silence. I am once again unsure whether I am required to reply.

'You paid by cash. You obviously did not want your wife to know where you were.' It is DC Rashid. She is desperately trying to allay the suspicions that DS Brookes perhaps betrayed about her with such subtlety.

'I was at a science lecture on that evening,' I reply.

DS Brookes mumbles inaudibly under his breath.

'You have a remarkable memory for dates, Mr Taylor.' It is DC Rashid in her continued attempt at rehabilitation.

Or is she feeding me lines?

I wonder for a split-second whether she believes me or not.

'It was the first Wednesday of the month. It is a regular occurrence. I am good with dates. It is what I can do well,' I reply.

I feel slightly out of breath as a temporary quietness envelops the room.

DS Brookes eventually shifts his bulk in his chair and plants his elbows on the desk. He glares at me slightly open-mouthed. 'I'm afraid I do not believe you, Mr Taylor.' It is a polite, precise and emotionless comment.

I contemplate an answer which I deduce should be some brand of denial or resistance. 'I paid by card for the lecture,' is my entreaty. 'Check it out, detective.'

DS Brookes keeps his elbows on the desk and smiles. 'Oh, we have, Mr Taylor, but it does not prove you were there though, does it, Mr Taylor?'

He grabs the top sheet of paper in front of him and looks at it with great care. 'We have tried to find somebody who may have seen you there,' he pauses almost dramatically, 'and guess what? Not one person could confirm it. Nobody at the so-called science lecture can recall you being there, Mr Taylor. Isn't that rather odd?'

He looks me straight in the eyes. I know he is trying to provoke a reaction from me. I look away. 'I was at the lecture,' I tell him with a surprising calm.

DC Rashid clears her throat. 'Let's take a quick break,' she suggests. 'I need to get some fresh water and powder my nose.'

DS Brookes grunts and pushes away his chair. 'Sure, like you, I need a piss anyway.'

'Me too,' I say.

'I guess you better come with me then, love,' DS Brookes replies. 'It's what us ladies do, after all.'

He smiles. It is un-PC and I suspect it is his attempt at disguising his true identity.

We are standing side by side at the urinals.

DS Brookes farts loudly as I hear him unzip his fly.

'I know you killed your wife,' he says nonchalantly and with a familiar chesty chuckle.

I glance in his direction. He is concentrating his attention fixedly on the urinal.

It is almost as if it was a spoken thought.

I walk away to wash and dry my hands. 'Give me a moment, I am an old man,' he shouts without menace. 'The prostate and flow are not the same nowadays.'

'You read *The Guardian*,' I reply, as I approach the taps and hand dryer.

He laughs out loud and then begins to cough deeply.

We are back in the white room.

DC Rashid appears not to have moved, but I know she left the room when we did.

The water jug is refilled and so are our glasses.

I sip the water in my glass. It is thankfully icily cold but has a strange hint of cloudiness.

I place it back on the desk and slowly look up at my fat tormentor.

'This seems to be utterly pointless, DS Brookes, and a chronic waste of my time,' I uncharacteristically forthrightly pronounce. I almost squirm with embarrassment at such a show of boldness.

DS Brookes glances at his assumed colleague.

'Just one more thing, Mr Taylor, and you will be able to go off on your merry way,' he quietly and sarcastically replies.

DC Rashid places her left hand in front of her mouth, I suspect, in an attempt to stifle a laugh.

It appears clear to me that DS Brookes likes playing to his assumed nickname.

I feel myself nodding in acceptance, although I had determined on my walk back to the white room that I would leave without further questions or answers.

DC Rashid delicately clears her throat but otherwise remains mute.

DS Brookes studies his refilled glass and snorts an obvious disapproval.

'Tap water,' he mumbles under his breath and takes an uncompromising swig, followed by the slamming of the glass on the desk.

DC Rashid awkwardly smiles and very slightly edges away from her partner.

I hear loud laughter from the office outside our temporary coffin and sense a sudden panic from my enclosure.

I do not like bounded spaces. They tend to grow smaller as time elapses. I grab the edge of the desk and squeeze it with intensity.

DS Brookes mumbles and then says, 'How did you meet you wife, Mr Taylor?'

I am taken aback. It is as unexpected as it is annoying.

I remain silent and consider standing up and leaving.

DC Rashid notices my intention.

I suspect DS Brookes does too.

My temper, such as it is, finally exhausts. 'DS Brookes, I have politely sat here for far too long a time attempting to cooperate with you and your pointless questions,' I begin.

I take a deep breath and try to overcome a sudden affliction of self-consciousness.

I want to avoid the attention that my outburst has attracted.

'I have tolerated this for long enough.' I pause and spy DC Rashid shifting uncomfortably in her seat, 'and I cannot for one nanosecond understand how you think my wife could have been murdered, when she fell from a balcony from a house that had all its doors locked from the inside, with windows all locked from the inside and no sign of a forced entry.' I pause once again and squeeze my hands together, pressing my nails painfully into my flesh. 'And since you presumedly believe it was me who did it, how is it possible for me to have been in London *and* at home at the same time? Do tell me! I am intrigued to say the least.'

I unclasp my hands and place them on the desk in front of me and lightly shake my head and ask loudly, 'Do you really think it is possible for me to have killed my wife?'

I stop and notice DS Brookes smile broadly. I smell his tobacco breath and a whiff of alcohol. I suspect he has a bottle in his office desk drawer.

DC Rashid remains impassive.

'You make it sound like a John Dickson Carr novel, Mr Taylor,' he utters, his smile undiminished, 'or I guess it would be *Jonathan Creek* or *Death in Paradise* for your generation.'

'A locked room mystery,' I hear DC Rashid interject with a hint of mockery.

'I love John Dickson Carr novels, DS Brookes,' I reply.

The DS Brookes smile remains. 'I bet you do,' he almost whispers. I deduce that he does too.

'Although he was very right wing,' I supplement.

DC Rashid looks on with a mild state of confusion. I guess she is not a fan.

'I bet you do,' he repeats, his voice vaguely raised, 'I bet you do, Mr Taylor.'

I stand up and politely ask to leave.

DS Brookes inclines his head almost in slow motion. 'Show him out, detective constable,' he instructs his fictional inferior. 'We will speak again, Mr Taylor,' he mumbles as he stands up and walks from the room.

I look up at the ceiling and notice the spider has devoured its prey.

It is two days after the funeral and I am walking to my carport to drive to the school to collect Matilda.

Joan Maxwell is unloading something from the back of her car.

'Hello Joan,' I say.

'Just been to the garden centre to buy a plant pot,' she tells me, 'to replace the one that was broken on my balcony.'

'Oh,' I reply.

'Yes, no idea how it was broken, seemed to happen on the day…'

She stops and looks embarrassed and sheepish.

'Sorry,' she says.

I nod an acknowledgement of her regret and jump into my car.

DC Rashid offers to drive me home. I accept. She asks me to wait while she collects her things, whatever they might be.

I am left sitting in the police waiting room.

It is grim. The floor is covered in cigarette butts and at least three copies of redtop newspapers. The walls have peeling grimy paint. It stinks of cigarettes and I wonder why, since smoking inside is supposed to be illegal.

It is like a blast from the past and I wonder if I am on the set of *Life on Mars.*

I recall that there may be a twin universe in which time travels backwards.

I wonder if I am now living in it.

I close my eyes.

I recall meeting Rachel for the first time.

I was at Peter's Advanced Puppy Training Class. She was accompanying a friend. Her friend had a German shepherd. It hated Peter.

This is going backwards.

It feels like a place you should never go.

I open my eyes.

The floor is clean and the stink of tobacco has dissipated.

I am sitting in the passenger seat of a car. DC Rashid is driving. I do not recall getting in the vehicle, but looking in the side mirror, I notice the police station in the near distance.

'Prisha Waring,' she bizarrely announces.

I grunt a lack of understanding.

She laughs lightly, titters. 'My real name.'

'Possibly,' I sharply reply, as a tremendous torrent of rain begins to clatter on the car window screen.

'He thinks you hired a hit man to kill your wife,' she states. 'He has spent months trying to find the evidence.' She stops talking and swears loudly as a car brakes sharply in front of her

I contemplate a reply.

'He could look for the rest of his life and find nothing,' I finally declare.

There is a silent pause. 'I know,' the newly christened Prisha Waring finally replies.

It does not surprise me.

We appear to have travelled out of town. The journey is a void. It is continuing to lash down with rain.

'Climate change,' I pronounce to break an awkward silence.

Prisha Waring is concentrating intensely while looking out of the car window screen, desperately searching for the optimum view through the intense array of raindrops. 'Hugo Coles,' she says, without averting her stare into the abyss outside.

I wait for her to continue, but a silence ensues. I ponder her obsession with Hugo Coles.

I know him as a very old man who is kinder than kind to my daughter, Matilda.

'He brings my daughter presents every time he visits Joan,' I explain. 'He always makes the effort to see Matilda,' I continue.

I pause but get no response. 'Joan often has to wheel him all the way round to our house. She is often very red in the face and panting with the effort.' I smile in recollection of Matilda's joy at seeing her 'old man friend'.

I am suddenly thrust forwards by the swift braking of the car. This prompts Prisha Waring to swear out loud and to bang on the steering wheel.

'Fucking moron,' she shouts and presses hard on the car horn.

I do hope she is not addressing me.

I find myself sitting in a bar.

There is a half-full glass of sparkling water accompanied by a half-empty bottle of sparkling water at its side.

There is a constant irritation of background 1980's music.

It is inane pop music from a bygone age. My brain hates such an intrusion and I grit my teeth and breathe deeply.

Prisha Waring is sitting opposite me cradling a glass of unidentifiable white wine.

I expect that it tastes bad.

She is looking me straight in the eye.

I judge it as a look of confusion.

'You were somewhere else there for a while,' she utters with a minor hint of concern.

She smiles with her sparkling teeth and quickly takes a reluctant sip from the glass of wine.

I spy a theatrically covered-up grimace.

I deduce that a smile in return is the norm and oblige somewhat over enthusiastically.

She rapidly takes a second sip and averts my gaze as she places the glass on the table.

'I was saying that DS Brookes will not stop pursuing you,' she explains with a hint of irritation; it is as if she is speaking to a small child.

I acknowledge her comment with an incline of my head.

I grab at my glass of water and take a gulp of the fizzy liquid. It is refreshing and allows me time to assess my reply. I would have preferred still but presume I must have requested it.

'He is wasting his time,' I judge to be an adequate response.

Prisha Waring shuffles her bottom in the chair and leans towards me, cradling her hands under her chin.

I instinctively move away but not before she whispers, 'You didn't do it, did you?'

It is a matter-of-fact comment, but she looks serious.

I judge that a smirk is necessarily supplemented with a fabricated chuckle. I treat the comment as a joke.

There is silence and it becomes clear that she is awaiting my denial.

I swig my glass of water. 'It is infinitely unlikely that the great detective Brookes will ever prove anything,' I reply with a hint of contempt.

I am deliberately ambiguous.

Prisha Waring wriggles her nose. She appears unconvinced.

She edges further towards me by shuffling her elbows. 'I need to know whether you want us to put a stop to his ridiculous investigations,' she whispers conspiratorially.

The comment is barely audible over the continuing irritation of the background music and chatter from fellow drinkers, but it is clear that she knows that I heard her.

She leans back in her chair and looks around the room. It is evident that she is willing and capable of what she is suggesting. It does not surprise me.

I clear my throat of an annoying tickle. 'He is wasting his time,' I repeat, 'I did not touch my wife and you know that is clear and true.'

I pause and contemplate continuing.

She interrupts. 'You will not be astonished to know that we have looked into the case and found nothing at all to suggest that you had any hand in your wife's death.' She pauses for a moment and scans the room, 'It is beyond my reasoning why the DS is so insistent, but, as I said earlier, he does appear to get obsessive about some cases and will pursue them to the absolute end.'

She glances at me. 'You want us to put a stop to him, don't you?'

I contemplate an appropriate reply and finally determine that a nod is adequate.

She nods back. 'Take it as done, Mr Taylor. DS Brookes will no longer be speaking to you.'

I am sitting on my sofa. I am at home. It is quiet, although I notice Hugo Coles sitting in his wheelchair opposite me. He has a glass of wine cradled in his arthritic hands which shake noticeably.

Hugo Coles is stick thin but, despite sitting down, it is clear that he remains a very tall man. He maintains a thick shock of grey hair that sticks up despite any attempt to control it with some kind of grease and a parting. His face is deeply lined and sports a large thin nose and square chin. He exudes an air of confidence and control that belies his infirmity and age.

I like Hugo and so does Matilda.

'How are you coping?' he asks me. He has an accent that I have never been able to place.

Joan Maxwell has taken Matilda to the local park to play with her grandson.

I shrug my shoulders, a gesture that Hugo Coles appears to interpret.

'I feel forlorn for Matilda's generation,' he continues. 'It will all change for the very worse you know. It is so sad that your leaders cannot see this.'

He closes his eyes, hums quietly and appears to lightly rock his head from side to side.

I am lying in bed.

Priya is by my side.

She is sound asleep and slightly snoring.

It is quiet but for a distant hum of motorway traffic in the far distance.

It keeps me awake.

Peter is asleep in the corner of the bedroom and the full moon squeezes an intrusive beam of light between the gap in the closed curtains.

I continuously recall my latest conversation with Prisha Waring.

I feel ashamed.

'I 'member seeing Chris'as lights shining in Mummy's eyes', I recall Matilda telling me. 'They looked very, very pretty. Just like mummy.'

I wanted to correct her English but instead stifled a sob and desperately pushed shameful memories away.

I am sitting on the train and thinking that I would much rather be walking Peter.

'Ever thought about whether we are all simulations,' the amazingly pretty, young, blonde-haired woman sitting next to me asks all of a sudden.

'Very often,' I reply with a hint of irritation at my quiet reverie being intruded upon.

'If intelligent beings in one world in a million were to survive…' she continues with a jollity that bellies my cool response.

'…Environmental catastrophe, nuclear war, or a pandemic are likely to kill off most intelligent species,' I cannot help responding.

She giggles. 'And then that world species reaches a very high-tech stage in evolution, and I mean way beyond where we are at the moment.'

Her voice is evocative and she has a whimsical allure.

'One in a million of these high-tech species could then have the urge to make simulations of themselves, their planet and universe,' she almost sings.

'That would be most interesting but unlikely,' I respond with a touch of confusion.

'Not if you use your imagination and have a little insight,' she chuckles and looks around at me for the first time.

'Or open your mind to what might be possible,' she persists as she flutters her eyelashes and grins.

'Really, do you really think a hyperintelligent race would waste all their time and resources making a simulation of themselves?' I ask her.

'Maybe,' she giggles.

A pause follows. 'This is my stop,' she says as she stands up, 'but I would like to bet that we are a simulation, the maths tells you this is likely. Think about it Mr Nice Man. Bye, Bye. Nice talking to you.'

'DS Brookes has taken early retirement,' Prisha Waring explains as I hold my mobile as far away from my body as possible.

I do not want my health bothered.

I uncomfortably ingest this information. 'That was a bit abrupt,' I reply.

She coughs loudly before replying. 'He refused to drop the case. His superiors had no choice after we put a tiny bit of pressure on them. He is a very stubborn man,' she says.

'You mean you people had no choice,' I respond. 'It is important to be factually correct.'

She makes an unintelligible noise but does not counter my assumption.

'I understand that he spent over four hours trying to persuade his boss that you were guilty of killing your wife,' she tells me.

I am unsure whether it is necessary and whether I want to hear it.

'They had to literally throw him out of the building in the end,' she says.

I wait for her to continue as I have no useful response.

'He told them that he had worked it out but would need to demonstrate it at your house,' she pauses, 'and he would not tell them how you were supposed to have done it.'

There is a pause and a wave of guilt envelops me.

'Could they not have just moved him to another job?' I ask.

Prisha Waring sighs heavily enough for me to hear her with my mobile at arm's length. 'The stupid man would not have moved to another job, Mr Taylor,' she responds with a hint of exasperation.

I suspect that arranging for people to lose their jobs is an everyday occurrence for Prisha Waring and her compatriots.

'We just cannot let him continue to pointlessly pester you,' she says and stops for a moment while I hear what sounds like her muffling her mobile and speaking to somebody else. 'We cannot allow a desperately sad man to make a nuisance of himself and disrupt our vital work,' she finally continues.

I intake a deep breath. 'Desperately sad,' I incredulously repeat.

It is not an impression I had of the detective sergeant.

'Oh yes, his wife left him a few months ago,' she explains nonchalantly. 'I guess his work obsession is a way to alleviate the pain of it all.'

This seems rehearsed, not totally honest, and an idea begins to form.

'Did this have something to do with you?' I ask contemptuously.

She chuckles nervously over the phone.

She does not need to confirm her complicity.

There is once again a pause and I contemplate throwing my mobile afar.

I did not dislike DS Brookes.

'We could not let him pester you,' she suddenly interjects. 'The work you do is far too important.'

I lightly cough with a hint of embarrassment. 'I am a hacker, Ms Waring, I am sure there are many, many more with my skill set that could take my place,' I angrily shout down the phone. 'I do not want to be responsible for wrecking a thoroughly decent man's career and life.'

I throw the mobile phone halfway across the garden and wince as a muscle in my arm tweaks.

I walk swiftly indoors and slam the door.

$E = MC^2$.

What does this mean?

In simple terms, energy is equal to mass multiplied by the speed of light squared.

Simple, isn't it?

So why do the young have so much energy, I contemplate, as Matilda runs round and round our garden, followed by an eager panting dog.

I conclude that Einstein forgot to factor in age.

'Your mobile phone thing is in the middle of the grass, Daddy,' I hear her say.

I notice the dog stop his pursuit and sniff at the mobile phone and then begin enthusiastically licking it.

I catch myself wishing he would eat it up.

We are back inside the house.

Matilda is sitting at the dining table eating a snack of avocado, sun-dried tomato, corn cracker and cheddar cheese.

I am sipping at a glass of lukewarm metallic-tasting water.

'Uncle Hugo told me that the world is going to get very, very, very hot,' she says with a seriousness beyond her years while chewing vigorously at a lump of cheddar cheese. 'He called it climate change and then changed it to climate cat something. He saided it is because we are burning lots of carbon and cows have a lot of wind.'

She pauses and takes a hefty bite from her cracker.

It is all so matter of fact, her childlike lack of understanding unerringly mirrors that of the great majority of the general population of the UK and beyond.

'Catastrophe,' I correct or tell her. 'Uncle Hugo is very concerned about the planet, and wants it to be good to live on, for you, Luke and all the other children,' I explain.

I find it easier to talk to Matilda than I do with adults.

She looks at me with an expansive smile, although her eyes hint at a deeply hidden underlying sadness.

I notice small morsels of cheese lodged between her teeth, and, thankfully, a small sparkle of joy in her eyes as she sees Peter walk into the room. It is an effervescence that has gradually returned since the loss of her mother, and one that Hugo Coles has nurtured back with a skill beyond me, on his few encounters with her.

'Uncle Hugo gave me this.' She pushes a small postcard towards me.

The card has a picture of a stunningly beautiful tiger and some prose underneath.

I read it with a hint of recognition:

'Surely it is our responsibility to do everything within our power to create a planet that provides a home, not just for us, but for all life on earth.'

'Uncle Hugo said I should keep this until I am a grown-up big girl, and I will understand it much, muchly better,' she explains, with crumbs ejecting from her mouth and spewing in all directions.

They are the wise words of Sir David Attenborough.

'Yes, that sounds like a very good idea,' I reply.

She nods her head with great enthusiasm. 'He has given Luke one as well too,' she splutters. 'Uncle Hugo seems to knows everything about the future. He is a very, very, very clever man.'

I nod my head in agreement. 'Yes, he is a very wise and gentle old man,' I tell her.

'And very, very, very nice too,' she says with an expansive smile.

I find myself stuck in an irritatingly long queue of stalled traffic.

This is not at all unusual, but it always causes me undue stress. The roads are disintegrating into rivers of potholes due to lack of care, or austerity, as the local council would have us believe.

My stress is confounded because I am travelling to collect Matilda from school.

I do not want to be late. It upsets her. It upsets me. It used to upset her mother too.

There is an inordinate mass of life and planet-threatening pollution spewing from the array of vehicles surrounding the oasis of my non-vomiting electric car, and I scoff at the latest opinion poll being discussed on the radio that tells us the general public are most concerned about immigration and the climate catastrophe doesn't even register in the top ten. I smile as I imagine Hugo Coles quietly dismantling the ineffectiveness of the UK media. He believes they are complicit and I find it difficult to disagree.

'Fracking fools,' I shout.

It is clear that I will be late for collecting Matilda.

I call the school on my mobile phone, and after a distressingly extended wait for a reply, I arrange for Matilda to stay in the after-school club until I arrive.

I know she will not be happy. She likes routine, as do I.

'A big fat man spoke to me before I went to after-school club,' I am told as I drive Matilda home. 'He said that he know'd you,' she continues, while chomping a raw carrot stick.

'Knows.' I am unable to stop myself correcting her.

'He tolded me not to wear a purple top, dress or hat,' she says.

She instinctively filters out my need for linguistic perfection.

My skin prickles with alarm. 'Who was this man?' I involuntarily shout.

I look in the rear-view mirror and spy Matilda squirm in her car seat. Her face is screwed up in alarm, she has dropped her snack and looks as if she may start to cry.

She is unused to me raising my voice.

She begins to cry.

'He was smelly, he smelled of smoking sticks and had very grotty brown teeth,' she sniffles, while trying to hold back sobs.

I grip the car steering wheel hard with anger, and angrily vow to call Prisha Waring as soon as I am on my own.

I am sitting on the train to London.

I have arranged a meeting with Prisha Waring.

I have grabbed my usual window seat and, as required, have emptied out my breakfast, a bottle of water and a copy of *Underworld* from my bag.

It has to be in that order.

It is necessary for me to eat something, and then to start to read after the second stop.

I also need to be in the quiet coach.

Constant chatter and the ringing of mobile phones would exasperate me.

I am eating a peanut butter sandwich, my usual and only possible breakfast on the train.

I notice a large figure approach the seat next to me and slump surprisingly gracefully into it. I sigh with annoyance and edge as close to the window as possible. I hate people sitting next to me.

The figure reeks of tobacco and immediately invades my space by leaning on the armrest separating the two spaces. I glance to my side and notice a copy of the *Daily Mail* being placed loudly on the shelf in front of the intruder.

'*Mail* readers say unemployed benefit scroungers to blame for the financial crash' is the headline in large bold lettering.

'What a load of shit,' I quietly mumble to myself.

I silently wonder why anybody would wish to read such rubbish.

'I agree,' DS Brookes, or to be precise, ex-DS Brookes, replies quietly as he chuckles.

We are sitting in a coffee bar at Waterloo station.

Jonah Brookes is sitting opposite me gulping at a plastic cup of coffee, and beholding, with lust, a large iced bun sitting on a not too clean plastic plate in front of him.

I have a bottle of still water and an empty plastic cup in front of me.

I am intrigued, alarmed, by the vociferous use of plastic, but I am not stupefied that the chain of a tax-avoiding corporation should show so little concern for the environment.

'You upset my daughter,' I growl and admonish the large man sitting opposite me.

He ignores my comment and grabs the bun, and then takes an enormous bite from it.

He chews it with an unnecessary loudness and a look of great satisfaction and desire.

'And you do not read that fucking shit newspaper,' I conclude.

It takes a while for him to empty his mouth and he then swigs deeply from his coffee cup.

I do not take my eyes from him as he does this.

He wipes his mouth with the back of his hand and smiles with his horribly yellowed teeth.

'She seemed fine when I left her,' he finally responds nonchalantly. 'I am sure that the death of her mother upset her very much more than I did, Mr Taylor.'

He continues to grin.

'We were discussing children's television programmes. I hadn't a clue who Pepper Pig or the Teletubbies are, but she seemed enthralled by them,' he says.

I ignore him and grit my teeth.

'I'm more a *Trumpton*, *Blue Peter* or *Camberwick Green* man myself,' he continues with an infuriating grin and a wink of his left eye, 'and *Play School* of course.'

I seriously want to punch him.

It is not something I am able to do.

Violence affronts me.

Instead, I remain calm. 'What do you want, Mr Brookes?'

He leans forward and annoyingly invades my space.

He licks his lips. 'I want you to admit that you killed your wife, Mr Taylor.'

He pauses and leans even closer. 'I do not care that you arranged for me to be sacked from my job. I do not care if you get away with it. I just want you to acknowledge that you did it. I want you to tell me I am right.'

He sits back in his seat and grabs hold of the bun and once again, with a grin, takes a large bite.

'What were you doing at my daughter's school,' I enquire angrily.

I do not want to give credence to his statement and so ignore it.

He leans back and takes a further gulp of his coffee while his mouth appears to still be full of the sugary bun.

'I am retired,' he smirks. 'I have volunteered to teach the children how to keep safe in this dangerous, unjust world, and to teach them a little bit of Christianity on the side.'

He leans back so far in his chair that I fear, or, to be honest, hope he might tumble backwards.

My concern and hope are irrational but exist.

I look at him with surprise. I did not imagine him as a believer in any gods.

'What will you say to God if he does happen to meet you when you die,' I randomly ask.

It is mischievous, but I am genuinely intrigued.

'Thanks for the chance,' he whispers without thought. 'I guess you are an atheist.'

I nod my head slowly in response and he smiles broadly and winks. 'Me too, Mr Taylor, me too.'

'What will you say to God when you die, Daddy?' I recall Matilda asking me.

It is the day after Rachel's funeral, and Matilda believes she has ascended to heaven, and is being cared for by a kindly God figure.

I do not believe this but am happy to see Matilda comforted by it.

Matilda is sitting up in bed, and I have just finished reading her a chapter from *Esio Trot* or 'the backwards tortoise' as she, and many others over the years, have christened the book.

I recall a quote by Stephen Fry but do not repeat it.

'I will thank him for looking after Mummy while I was still alive,' I begin, 'and I will ask him to make sure you are happy while you are still alive, and to lead you to me and Mummy when you die, so we can all then be together again.'

She sniffs loudly and then begins to sob. 'I want my mummy back,' she gasps. 'Daddy, can we please, please, please, please ask God to bring Mummy back to us.'

'I was watching a TV programme a few nights ago,' Jonah Brookes recalls.

He appears to have another iced cake in front of him, but I do not recall him buying it.

I know that I am tempted to just walk away from him but cannot find the inclination.

'This plump middle-aged guy walks into the office of his manager, and there is a clock above his head. It is very prominent.'

He pauses and wipes his sticky lips with the sleeve of his shirt. I notice the shirt is grubby and in need of a wash. I also note that his left eye appears to be inflamed.

'The time on the clock reads 10:03; it barely registers in my tiny mind.' I am not averse to his self-mockery. I am not deceived.

'I happened to look up at the clock above my television set, I do not know why, I guess it is something I do often.'

He pauses and takes a bite from the cake.

It appears to be a piece of chocolate cake but could just as easily be a dark coffee cake.

I am intrigued by why this should concern me.

'My clock told me it was 10:03.' He almost whispers this denouement to a story that I was barely taking any interest in and one I have heard before. 'Coincidence, Mr Taylor,' he raises his voice, 'a bit like your wife dying just when it suited you.' He once again lowers his voice and broadly smiles.

He licks his lips with his tongue and then again soils his shirt sleeve as a parting shot.

I remain mute.

He smiles, revealing his brown teeth, with the remnants of his cake lodged between them.

I restrain a smile out of a feeling of pity.

I know he is an intelligent man; to me it is clear, but he is a universe away from my mind.

I stand up and walk away without a further glance, and hear him lightly laugh.

I am standing outside Matilda's school with Peter when I next encounter Jonah Brookes.

He is standing outside the school smoking a foul-smelling cigarette. It is his rattling cough that attracts my attention.

It is clear that he has seen me. He walks casually in my direction and exhales his fumes as he reaches me.

'Put that fucking thing out,' I scold him. 'There are young children around who should not have such harmful pollution inflicted on them.'

He smiles and throws the cigarette to the ground, crushing it with his immaculately polished right shoe with surprising care.

'And what about the just-as-harmful shit spewing from all the cars?' I hear him respond antagonistically.

He is right.

He leans over. I flinch, but he only gently pats Peter on his head.

'Nice dog,' he says casually. 'Wouldn't ever have thought of having a poodle for a pet,' he continues. He is looking at the dog with infinite interest while Peter laps up the attention, 'I've heard they are supposed to be very clever dogs.'

I do not respond.

'Guess you could teach them to do anything you wanted,' he continues.

He coughs loudly and spits onto the ground.

I shake my head and spy Matilda walking towards me.

She smiles broadly as she spots me and then scowls as she sees Brookes standing next to me.

Brookes walks away without a further word before she reaches us.

I detect him lighting another cigarette and throwing the match to the ground.

'Yuck!' I hear Matilda exclaim, 'That man is fat and smelly.'

'A strange big man came round here today,' Daniela my diligent Ukrainian cleaner tells me. 'He wanted to speak to you.'

Daniela fled from Crimea when the Russians did their dirty deed in 2014. She was a student at that time but now scrapes by cleaning houses. Such a waste. Fuck Putin!

She is talking about Brookes of course.

'He was wearing the most ridiculous purple coat,' she continues. 'And he called Peter as soon as he had barged into the house.'

I am seething.

She grins. 'Peter jumped up at him and growled. The fat man looked scared for a moment but then laughed loudly.'

She shakes her head with an air of incredulity. 'He left when I told him you were in London, but he seemed very pleased with himself, patted Peter and thanked me for my time.'

'He would do,' I reply. 'Please don't let him in the house again, Dani.'

'No, I will not, Mr Taylor,' she replies.

My mobile phone rings as I drive home from taking Matilda to school. The weather is foul, rain sheeting down. I am having difficulty seeing through the fogged-up window screen.

Alt J are warbling from the CD player, 'I would like to be the wallpaper on your bedroom wall', or something to that effect. It sounds like a teenager's wet dream.

The mobile is hands-free.

'Can you talk?'

It is Prisha Waring.

'As much as usual,' is my poor attempt at humour.

There is a pause as a large lorry succeeds in splashing a tsunami of filthy water over the side of my freshly cleaned car.

'Do you want Brookes dealt with?' she continues casually. I guess this is normal in her line of work.

I do not respond.

'He will not be at your daughter's school any more. He will no longer speak to your daughter, and you will not see him again,' she persists.

It is said with an almost disturbing calm but also with a corresponding immense conviction.

I glare through the stubborn fogged-up window screen with a sense of relief.

'We could have him eliminated, if necessary,' I hear her shockingly pronounce.

My senses tell me that I have imagined it, but I respond loudly, 'No!'

I hear what could be a high-pitched chuckle in the background, but I remain unsure as she replies, 'Just to let you know that we would consider it if Brookes continues to be a problem to you.'

'No need,' I retort loudly and firmly. 'I guess and hope your warning to him will suffice on this occasion.'

There is a hiatus as I barely perceive Prisha Waring talking very quietly to somebody else.

'No problem this time,' she finally replies, 'but you know what we can do if you need it.'

I feel a shiver down my spine, my skin tingles and a dizziness destabilises my consciousness.

I shake my head and wipe the car window screen with a damp cloth.

'Goodbye, Ms Waring,' I say.

'Goodbye, Mr Taylor. Do take care,' she quietly replies.

I suspect I will never see or hear from her again, but who knows?

I am sitting on the train thinking about how Peter is coping in my absence.

'May I sit here?' a voice asks, and I look up.

It is the young pretty blonde woman who spoke to me about simulations a week or so ago.

'Sure,' I reply, although I know it will cause me distress.

'Sorry,' she giggles as she almost floats into the seat next to me.

'Ever wondered whether we are living in only one of many universes?' she asks as she fixes me with a sensuous smile and flutters her eyelashes.

'Do you?' I ask her, feeling distinctly uncomfortable.

'What do you think? Tell me what you think before I let you know my views, cheeky,' she replies with another flirtatious giggle.

'Actually, as it happens, I do believe in the multiverse theory,' I reply a little hesitantly and likely a touch impatiently.

'Really, then I presume that you must go along with the theory of cosmic inflation,' she responds with a touch of what I assume is disbelief.

'Don't you believe in cosmic inflation?' I reply.

'Sure,' she giggles, 'there is lots of evidence to prove that the big bang was preceded and set up by a prior phase,' she says enthusiastically and possibly a little loudly.

'Keep it down. We are in the quiet coach,' the man in the opposite seat next to the blonde woman suddenly angrily says in a loud whisper.

'I do apologise,' she giggles while fixing the man with a murderous stare.

'Let us continue, shall we?' she says quietly and looking back in my direction, as the man begins to cough uncontrollably.

'Look, the prior stage is likely to have been cosmic inflation,' she continues as the man stumbles from his seat and heads in the direction of the toilets.

Everyone in the coach appears to ignore the man's discomfort and I, only for a fleeting moment, consider asking if he needs help.

'Do you think we should help him?' I ask her before she is able to continue with her physics lecture.

'Think he will be okay,' she smiles. 'In fact, I am sure he will be.'

'He didn't look great,' I shyly and embarrassingly mumble.

'Everything will be fine with the silly interfering man,' she snaps, and then, as if regretting a minor show of temper, smiles broadly.

'Perhaps I should continue,' she then giggles, after an awkward pause.

'Okay,' I dishonestly reply, hoping my stop is not too far away.

'Anyway, for the universe to be as it is, something else has to come along for the ride,' she continues, as if the incident with the man had never occurred.

'Could that something be the multiverse?' I ask, although I know I am right.

'Here are the reasons why most physicists now believe in a multiverse,' she says as she hands me a book.

Easy Ways to Explain our Universe Amongst Many More Universes is the title on the front of the book and it appears to be written by a woman named Olivia Bartholomew.

'Really,' I respond as I take the book from her. 'That is most kind.'

It is fifteen days later, and I find myself staring at the wall in my office. There is a spider edging upwards with no seeming purpose. But I know better.

I hear the doorbell ring and hesitantly tiptoe down the carpeted stairway towards the offending and inconvenient noise.

It is the postman, a man who has complained of Peter jumping up at him in the past. I restrain Peter, whilst attempting to make small talk, and sign for a large parcel. The postman grunts approval and sneers in the direction of Peter. I close the door, no longer feigning any interest.

The parcel is quite heavy, and for a moment I find myself hesitating.

The address label is grubby and has a barely readable scrawl indicating my name and address. I suddenly develop a newfound admiration for the Royal Mail.

Peter has lost interest and trots up the stairs as I stare at the parcel in trepidation. I know who it has come from and wonder what the fuck he is attempting now.

I wait two hours and thirty-one minutes before ripping the brown paper away from the contents of the parcel. It is a pile of paper. The top piece of paper also has the barely readable scrawl inhabiting it. I sit down and take the top piece of paper from the pile and attempt to read it:

'Dear Sir,

'You may find the enclosed of interest since I know that you take a great curiosity in the mystery genre!!! After you have read the document, please do let me know what you think! In the meantime, I will get back to reading *The Sun* newspaper, or the *Daily Mail* if you prefer, and, thanks to you, seeking a new career. Yours as ever, Jonas'.

I contemplate on whether to read it while listening to some neighbours shouting at each other in their garden. I notice a murder of crows swoop over the nearby country park. It is as if dark clouds are falling to earth. I carry the papers to my office and then, noticing the time, I leave to collect Matilda from school.

It is five hours and forty-two minutes later, and Matilda is in bed. Since Brookes has clearly failed to heed his warning, I contemplate contacting Prisha Waring.

But I sit down in my armchair, turn on the radio, decide to read the paperwork and tell Peter to go and sit down.

'How useful going out does it do in time,' the radio announcer inexplicably says two hours later. I guess he has muddled his words. Shaking my head, I switch off the radio, drink a glass of water and go to bed.

A cross and a tick and a solution come to mind as I lie awake a few hours later.

'What the fuck!' I shout.

Chapter Five

A Letter and a Mystery Parcel

Dear Jonas, or Mr Brookes, if you prefer a touch more formality,

My uncle, James Corbett, suggested, well, to be honest insisted, I contact you. I do so hope you do not mind such an unexpected intrusion on your, no doubt, invaluable time.

We thought you might be interested in looking at this (the parcel enclosure!), given your interest in unsolved mysteries. I understand (from James) that your ex-colleagues in the force used to call you Columbo, so this should certainly be of interest.

The transcript, enclosed (photocopied. I have the original if you wish to see it at some point, although I believe little could be gained from this) with this letter, was discovered in the attic of a small cottage owned by my late great-aunt, who lived in a small, very remote, village (Chudleigh Knighton, I believe, but I may be incorrect) in the heart of the beautiful County of Devon, all her life. It is of a reasonable quality, a bit muddled and strange, and could likely benefit from a bit of polishing up (maybe, for I am no editor!) and expansion, if it is meant to be the transcript of a novel!

The author's identity is unknown (although some clues may be found in that my great-aunt was in possession of the manuscript), and the narrator of the story appears eccentric to say the least. My preliminary investigations, however, appear to indicate that the events (mostly) seem to have taken place but were hardly reported at the time and thereafter.

Anyway, Jonas, or Mr Brookes, I will say no more in fear of prejudicing the impression that you draw from the manuscript, but I would at some point like to meet up to discuss your conclusions.

Yours faithfully,

Alan Corbett-Hemingway.

PS. One more thing (sorry!) I would be very happy to accompany you to Chudleigh Knighton (or wherever) if you would find this helpful.

PPS. Jack didn't die!

Chapter Six

A Most Odd, Mysterious and Dog's Dinner of a Manuscript

Locked Room Problem

Oh Lord, a bad start to the evening.

My master, Detective Inspector Clive Lewis, was sitting in the only interview room in the small village police station when Constable Abel, a fool of a man (in my opinion, which in my opinion is worth a great deal!) with a deep southwest accent and very red, ravaged face, prematurely aged by smoking, showed the lady in.

She was elderly, stick thin and looked well into her eighties. From my vantage point in the corner of the room, I could see that she was dressed in an immaculate blue wool coat and wore a velvet purple boater like hat with a small white feather sticking out of the left-hand side. The coat betrayed thick stocking-covered shins while her feet were dressed in demonstrably bright purple shoes with shiny gold buckles. To be honest, I only wished that I could have laughed. Her face was made up thickly in what I guessed was a failed attempt to conceal the erosion of age and she wore gold round-rimmed spectacles. Her attire was topped off with a large lavender handbag which she held firmly and protectively in both white-gloved hands.

'This is Miss Hemingway, sir,' the red-faced idiot Abel announced with a hint of glee and a smirk, which he hid from Miss Hemingway with surprising alacrity, and without need, since my master was quite aware of who she was.

My master acknowledged Abel with pleasing contempt, and then smiled in the direction of Miss Hemingway, whose scowl could have scared the bravest of poodles. I decided it was best to keep a low profile, and curled up in my given corner of the room, and feigned disinterest.

'Take a seat, Miss Hemingway,' my master politely said, while indicating the chair opposite him to the shuffling wreck. She minced her path to the seat, taking short, careful steps and betraying an unsteadiness that I suspected may have originated from far too many glasses of sherry or gin. Funnily enough though, I did not smell any alcohol on her breath as she slowly bent down and sat in front of my master. Then, as she placed herself on the chair, she winced with, what I suspected was, disgust, and continued to clutch her distasteful bag which she had placed on the desk. She then myopically squinted in my master's direction, with her apparent nervousness making her dentures lightly chatter in her quivering jaw. I feigned a yawn in order to adjust my view, and then awaited Miss Hemmingway's latest complaint; there had after all been many in the past. I yawned again at the remembrance but pricked up my ears anyway.

My master, with a hand waft, gestured for Abel to leave, and he watched contemptuously, to my enormous approval, as the fat clown slumped out of the room. What a fool!

'Miss Hemingway,' my master began with admirable patience, 'how can I help you on this occasion?'

Miss Hemingway shifted uncomfortably in her chair and clutched her handbag with renewed vigour. I was sorely tempted to grab it and root inside for any semblance of food, but admirably resisted.

She took a deep breath, and coughed demurely. I sniffed in amusement, and shifted my head minutely, in an attempt at getting an even better view of the proceedings.

'I, I, saw a man appear from nowhere in my cottage garden,' she eventually stuttered. 'He looked very strange and big.'

I admired my master's straight face, while stifling a laugh.

She stopped abruptly, slowly shook her head, and then groaned barely audibly.

My master remained silent for a moment, more than likely already contemplating an exit strategy for the interview.

'When was this?' he asked, surprising me with the amount of patience his voice evoked.

Miss Hemingway fixed her attention on my master and finally stopped shaking her head.

'This evening, sergeant. Did your colleague not inform you of the situation?'

She appeared upset that my master was not as well informed as she expected, and made a slow whistling noise.

Disturbing in the least!

My master in response adjusted his ample backside in the chair.

'I know it was this evening, Miss Hemingway,' he finally replied.

My master appeared to realise that he had raised his voice, as Miss Hemingway backed away from him but remained clutching her bag for dear life.

'I just wanted to know the time.' He appeared to deliberately tone his voice down, and then added with what I imagined to be a conciliatory tone, 'just to make sure all is as accurate as possible.'

Sitting and smirking in my corner, I couldn't help but admire his patience.

There was then a silent break, and I took the opportunity to yawn loudly, but unfortunately nobody seemed to notice.

Fail!

Miss Hemingway mumbled to herself, and then nodded her head just the once.

'What time was it, Miss Hemingway?' my master finally prompted with admirable calm.

There was then a further pause, and I loudly, well sort of, adjusted my recumbent position, but was once again ignored.

'About half past seven,' she finally explained with a large hint of reluctance, 'and he was dressed funny all over.'

I looked over with disdain, and restrained further remonstration.

'How so?' my master once again prompted, while, I guessed, he was desperately trying not to prolong what he judged to be a pointless diversion.

She mumbled again, and then nodded her head up and down slowly, as if in tune with her voice. She really was insane, well, in my extremely well-informed judgment anyway.

My master breathed heavily with what I sympathetically judged to be frustration, and then as if nothing untoward had happened, Miss Hemingway continued. 'A silver all-in-one overall type of thing,' she almost whispered, 'and his hair all gone,' she paused, 'and he looked shocked, and his face was bruised, and he had funny purple boots and…' she tailed off and clutched her bag with renewed vigour. 'It was so scary I almost screamed.'

So, did I!

My master digested the ramblings and appeared to silently work out a response. It was clear to me that Miss Hemingway was delusional or, if I was feeling kind (which I wasn't), just seeking attention.

'What did this man do?' my master, to my great frustration, encouraged.

She did not immediately respond, screwing up her face in a show of concentration instead. I screwed up my face in utter vexation.

'He looked around as if he was completely shocked to be in my garden,' she continued, 'and then crouched low as if he was a soldier or something. I have seen them do that in films, but they were not dressed like this man,' she paused and gasped for air, 'and then he ran away very quickly. He jumped my back gate like a deer.'

To be honest, I am sure I would have been shocked to be in her garden too!

My master sighed lightly and feigned making a note in his notebook, an old trick which he tended to employ every time Miss Hemmingway showed up for one of her regular rambling reports.

'He jumped the gate,' my master repeated, 'he jumped the gate.'

He really sounded fed up, and I didn't blame him. I grunted, stood up and stretched in hope that it would encourage an end to the lunacy.

She nodded enthusiastically, her cheeks finding colour at the activity.

'He did not see, or threaten you?' my master frustratingly persisted.

She shook her head vigorously. 'I don't think so, but I did quite quietly say, "Who goes there?" when I first saw him.'

I presumed she was answering his first question and as a consequence the second.

I was feeling very tired and yawned once again.

'I think we will leave it for now, Miss Hemingway.' He, about time, began his exit strategy, I almost jumped for joy. 'I will arrange for you to come back tomorrow to sit with a sketch artist so that we might get a better picture of our intruder.'

She looked at him with surprise and began to mumble what could only be interpreted as an objection of some kind, but thankfully she took the hint and began to stand up.

Thank God. Did she really say 'Who goes there?' to the imposter!

Right, an even worse ending to the evening

My master arrived at Little Whittingham Hall at 8:33 pm. Why so precise? It is one of the things I have to do, accuracy is important for me.

He had received a telephone call from a distraught man servant/butler type at 8:23 pm and was told rather incoherently that Lord Irvine Marshall-Atwood had been shot in his study.

My master knocked vigorously at the oak door, rather too ornate for my taste, but typical of the boastful aristocracy, while I sat next to him recovering from a rather rushed journey. He glanced at me and found time, annoyingly, to pat me on the head. Rather demeaning, but it keeps him happy since he thinks it makes me happy.

We waited for over a minute before the door was opened by a rather, well, extremely fat, hairless, well, totally bald man, dressed in a penguin-like suit. I had seen him before and I knew it was Ecclestone, the sweat-and-mothball-smelling butler, or whatever his title may be. He was, almost amusingly, well, extremely amusingly, very red in the face and I failed to understand a word of the babbling and heavy breathing that was emitted from his small-lipped effeminate mouth. However, my master seemed to decipher it all and we resultantly followed the waddling wreck through the door and into a hallway that appeared larger than my master's whole house. Such social inequality, which I am certain will be addressed in the near future!

I inspected the floor, seeking out food of course, as I followed the comical cast, and fortuitously came across a spot of sweet nutty ripe-smelling liquid. It was clearly recently deposited human blood. I stopped and sat down next to it, pointing with my nose in an attempt to indicate to my master that there was something of interest. He stared at me, nodded his greasy head, gave the floor a perfunctory glance, and I hope noted down for further future investigation.

The obese Ecclestone had paused, and then with a definite display of annoyance led us to his employer's study which, he babbled, was the scene of the 'terrible, terrible, outrage'. I jumped up quickly, and as Ecclestone opened the door, kept close to my master's legs, in the hope of getting a good view of a juicy scene of delicious blood and gore.

However, looking through my master's legs, I was disappointed, I noted a bundle of clothes on the floor, that I quickly gathered was the prone body of the victim Lord Irvine Marshall-Atwood. There was a bushy-haired middle-aged man bending over the said bundle. This was Dr Norman Gatewood, or Gaters as my master, an old school chum, nicknamed him.

There quickly followed a pointless human acknowledgement and, while this nonsense ensued, I crept stealthily from around my master's legs, and purposely began to wander about the room. I noticed the window was open, and almost sneezed at the acrid smell of what was likely to be the residue of a gunshot, although it did also curiously smell somewhat like a firework.

I continued to diligently sniff around the room as the stupid humans continued their pointless chatter. The search was in the hope of finding some food, but for curiosity's sake, I was also seeking out something to connect to and solve the crime.

Whilst sniffing, I cocked my ears and overheard Gaters tell my master that his Lordship had been shot in the left shoulder and that the likelihood was that he would survive. So unfortunately, it wasn't to be a murder case, so it appeared that it was back to reading the latest Agatha Christie to satisfy my blood lust.

Suppressing this bad news, I decided to continue sniffing for clues. After all, somebody had shot his Lordship, so it was at least halfway to a juicy murder. My sniffing and snuffling quickly led to another nutty-smelling spot by the entrance door and it was clearly the same smell that was emanating from the prone body of his Lordship that was just as clearly still in the process of bleeding.

I glanced up and noticed that my master had apparently exhausted his chit-chat with Gaters, and was now casually looking around the room. He appeared to find the open window of interest but would not be attracted to my find by the door, despite my hopeless attempt at gaining his attention. I gave up, and continued the enjoyment of so many new smells that emanated from the room. Latching on to his Lordship's odour, I followed a trail to the open fireplace where the fire was almost exhausted. There were grey embers, some singed wood, papery ashes and a few still-hot coals, and I couldn't help thinking that Ecclestone had been surprisingly very remiss in his fire-laying duties. I couldn't help thinking that the fat servant was losing his touch.

I then decided to give the window a look to try to gather what my master found of interest, but apart from a thread of wool or something similar caught at the edge, there appeared nothing of great interest or curiosity.

'Sir.' I was suddenly shocked from my investigations by the deep southwest-accented Constable Abel, a most inappropriate surname, Harry to his friends (not me), of which there seemed inexplicably to be many.

We all instantly looked around to the source of the voice by the entrance, except of course his Lordship, and witnessed a very red-faced Ecclestone accompanied by an equally red-faced Constable Abel.

'Abel,' my master snapped with more than a hint of irritation.

I suppressed mirth and amusingly noted Abel's shock at seeing the prone body in the middle of the room. I thought for a moment that the idiot would faint, but he unfortunately averted his gaze while losing any visible colour from his chubby face.

'Yes, Constable Abel,' my master once again prompted while I sniffed around feigning indifference.

'Sir, we have another death,' Abel finally incorrectly stuttered while I pricked up my ears and smiled with the delicious anticipation of a dead body and hopefully plenty of gore to get my teeth into.

We arrived at the house of Sir Terrance Edwards (or Ted, as I called him) within ten minutes of Abel's white-faced stuttering announcement. My master had left Abel to protect the scene of crime at the Hall (heaven help us) and agreed that Gaters would get his Lordship to hospital, while I had jumped in the back of my master's car without waiting for an invitation. Anyway, he didn't seem to object.

Ted lived in a large cottage (Old Moss House) on the outside of the village and we were met by my master's other, slightly more efficient, Constable Roddy Bell (ding-dong, I know, not very original and a bit pantomime but the best I could come up with) who was waiting outside the ornate wooden entrance door.

My master parked the car, opened the door and in my usual enthusiasm I barged into his legs and pushed past him, shot off at breakneck speed and then waited unobtrusively by the door to the house. It was a mild night and my master appeared to not need a coat. By the door stood a shotgun and tied up next to it a scruffy, unattractive and most unintelligent dog. I casually sniffed around, ignoring the attention of the ignorant dog, smelling the dreadful odour of Ding-Dong, the unmistakable smell of a cat and once again the familiar nutty smell. However, as I attempted to investigate further, I was rudely pushed aside by Ding-Dong, who led my master into the house. I shook, and followed them at very close quarters since I did not want to be left outside and miss the impending fun and games.

In an elaborate hallway, which somehow seemed out of place, stood a shivering soppy girl, Ted's daughter, Carillon, sobbing her heart out, and the Poacher (allegedly), impassively making it look as if everything really was fine and dandy. I nearly felt sorry for her, well, not really, since the lure of a dead body was far more appealing. I pushed myself past the stupid blustering girl and the guileless Poacher and, as my master uttered some words of comfort, I resumed some wholesome sniffing while looking around in the hope of encouraging some action. They had all started in my wake and as the girl glared at me, I responded by sticking my tongue out at her, but she just ignored me and continued her pitiful sobbing.

'It's in the study,' Ding-Dong announced rather loudly and with a great deal of insensitivity considering the girl was with us. For once, I had to admire him.

'It?' my master snapped at Ding-Dong. 'Take Miss Edwards to the sitting room, Bell,' he then instructed.

Ding-Dong complied with a louder than necessary 'sir' and, aimed at the soppy girl, 'miss', and as if by magic, the girl shuffled along in his wake. I just salivated in anticipation of seeing the blood and the delicious dead body.

My master paused as I continued to sniff along the corridor, smelling a familiar but unrecognisable human odour.

My master turned to the Poacher who stood gazing in the wake of the girl and was looking distinctly ill.

'Tell me what happened,' my master prompted the tall muscular twentyish Poacher.

The Poacher breathed in heavily and appeared to wince with a pain of some sort.

'I heard a gunshot as I was walking past the Edwards' house,' he began in an emotionless quiet drawl. 'I then heard the Edwards girl scream and I rushed to the door and knocked loudly.' He paused again and took another deep breath. 'She, the girl, answered the door and blurted something about the shot coming from her father's study and that she was scared to go in there because someone might shoot her. I then went to the door and tried to open it, but it was locked, so I kicked it in and found the, you know, body sitting slumped in the armchair.'

'Thank you. I think we can take it from here, but of course we will need a statement later,' my master replied.

The Poacher nodded his head gingerly. 'I will go home then if you want no more from me,' he almost whispered and without further ado took his leave.

He seemed rather nervous to me, but my master appeared not to notice.

After a few moments of further sniffing, I was distracted by the return of Ding-Dong who proceeded to point us to the right of the corridor where we were confronted by a half-open door with footmarks indenting the outside. On inspection I noticed that the inside of the doorframe on the right-hand side was splintered off but was prevented from further investigation by a firm, 'Leave it', from my master. I reluctantly did as I was instructed, sat down and sniffed the air nonchalantly.

'I found the door like this when I arrived,' Ding-Dong pronounced officiously, clearly oblivious to my reprimand. 'I went in, trying not to touch anything,' he continued. 'I did not know if Sir Terence was in need of help, and his daughter was extremely anxious,' he continued annoyingly with a pre-emptive defence of his actions. 'Miss Edwards had already told me that she had tried knocking on the door when she arrived home, and had not been able to get a reply from her father. The Poacher had helped her get in and then she had called the station when the Poacher found it, the dead body.'

My master acknowledged Ding-Dong with a nod of his head and a largely disguised mumble. He stared at the door for a moment, glanced at me, probably to confirm that I had obeyed his command, and then he asked Ding-Dong to go and sit with the girl while he had a look inside, and to make sure the doctor was on his way.

Ding-Dong, although I sensed disappointment that he had once again been given babysitting duties, assented with a louder than necessary 'Sir' and trotted off in the direction of the sitting room.

I then snuffled into my master's legs in an attempt to encourage some action. It seemed to work as my master opened the door gently and, not interested in any ceremony, I barged past and trotted in front of him to enter the room.

My master immediately leaned down and studied the door. I took a glance myself and noted that the wood around the frame had been split away where the keyhole would have been placed when locked. I then sniffed around the inside of the door and found a sharpish piece of wood lying by the door that appeared to have broken away from the frame. I noticed my master give it a perfunctory glance but no more. I was surprised that it was so close to the door, but who knows what damage the Poacher and Ding-Dong did when they entered the room!

My master then rudely shooed me away and closed the door. I kept as close as I could and I noted that the lock was still in place and also that there was a large indent in the carpet inside the door, as if something had been dragged or pushed along it. My master kneeled down and looked at it and then stood up without reaction or comment.

We then approached the chair in which the recently demised Sir Terrance sat. By the chair on the right-hand side stood a small table upon which sat a half-drunk glass of, what my nose told me, Scotch, and a notebook and pen. Sir Terrance himself was as white as a ghost (No pun intended!), surprisingly sitting erect with a trail of blood seeping out through his left temple. I investigated the floor and noticed the offending gun had dropped to the left of his seat, and smelt the still-strong residue of a gunshot.

'Clear case of suicide,' I heard my master mumble, and a shout of, 'Leave it,' as I tried to get a closer look at the gun.

I put my head in the air and sniffed loudly in protest and then had a further look around the room. The one window appeared to be closed, and upon closer inspection also appeared to be locked, the presumption of which was rapidly confirmed by my master attempting to open it. I then wandered over to the fireplace that housed a glowing fire and I quickly deduced that any possible assailant could not possibly have entered or left by the narrow smoke-filled chimney. The fire appeared to have been made up quite recently since it was still aglow with amber coal, a large log and what appeared to be some scorched hair underneath.

My master seemed to be following me, since I looked around to find him approaching the fireplace, where he gave it a perfunctory glance, sniffed as loudly as I had done a few minutes previously, and pronounced, 'Suicide, no doubt, the room was locked, let's go and speak to the daughter.'

A few minutes later we were walking into the sitting room. Ding-Dong was slumped awkwardly in an armchair opposite the sniffling girl and an unlit fireplace.

'Miss Edwards, I know this is not an ideal time, but I really need to ask you a few quick questions,' my master pronounced with a fake schoolmasterly authority.

The girl sniffed meekly and barely nodded her head.

'Constable Bell, make your way to the scene and await the doctor,' my master almost barked.

Ding-Dong jumped as if stung by a bee. I had the impression he was more than keen to escape his childminding duties, but this was tempered by the prospect of minding a dead body.

My master waited silently for Ding-Dong to leave the room and close the door, which he did rather more forcefully than was necessary. My master then sat down in the armchair opposite the girl and I followed by lying down next to his chair. The girl afforded me a smile of some sort and I reciprocated with a sniff and a sneer.

'Miss Edwards, I know you are dreadfully upset,' my master began with his most caring, but perhaps not very convincing, manner, 'but I really do need you to clarify what occurred here tonight.'

The girl began to sob in response, and I yawned loudly. 'The Poacher found my father dead in his room,' she managed to babble pitifully.

Nothing like stating the bloody obvious!

My master gave her a look of what could only be determined to be fake sympathy. 'Let us start at the beginning, Miss Edwards. I understand you had been out most of the early evening.'

There was a short silence as the girl appeared to be gathering herself. 'I, I had been at a friend's house for a while,' she then managed to splutter. 'Norma Jenkins. I always go round to hers on Tuesdays,' she added meekly and almost apologetically.

My master made a sort of sympathetic noise and then said, 'What time did you arrive home, Miss Edwards?'

The girl appeared to think for a moment. 'It, it must have been, eh, about half past eight, it's the time Daddy insists I get home,' she managed to whisper and then began to sob some more.

'And then what happened?' my master prompted after an appropriate (unnecessary in my view) pause to allow the stupid snivelling to die down.

'I let myself in and noticed my father's study door was closed, which often meant he was busy and did not like to be disturbed, so I went to my bedroom to read,' she began, paused a moment, began to sob a bit more and through the sobs, 'It was then I heard the noise, the, eh, shot.'

My master remained silent and I decided to grunt loudly, mainly out of frustration at the tedious slowness of the progress of the story.

'What did you do then, Miss Edwards?' my master enquired after glancing disapprovingly in my direction.

The girl once again seemed to think for a further amount of time. 'I was not sure if the shot had come from outside, but it did sound very close, and while I was standing thinking about this, I heard a loud banging on the door, and somebody shouting outside.' She glanced at me for a moment for no explicable reason. 'It was The Poacher.'

'And then what happened?' he prompted with a hint of frustration.

'I knocked on Daddy's study door, got no answer and so I went to answer the front door,' she wavered, 'and the Poacher asked what had happened. He sort of mumbled something about hearing a shot from in our house, and then asked where my father was. I said he was in his study, he asked where it was and we ran to the door. He then tried to open it, said it must be locked and then he kicked the door in.'

The girl then broke down with uncontrollable sobs as there were suddenly, as if comically coordinated, loud knocks on the door to the sitting room.

What delicious coordination, I thought!

It was, of course, Dr Gaters, our hopeless medic.

My master left the girl in the (incapab-) able hands of Ding-Dong and then led Gaters to the body. I, of course, followed unobtrusively.

Gaters gasped as he spied the body, and I detected a distinct feeling of unease from the good doctor. He was clearly not used to dealing with dead bodies, although I suspected that he was likely, inadvertently, responsible for quite a few.

'Clearly a suicide, Norman,' my master pronounced with a little less confidence than before, and a hint of a question.

Gaters bent down and proceeded to study the body while my master looked on silently.

I took the opportunity to sniff around, and recognised a faint odour from earlier, that of his Lordship; it certainly seemed to have lingered from their earlier meeting at the Hall.

'Shot through the left temple,' Gaters finally announced the obvious. 'He also has a nasty bump on the back of his head,' he further elucidated, 'and it looks pretty fresh.'

My master moved closer, and investigated the bump, which I also tried to do but his hair obscured any view I may have had from my lowly position.

'How fresh?' my master said, finally finishing his investigation.

Gaters appeared to think for a moment. 'Last few hours, hard to say other than that, may be older,' he finally, less than convincingly, pronounced.

Down to business the next morning

We were once again met by the fat Penguin Ecclestone as the door to the Great Hall was opened. There was a bead of sweat dancing on the butler's fat face as the early morning sun began to up the temperature. My master was met with a badly accomplished smile, while I was met with a well accomplished genuine look of infinite distaste. I glared back, and the beetroot-faced Penguin rapidly looked away.

We were led to the sitting room by the waddling butler and as we entered my master was offered a drink of indeterminate style, which he sensibly declined. My master, uninvited, sat down in a plush armchair and motioned for Ecclestone to sit opposite him. I slumped, uninvited, onto a comfy-looking multi-coloured rug which proved to be as luscious to lie on as it appeared. I noticed the Penguin glower at me, but he refrained from any comment.

My master then, after an uncomfortable silence and the Penguin failing to sit down, gestured once again for Ecclestone to sit down, and eventually with a moment of hesitation and an almost indefinable sign of petulance sat his ample rear down in the almost groaning seat.

'Now, Ecclestone, I need to know what you witnessed last night,' my master quietly announced, which gave me the opportunity to stare unblinkingly at the Penguin in the hope of unsettling him, but unfortunately, he quickly looked away from me again with a hint of disdain.

'Yes, sir,' he replied whilst pinching a quick glance at my continued stare. There was a pause, and I took the opportunity to sniff the air, and almost sneezed at the odious odour emanating from the Penguin; mothballs mixed with sweat and some cheap perfume, if I wasn't mistaken. Not a recipe to be recommended.

Ecclestone shifted his ample backside, I sneezed snot onto the rug, which he ignored, and he then began to narrate the previous evening's events.

Apparently, his Lordship had left for a prior meeting (no details given) that afternoon and had told Ecclestone that he would be back by eight o'clock when he had arranged to meet the now cadaver (No, he didn't say that bit!), Sir Terrance Edwards. When pushed, Ecclestone did not know the reason for the meeting but considered that he had got the impression that it had some importance. When further pushed by my master, he made it clear that he had not asked and that curiosity of any form was not what he was paid for. His Lordship, before leaving, had then instructed Ecclestone to light a fire in the study prior to eight o'clock, and on his arrival, show Sir Terrance into the study and leave him be if he had not arrived home in time. Ecclestone then confirmed that this was not an unusual request as his Lordship often arrived home later than intended and on occasion had objected to Ecclestone 'harassing' his guest while he was absent.

There was then a pause as my master scribbled something down in his notebook.

'So, what happened next?' my master prompted in an attempt to break what had become an embarrassingly long hiatus.

The Penguin appeared irritated by the question and blinked unusually quickly. I remained very still and silent in anticipation of some deliciously gory details.

'That man,' Ecclestone paused with a look of strong distaste (even stronger than his usual reaction to my appearance), 'arrived at about five minutes to eight, and with little fanfare I showed him into the study,' he paused and then spat out somewhat defensively, 'as Lord Marshall-Atwood had specifically requested I should do.'

My master nodded his head and, expressionless, prompted with a firm, 'and…?' (One of his specialities, particularly when he was impatient.)

'Lord Marshall-Atwood arrived about fifteen to twenty minutes later, I am not totally sure, looking a bit flustered and dishevelled, no doubt from rushing to get back on such a mild evening,' Ecclestone almost whispered, and then in a much louder and somewhat annoyed fashion, 'and angrily refused to let me take his coat from him.'

'And then…?' I wanted to prompt, but my master and I remained silent and waited for the Penguin to continue his little tale.

The Penguin shuffled his ample backside once again, cleared his throat and then seemingly less annoyed, continued, 'I offered him a drink, but he refused and said, rather short of breath, that he would go and greet his guest since he had left him waiting for a rather rude period of time.'

The Penguin once again paused and then added, 'Lord Marshall-Atwood was as white as a ghost and I was very concerned about him, but, of course, did as I was asked.'

I wanted to laugh but remained impassive.

My master, who had been noting something down in his notebook, then looked up and prompted, 'Did you follow him to the study, Mr Ecclestone?'

Ecclestone's neck wobbled as he appeared to be attempting to reply, or more likely racking his meagre brain for a recollection. 'No, I was told that I could finish off for the day and that Lord Marshall-Atwood would show that man out when they had finished their business.'

'And then…' my master once again prompted.

'I heard the two men greet each other and then went to my room in the basement, hoping to enjoy a relaxing evening,' the Penguin replied. 'Of course, the sound of a gun firing put an end to any hope of that,' he continued sadly.

'Of course,' my master feigned (I guessed) sympathy, while I just choked back a laugh and then decided to have an unobtrusive sniff around in the hope of finding a scrap or more to devour.

As I sniffed around, my master decided to change tack. 'How did Sir Terrance seem when he came to see Lord Marshall-Atwood?' he enquired.

I pricked up my ears, wondering if my master really was less thick than I had thought.

The Penguin hesitated. 'Hmm, well, not very talkative,' he replied thoughtfully (which was some achievement for such a feeble-minded human). 'To be honest, I wondered if I had offended him in some way.'

I almost choked for (in my opinion) the sight of the Penguin was enough to offend anyone.

'How so?' my master interjected with an admirable straight face.

The Penguin once again hesitated and, unusually for him, had a semi-thoughtful expression. 'Hmm, well, he refused to give me his hat and coat and stamped to the study without wishing to engage or even look at me,' was the affronted reply.

'And this is out of character for Sir Terrance?' my master queried with a hint of irony.

'Yes, most certainly,' without hesitation the Penguin replied, his jowls shimmering with affronted rage. 'He was usually most obliging,' a slight pause and then, 'but of course his behaviour is now, in hindsight, easily explained by what was to come later. He was clearly not of a sound mind.'

'Quite!' my master almost barked. 'There was clearly, for some reason, some animosity between the two men.'

Ecclestone nodded his head and appeared to calm down while I shifted my posture as quietly as was possible. 'Yes, yes,' he replied, 'that is clear in retrospect.'

'Did you hear anything before the gunshot?' my master, voice now calm, enquired almost nonchalantly.

Ecclestone thought for a moment. 'I think I heard raised voices, but I was a good distance away with the door to my room being closed. And with the study door being closed, I cannot say for certain what was occurring.'

My master noted something down in his famous notebook and then with a mumble almost to himself, 'But it would have been likely, wouldn't it?'

'I guess they must have had a disagreement of some kind,' the Penguin mused (nothing like stating the obvious). 'It is all so unfortunate. They were on good terms until the daughter started working here part-time.'

My master ignored the comment and I wondered why. 'I don't suppose you noticed whether Sir Terrance was carrying a gun when he arrived,' he paused, 'or whether he often carried it with him.'

Ecclestone thought for a moment and then spluttered, 'No, no, he was wearing a large checked coat, so he would have likely hidden it inside that if he was carrying it. Well, he must have been carrying it, but I do not ever recall seeing him with a gun in the past. He was very much an anti-hunt, anti-country sports man, if you know what I mean,' his face gradually getting redder and redder with the exertion, 'not a real country gentleman in any way.'

'Yes,' my master replied, 'I saw the same said coat hanging up in the hallway at Sir Terrance's house.' He hesitated and then said quietly to himself while once again writing in his notebook, 'Probably means he meant to shoot Lord Marshall-Atwood when he arrived and was somewhat waylaid by circumstances.'

So, it was likely not a violent response to an argument, likely premeditated. Curious I was really, oh, all right, extremely curious to know why, and I had feeling that I had missed something relevant in the past few minutes. Maybe!

'He always wore it in cold weather,' Ecclestone mumbled, 'the coat, not the gun,' he clarified.

I pricked up my ears, curious. It could hardly have been classed as cold on the night of the shooting. Could it?

My master seemed to ignore the comment once again. 'What did you do when you heard the gunshot, Mr Ecclestone?'

Ecclestone wiped his wet and red blubbery forehead. 'I was reading a book, Agatha Christie's *Murder of Roger Ackroyd* (Too much information, I think!), and stood up with a start.' I doubted that was possible given his size. 'And then rushed (Please!) out of my room towards the study.'

He stopped and I noticed a tear appear from his left eye (what a devoted and misguided fool the Penguin was), and I held back a roar of laughter by sniffing vigorously at the floor.

'I ran as fast as I could,' he continued (I was glad I wasn't there to witness it; it must have been a rare sight to behold), and almost fell into the room as I opened it,' he continued with some undignified and unnecessary spluttering.

He was genuinely upset and despite my distractive sniffing, I could not help smiling broadly.

'Take your time, Mr Ecclestone.' My master attempted to some show concern, but I am not sure it was particularly convincing.

The Penguin took a multitude of deep breaths, wiped his eyes with a miraculously produced blue-and-white checked handkerchief and finally appeared to compose himself.

'What did you see?' my master asked. A deliciously bloody body on the floor, I stopped myself from shouting out, and instead slowly rose to my feet, and began to inconspicuously sniff around the Penguin's feet.

The Penguin hesitated and coughed effeminately. 'The first thing I saw,' he hesitated again furrowing his temple (Surely not thinking!), 'the window was wide open and I felt a breeze coming in,' once again a hesitation, 'and then I looked down and saw Lord Marshall-Atwood lying there on the floor with blood all around him.'

He stopped, took a massive gulp of air, and his face swiftly changed from red to a ghostly white.

I took the opportunity to sniff around a bit more, but to my chagrin found nothing of the edible variety to eat.

Ecclestone suddenly started to converse again and I perked my ears up. 'I smelt cordite, or something like that, and assumed his Lordship must have been shot by the Edwards man,' a slight pause for a further gulp of air, 'I rushed to him, he mumbled something about Edwards and I then rushed to the telephone to call the local doctor, Dr Gatewood.'

My master remained silent, wrote something in his trusty notebook while I slumped down on the floor by his feet, readying myself in anticipation of some delightfully gruesome details.

'I then did as I was asked.' The Penguin broke the silence, hesitated and then stuttered, 'I also called the police,' once again a pause to wipe his sweaty forehead. 'The doctor asked me not to move his Lordship and to just wait with him until he arrived.'

My master nodded his head studiously, thought for a moment and then, 'Did you see Sir Terrance Edwards leave the house, Mr Ecclestone?'

Ecclestone shook his head vigorously, well, as vigorously as was possible for such an obese human creature. 'No, no, no, I did not,' he almost squeaked and then somewhat calming down, 'but I guess he would have fled very quickly after doing what he did to Lord Marshall-Atwood,' he paused, 'and of course I did have quite a long way to run (A joke, surely!) prior to arriving at the study. He would have had plenty of time to flee from his heinous act.'

My master mumbled something in contemplation, 'Yes, it would have given Sir Terrance ample time to escape through the window.' (Surely it would have given him plenty of time to get home, put on his slippers, light his pipe and sit down in his armchair, but of course my master was far too polite to say what I was thinking).

My master then had a long look at his notes while Ecclestone waited rather dejectedly opposite him (I almost felt sorry for him!).

'You are sure it was Sir Terrance Edwards who you showed into the study?' my master finally asked.

Ecclestone hesitated for a moment, I guess, taken aback by the question. 'Yes,' he whispered appearing to choke back a sob, 'yes, of course, I had seen him in that coat and hat many times before, and, of course his beard was unmistakable,' he paused, appeared to think deeply, 'and of course, his deep booming voice is positively unmistakable,' he paused again, now appeared flustered, 'I mean he was unmistakable, an unmistakable figure.'

'I guess he was,' my master replied with a dubiousness that almost impressed me.

'Next stop, Dr Gatewood,' my master announced as we walked back to the car. I sighed and squirmed at the suggestion.

The good doctor's house/surgery was a ten-minute drive away. On arrival we were shown into his office. The doctor's maid tried to stop me following him but severely underestimated my ability to overcome such unwelcoming rudeness.

My master sat opposite the doctor before an elaborate mahogany desk while I unobtrusively crept under the selfsame desk, and slumped silently by my master's feet.

'Now, inspector, I guess you have come for some preliminary conclusions on our two very unfortunate incidents last night.' (He really was an officious oaf).

(Just a point of order at this juncture, but since I was lying under the desk, I can only recount what was being said from hereon; facial expressions and hand gestures are left to your imagination.)

'Shall we dispense with the formality, Norman? No need for the "inspector" business, just call me Clive,' my master replied with a hint of amusement.

'Clive it is,' Gaters (time for me also to dispense with formality) retorted, 'and if we intend dispensing with formality, I think a good drink of Scotch is in order. What do you say, old boy?'

He didn't appear to await a reply as he walked over to, what I guessed, was a drinks cabinet, and from the sound of it poured some whisky into two glasses. I was now regretting my unobtrusive entrance and wondered if it was possible to get a sip at some point.

I heard him walk back to the desk, knees cracking as he sat down, and then I heard the clinking of glasses and a mutual, 'Cheers, old boy.'

'Let us start with the live one,' Gaters almost chuckled.

'And is he likely to remain that way?' my master countered.

'Oh yes,' Gaters replied, before taking a noisy gulp from his glass, 'his Lordship will likely be back on his feet within the week.' He took another gulp. 'He was shot in the left shoulder, not nice, but he should have no problem returning to good health, and being right-handed, the injury shouldn't inconvenience him too much.'

'Good, good,' my master replied. 'He was very likely a lucky man to escape so lightly.'

'Couldn't agree more. He was shot from very close quarters, and was very fortunate that the assailant failed to get a more telling shot at him. I guess he put up a fight, and scared the criminal into rushing his assault, or something like that anyway.'

It sounded pure speculation and my master failed to respond to it.

'How about the dead one?' my master asked.

'Shot through the left temple, close range, typical suicide,' Gaters replied, before gulping at his drink and smacking his lips in satisfaction. (And I thought I was the heartless one!). 'Looks as if it was the same gun used in shooting his Lordship, but we had better wait for confirmation before jumping to any conclusions.'

'Thought that might be the case,' replied my master. 'Must have thought he had killed his Lordship and preferred a quick death to waiting for the fuss of a trial and the noose.'

I stayed under the desk, but felt a tinge of confusion, wondering about left and right, things being the wrong way round and not knowing why, but for once it was not about food, although my stomach felt as if it was about to emit a massive rumble, which would do little to help my attempt at unobtrusiveness.

'Any idea why Edwards did it?' Gaters stupidly asked.

'Good question,' my master whispered. 'We shall have to see if his Lordship can shine some light on the proceedings when he is up to it.'

I somehow doubted it but remained silent.

After the two old chums had shared a second glass of Scotch, we made our way back to the police station. I remained much too thoughtful to think about food, and my master appeared to find it difficult to concentrate on his driving, which nearly resulted in him crashing into the rusty gatepost at the entrance to his place of employment.

As we entered the station, Ding-Dong greeted us, well, to be totally precise, he greeted my master.

'Sir, as asked, I have spoken once again to the daughter girl,' he almost screamed at my master as we walked towards his office.

'Not out here, Constable Bell,' my master snapped, 'and it is Miss Edwards,' he admonished.

I smirked and delightedly trailed in the wake of my master's displeasure.

'Yes, ye—' Ding-Dong spluttered, but was interrupted by my master.

'Come into my office, constable. I would rather like to sit down and talk, if you don't mind.'

Ding-Dong nodded his head in reluctant supplication and shuffled behind us into the room. 'Close the door,' my master instructed, 'and sit down for God's sake, man.'

I took up residence in the corner of the room, with a smug smile of satisfaction at Ding-Dong's discomfort at having to bear the brunt of my master's displeasure.

My master sat down with a groan. 'Yes, constable,' he snapped pulling his trusty notebook from his jacket pocket, 'what of relevance did you discover from Miss Edwards that necessitated you ambushing me as soon as I stepped foot in the station?'

Ding-Dong hesitated, no doubt due to my master's apparent bad mood, and I was sure that he had difficulty recognising the concept of relevance or even understanding the word. 'She could add little to what she told us last night,' he began to explain, while in an attempt to derail the fool, I emitted a loud yawn. 'She was clearly still upset' (What a surprise!).

I glanced at my master who admirably didn't completely lose his temper but instead snapped, 'And, constable, what else? What necessitated such urgency?'

Ding-Dong shifted his great bottom in the chair and then said meekly, 'There was a small thing that she said was puzzling her,' he paused almost for effect, 'she said that she was surprised that her father had not locked the front door, which was almost an obsession that he had. She said he had recently been very security-conscious, well, something of the sort anyway.'

'But he did put the key in the door as he entered,' my master said, now with a much milder mannered interjection, while writing in his notebook and asking, 'anything else, Constable Bell?' without looking up.

Ding-Dong appeared to think for a moment (which was not a usual or familiar occurrence). 'She said she thought Lord Marshall-Atwood had been rather annoyed at her father a few days ago.'

There was a long silence, during which Ding-Dong looked everywhere but in my master's direction or in mine, while my master slowly nodded his head in deep thought.

Finally breaking the silence, my master asked, 'And what do you surmise from what Miss Edwards told you, constable?'

Ding-Dong appeared shocked that he should be asked to come to any semblance of a conclusion, and I decided to get up and sniff around his legs to add to his clear discomfort.

'Well, thinking about it,' (that would be a first) he began, while discreetly pushing at me with his right leg in a failed attempt to get me to move, 'I guess he could easily have forgotten to lock the door, considering his state of mind,' he continued to doubtfully offer.

'But he did think to place the key in the door after he had entered the house,' my master mused.

There was a moment of mutual silent thought, which was suddenly crushingly broken by the uncouth voice of Constable (less than) Abel, and a loud knocking and opening of the door. Abel slumped in and crashed down in the chair next to Ding-Dong. My master, used to such behaviour, looked on calmly, while I emitted a yawn of disapproval.

'You have something to report, Abel?' my master asked, while staring intensely at the scratchings he had written in his notebook. I suspected he was still puzzled by the key in the door, as was I, well, just for a moment anyway.

Abel, being a slob, released a loud alcohol-soaked belch. 'I spoke to a fair few of the villagers,' he began and, after an unnecessary dramatic pause, 'with very little success, I am afraid, sir.'

He then broke out into a broad smile, and before my master could respond, 'Until I ran into old Jack Broadstairs in the pub.'

He paused once again, and almost seemed to wait until my master was once again ready to speak, and then said, 'After a great deal of rambling, the old man claimed that last night he saw Lord Marshall-Atwood's car parked in a quiet lane not very far from Sir Terrance Edwards' house.' He hesitated, and after awaiting a non-existent response, added, 'He said it was about quarter past eight.'

'Interesting,' my master responded (very, I thought, if true of course), 'but how reliable is such a statement, considering it is Broadstairs, and it was dark at the time and he is as blind as a bat at the best of times?'

Abel shook his head with vigour. 'The old boy is, I must say, a bit short-sighted, but he does surprisingly have his wits about him, you know.'

'And it clearly makes no sense if we are to believe what Lord Marshall-Atwood has told us,' my master added.

'Any evidence from old Jack should be taken with a pinch of salt,' Ding-Dong suddenly interjected, 'lost his marbles a long while ago, if you ask me.'

I truly thought the oaf had fallen asleep, wished he had, and seriously wanted to bite his ankles in frustration.

My master scrawled something in his notebook. 'Did anyone you spoke to have a theory as to the motive?' he said, clearly ignoring Ding-Dong's comment and putting to an end the discussions about the Broadstairs' possible revelation. I was more inclined to not ignore Ding-Dong, but to, as usual and sensibly, take the opposite viewpoint on almost everything he said or concluded.

'Not a thing,' Abel replied, 'not an inkling.'

'I always thought they were good friends,' Ding-Dong once again interposed pointlessly.

'Appears not,' my master replied thoughtfully.

'There was a rumour I heard a few years back,' Abel suddenly added, his cheeks then reddening.

I pricked up my ears. (I love rumours, true or false, who cares!)

He didn't continue and my master prompted with irritation, 'Yes, Abel, do tell us your rumour!'

'Well,' Abel hesitated, and suddenly appeared uncomfortable.

I pricked up my ears even higher.

'This comes from a past lady friend of mine, so I can't be completely sure how true it may be,' he continued with even greater hesitancy, 'but, well…' I almost shouted at him to spit it out, '… she claimed that Lord Marshall-Atwood's wife visited Sir Terrance Edwards at his house a good many times and stayed for some time after the death of Mrs Edwards.'

Abel clearly appeared to intend the word 'visited' to mean something else, but I could not be sure if my imagination was running ahead of reality. 'This was of course before she had her terrible accident,' he pointlessly continued (I think it was clear to us, even Ding-Dong, that a dead woman could hardly visit somebody).

My master appeared to contemplate for a moment, and then addressed the room. 'Do you think there is any truth in this, Abel? And if so, whether they were purely innocent visits. Sir

Terrance Edwards had after all recently lost his wife and was likely in need of company and comfort from a friend.'

A daft question, but one that would need an answer at some point. 'It might be useful if I had a word with your lady friend,' he continued.

Abel smirked. 'That would be somewhat difficult, sir. She died last year!'

My master did not respond, but instead looked puzzled.

'The visits were just after Sir Terrance's wife had died, so were likely to be an act of kindness.' A moment of sense from Abel surprised the room, and I almost threw up on the rug.

'You are likely right,' my master finally responded. 'I think we need to ask Lord Marshall-Atwood what the argument was about, once he is well enough to talk to me of course, but it does look as if this is just a very tragic incident.' He hesitated, 'But it is important to make sure we have checked everything that needs checking before coming to a definitive conclusion. The likelihood is that it is an attempted murder and suicide, but you know me, I like to tie up all the loose ends and threads.'

There were nods of assent from the two constables (although they both looked worried that it might mean them having to do more work than they wished, or any work at all to be honest), and an enthusiastic sniff and yawn of agreement from me.

'Now, Constable Abel, did you speak to the Poacher?' my master enquired, I guess, already knowing the negative answer.

Abel smiled. 'Gave him a knock but no answer,' he somewhat dubiously replied. 'Bloody dog of his was kicking up a right fuss inside the house as well,' he added with a blank look on his face.

My master smirked and shook his head in resignation. 'Go back, Abel, and take Bell with you in case there is a problem. It is not like the Poacher to go out without that dog of his trailing in his wake.'

'Sir,' they echoed in unison. It was highly likely there would be a stop off at the pub on the way, from the look of delight on their faces.

I just sneered at the fools, and felt for the Poacher's dog. It must be just murder.

Down to Business in the Late Afternoon

The two fools returned to the station mid-afternoon. They were sucking mints to, no doubt, mask the smell of alcohol and seemed far too merry for a state of sobriety.

My master had spent most of the afternoon staring at the ceiling in his thinking mood, while I had been catching up on some much-needed shut-eye. I was woken by the crash of the station front door, and then an overexcited knocking on my master's office door.

My master hesitated before pronouncing, 'Come in,' and then he straightened up, and made out to be busy with the few pieces of paperwork on his desk. I just stayed lying down, and didn't bother to acknowledge the fools as they entered.

'Sir,' Bell almost shouted with a minor slur, 'we went around to see if we could speak to the Poacher but still got no reply.'

They were both standing just inside the door, giggling, and both looking somewhat sheepish.

'The dog was barking loudly, but the doors were all locked and the curtains closed,' Abel continued.

My master hesitated for a moment, and I wondered if he was going to ask them why it took them over three hours to visit a house which was a five-minute meandering walk away from the police station, but on this occasion, he seemed far too preoccupied to take the disciplinarian route.

'We need to break down the door,' Bell broke the silence, 'that dog sounded in deep distress.'

Too right you fucking do, I thought, and then barked and cried loudly.

Ten minutes later, my master and Ding-Dong arrived at the front door to the Poacher's house, and, as anticipated and forewarned, the noise from the dog was deafening and heart-breaking. My master duly ordered Bell to break down the door, which he did after three pathetically weak attempts, and then, predictably, the act was followed by a moan about the pain in his shoulder.

As the door was opened, the stink of dog pooh viciously invaded our noses and was followed by the dog fleeing at great speed from the house. My master glanced at Bell, and then led the way, seemingly oblivious to the smell. I followed, leaving Bell to hesitate about whether to pursue my master or the dog. He decided on the former.

The house was a mess, and not just due to the actions of the dog, housework was clearly not a priority for the Poacher at the best of times. I wandered off as my master poked his head into the ramshackle kitchen. I found the door to what I guessed was the sitting room, not much of a guess since it was a two-up two-down. I sniffed at the half-open door and sensed the unmistaken odour of death. Two in two days and a partial; it was getting out of hand, or should I say, more and more fun!

As I waited expectantly, Bell blundered down the hallway, yanked the door fully open, and then promptly, with a high-pitched cry, fled before entering the room. He then, with a few missteps, comically collapsed, like a dynamited chimney, to the floor. I trotted into the room and smelt the wonderfully familiar smell of blood. I walked around a tin bath which appeared to be full of now cold cloudy water and then went to investigate the body which was slumped on the filthy stinky sofa. There was a profusion of blood, which had seemingly emanated from the man's stomach, and had soaked the sofa and some of the carpet beneath it. It was the Poacher. His face was almost a caricature of torture and his trousers were strangely half-pulled down; he had been getting ready for his bath, I guessed. His shiny new-looking (which was a surprise) belt seemed to be pulled halfway from his trousers, while his shoes were lying on the floor next to the chair. It was almost as if he had decided to kill himself after firstly starting to undress for his bath. It really didn't seem to make much sense. Then what ever did in this godforsaken village full of idiots?

'Leave,' my master shouted at me, I thought, rather too loudly and unnecessarily, as I heard Bell groaning and gagging in the hallway. The oaf was certainly a liability in more ways than one.

Anyway, I made a pretence of 'leaving' and then surreptitiously resumed looking and sniffing around the tiny box of a room. Like the Poacher, the room was dusty. There was no smell of any other recent intruder, but there was the odour of rotting fruit whose source quickly showed itself to be a bowl of apples and bananas placed on a small table in the corner of the room. I noted that the window was stuck fast, and had probably not been opened in a short lifetime. No way in and no way out, so my master and his hopeless gang were bound to, probably incorrectly (Who knows?), conclude it was suicide.

There was very little else to see or do, so I wandered outside and sat in the diminishing sun for a while, fell asleep, and joyously dreamed of a strangled family and a fresh bowl of fruit soaked in blood.

Thirty minutes later and the esteemed Dr Gatewood was once again surveying a dead body. The fool Bell had been dismissed with the instruction to 'pull himself together' and to 'bloody catch the Poacher's dog', while my master had been looking around the house, leaving me to do a bit of further investigation and sniffing around.

'Stabbed in the stomach,' Gaters pronounced to nobody's surprise. 'Rather a thin knife but very deadly,' he continued in a desperate attempt to sound as if he knew what he was talking about, and, of course, the knife had been found in plain sight at the feet of the filthy victim.

My master mumbled something that I didn't catch and then, 'Could he have done it to himself?'

Gaters thought for a moment, a deep frown appearing on his large forehead. 'Possible, I suppose, but a damned funny way to kill yourself, if you ask me.' (Which he had!)

'The door was locked with a key on the inside, as were the windows,' my master pronounced. 'The only explanation, as far as I can see, is suicide.'

Gaters nodded his head. 'So it seems, so it appears, but bally strange though.'

I shook my head and daydreamed all things bananas, rooms and specifically the colour yellow, and wondered if Bell could have been responsible. Surely not!

A while later, my master drove back to the station deep in thought, no doubt wondering why the Poacher should want to kill himself in such a bizarre way, and why we should have two suicides in two days. Although I, for one, doubted this was the case. The case was certainly becoming more and more cryptic, but the clues were mounting up, for you and me anyway.

Into the Next Day

The next morning was one of great anticipation, since my master had been informed that his mighty Lordship would be able to speak to him. This resulted in an uplifting of the general mood amongst the happy team of total incompetents, while I couldn't stop wondering why Sir Terrance Edwards would want to kill his Lordship.

Such prolepsis and jollity were short-lived however for, as we entered the police station, we were met by the sight of a large ornate green hat under which sat the not-so-delightful, scowling Miss Hemmingway.

When we were nicely and comfortably ensconced in my master's office, he asked Miss Hemmingway how he could help her. I wondered whether the large bald man had made a reappearance, but unfortunately if he had, he had failed to take her away.

She clutched her handbag, as was her want. 'Before I tell you what I saw two nights ago,' she began with more than a hint of anger, 'have you found that man who so rudely invaded my garden and scared me witless?'

And with that she stared at my master with disturbingly pouted purple lips and rapidly blinking eyes.

My master shuffled some papers in front of him. 'We are still looking, Miss Hemmingway, still putting in the hard work to hunt down your intruder,' he lied with admirable acumen.

She breathed in heavily and started to sniff loudly and rapidly. 'Well, you really do need to work a lot harder, sir, or I will be forced take the issue to a higher authority than yourself,' she stuttered and growled. 'It really is not safe while that strange large man, who could do any number of things to a helpless old woman like me, is wandering around our village. Do you not agree, inspector? Do you not agree?'

I would have arrested her for wasting police time, but unfortunately my master has infinitely more patience than I do, and knows, for some unknown reason, that Miss Hemmingway inexplicably has the ear of his superiors.

'Yes, yes, we will put in some extra effort,' my master replied nonchalantly. And with a continued remarkable degree of tolerance, 'Now, what else can I help you with, Miss Hemmingway? You said there was something else bothering you?'

I stifled a yawn, and then didn't stifle a yawn, which drew the attention of Miss Hemmingway, who gave me a stare of pure death. She then, with a grimace and grunt, looked back at my master.

'What I saw two nights ago,' she paused, huffed, blinked, 'the night that horrible, and I thought he was nice as well, man, shot Lord Marshall-Atwood. Poor, poor man. Horrible, horrible, horrible.'

She then turned her attention back to me and stared at me with a look of utter disdain. I just ignored her, feigned a deep sleep and stuck out my tongue as she finally looked away.

'Yes,' my master prompted, 'do please tell me what you saw Miss Hemmingway.'

I opened one eye, and thankfully noted that she continued to no longer stare at me, and then closed my eye again.

'I saw that killer man!' she said and clung to her handbag, shook, and grimaced. 'Edwards, that Edwards man who shot our dear Lord of the Manor,' she continued with a disturbing slowness. 'I saw him the night he did it. I saw him.'

'You did?' my master once again prompted while, suddenly, and inexplicably enthusiastically opening his notebook and grabbing hold of his pencil.

Miss Hemmingway nodded vigorously. 'I saw the Edwards man, the evil man,' she repeated. 'I saw him. I did.'

'And what did you see?' my master once again prompted, but with a touch of impatience.

She looked reluctant to continue, and to be honest I wished she wouldn't. 'You will think this unbelievable!' she almost shouted while throwing her hands into the air. 'I really couldn't believe it myself!'

'No, no, do continue, Miss Hemmingway,' my master replied with admirable tact. 'Of course, I will believe what you have to say. It may well be very important to our investigations.'

I really had to admire him. Although he was not the smartest person in the room, he certainly knew how to elicit information from total idiots.

'He, he…' she stopped, swallowed noisily and clutched her handbag, 'he was driving Lord Marshall-Atwood's car past my cottage.' (I had to hand it to her; she was supremely topical with her insane little ditties).

'What time was this?' asked my master while writing something in his notebook. To his credit, he seemed to be taking it seriously, and lord knows how he kept a straight face.

Hey, ho, maybe he was right too, who knows how he deleted relevance.

Miss Hemmingway screwed up her face. 'It was,' she then paused, and paused, and paused.

'Yes, do go on,' my master again prompted while I feigned a sleeping cry, yelp and bark.

She manically glanced in my direction and then swiftly looked back at my master. 'Eight o'clock, or a little after, or maybe a little before,' she replied dubiously. (Just when Sir Terrance was in his Lordship's study. Crazy!?) 'It may have been a little earlier or later. My watch is not always very reliable.' (Or never! Who knows? And nor is she! Or is she? Who knows?).

My master appeared to play with his pencil, and there ensued a hiatus during which he fiddled and Miss Hemmingway quietly clutched her handbag strenuously. I just shook my head, and wished my master would dismiss the crazy timewaster (Or was she?).

'Are you sure this is what you really saw, Miss Hemmingway? Could it not have been Lord Marshall Atwood driving his car?' my master finally quietly broke the silence. 'Or could you have been mistaken? Could it have been somebody else in a different car? Could it have been a different day?'

Miss Hemmingway looked offended and pouted her lips in more than apparent disapproval at my master doubting her.

'It would have been dark at the time,' my master persisted. 'It would have been easy to be mistaken.'

She spluttered and sniffed rapidly, and then leaned forward in her chair, and with a disturbing degree of anger, said, 'Do you not believe me, sir! Do you not believe me!'

I jumped, almost pissed myself and with utmost stealth crawled under my master's seat.

'If this is the case, if you think I am mistaken, or even lying, I will be forced to speak to your superior,' she yelled, 'and report your utter,' she paused, 'utter, utter, utter incompetence, sir.' (Maybe she had a small point on this occasion! Who knows?)

I crawled into a tight ball, closed my eyes, gritted my teeth and wished the conflict would disappear.

'Firstly, you fail to catch a very scary and dangerous large man sculking in my lovely cottage garden, and now you disbelieve me when I try to assist your enquiries into a very, very serious crime against our Lord of the Manor!' Her voice was getting louder and scarier by the second and I rolled up into a tight ball and clenched my teeth.

I heard the sound of a chair scraping against the floor, some twinkling footsteps, and then the door to the office opening and slamming loudly closed. I heard my master lightly cough or laugh, heard the sound of his pencil scratching against his notebook, and I decided to remain curled in a ball until I deemed it safe to move, and to think deeply about what we had just heard. (Was she really as mad as we all thought? Who knows?)

I slept fitfully for most of the rest of the morning, and as far as I could make out, my master sat staring into space (He often does that when he has a case to think about and is hopelessly out of his depth.). However, as noon approached, he suddenly pushed back his chair, giving my ribs a painful nudge, and then prompted me to follow him (No apology!) to his car, and we set off to who knows where. I yawned and fell straight back asleep on the back seat.

After five or so minutes (I think), we arrived at a dilapidated old workers' cottage, the home of the infamous Old Jack Broadstairs. My master parked his car outside, and prompted me to follow him through a creaking rusty gate that was almost falling from its hinges. He stepped gingerly along the weed-infested pathway, and then knocked vigorously on the battered wooden door for what seemed to be an age, but in reality, was probably only a minute or two. The door was finally slowly opened to reveal a stick-thin bald-headed old man, Jack Broadstairs himself. He wore a filthy grey three-piece suit, a white-grey frayed-at-the-collar shirt and stank to high heaven of sweat, sour milk and alcohol.

The old man squinted in the sunlight while I suppressed a gag from the smell emanating from inside the cottage. Cats' pooh and piss, if I was not mistaken.

'Mr Broadstairs,' my master officiated, 'I am Detective Inspector Lewis, and I wonder if I might have a quick word with you.'

I was amazed that he appeared not to be in the least fazed by the smell.

'Mn, Mn,' I think the old man mumbled as he continued to squint, 'knows who you are. Comes down in.'

My heart sank at the thought of entering such a squalid stinking wreck of a house, but my curiosity only just trumped my disgust. I followed my master into the two-up two-down shambles behind the limping old man.

We followed Broadstairs into a small room, within which the only furniture appeared to be two ancient dust- and dirt-covered armchairs that I guessed had once been red, with the rest of the room covered with newspapers, empty boxes, cats and their excrement. I was tempted to have a taste of the pooh, but that was even beyond my prodigious, less than choosy, appetite. As we entered the room, the cats scattered and fled for their lives, I guessed it was due to me, but it may well have been my master's imposing figure.

The old man slumped into one of the excuses for armchairs with a loud groan and a twang from the chair (or it could have been his back). He then motioned for my master to take a seat in the other one. I decided the best course of action was to remain standing, and to watch carefully where I placed my feet. And to his credit, or was it stupidity, my master watched carefully where he stepped and sat down doubtfully in the second creaking armchair.

My master took from his jacket pocket his trusty notebook. 'I understand you spoke to Constable Abel yesterday,' he began while sitting forward in the chair, clearly in an attempt to prevent any unnecessary accidental contact with the back of it.

'Mn, Mn,' the old man responded.

'Constable Abel said that you told him that you saw a car parked by Sir Terrance Edwards' place, Old Moss House, on the night that he died,' my master continued with admirable patience and a badly disguised hint of 'going through the motions'.

I sniffed the foul air and almost choked, and then feigned chase as one of the mangy cats briefly contemplated re-entering the room. It stared at me, squealed and then fled as if its tail was on fire.

'Mn, Mn,' the old man once again responded.

It was like pulling teeth, not that he had any, as far as I could see.

My master scribbled something in his notebook, I couldn't imagine what, probably 'Mn, Mn or God help me'.

'Constable Abel said that you were able to identify the car,' my master continued with a good-natured and patient prompt.

The old man squinted myopically. '"Is Lordship,' emanated from his thin chapped lips. Well, I think it is what he said, but to be honest, who knows or cares?

'You are absolutely sure?' my master countered dubiously.

I was not sure the poorly sighted old man could actually see my master sitting opposite him, but, as always, I remained open-minded and tolerant!

The old man slowly inclined his head. 'Mn, Mn, knows that car well enough, and seens it parked in lanes before,' he continued, before dribbling from his toothless mouth. 'Usesed to cleans it years ago.' The dribble descended down his chin and he wiped it with the back of his filthy hand leaving a brown smear on the side of his unshaven face.

'And this was most definitely close to Old Moss House?' my master persisted, while scribbling in his notebook.

'Mn, Mn,' the old man mumbled, 'byse entrance to big old meadow.'

'At what time would this have been Mr Broadstairs?' my master enquired.

The old man seemed to contemplate the question for a long while, wiped his chin once again, and appeared to study the resultant slime on his sleeve. 'Eight ten, probly, fiftin latest would be.'

'You are certain?' my master persisted.

The old man once again seemed to contemplate his answer. 'Mn, Mn, constable, as cans be ats me age an all.'

We next stopped off at Old Moss House. The stupid girl was staying with a family friend or something of that sort, so we had the run of the house to ourselves. My master spent a good deal of time studying the scene of death, paying particular attention to the door and the carpet, and then trekked around the rest of the house while I took up the time searching for a morsel of food with, unfortunately, no success.

After this we went for a drive through the village, with my master dangerously slowing down as we passed the abode of Miss Hemmingway, but thankfully we did not see her. We then headed for the hospital, which was approximately five miles away from the village to visit milord himself.

His Lordship was sitting up in bed as we entered the hospital room. The room was large, clearly the best available, and was decked out with an assortment of flowers and a bowl of fresh fruit. I could not guess for a moment who would bother to provide such luxury but assumed there were plenty of sycophants all too ready to curry favour with the local royalty. We were shown in by a dragon of a nurse, who unsuccessfully and annoyingly failed to block my passage as I crept past her ample-sized legs.

His Lordship acknowledged my master with an almost imperceptive incline of his head as my master sat down next to the bed. I, in the meantime, unobtrusively lay down by my master's feet and sniffed the familiar odour of the patient, the whiff of death unfortunately no longer simpering through.

His Lordship was as white as a sheet, and impossibly appeared to have diminished greatly in stature.

'Take a seat Lewis,' his Lordship demurred, a bit late in the circumstances, but I am sure it helped maintain his self-importance, which had clearly been diminished by the present circumstances.

'Of course,' my master replied from his seated position. I sniffed loudly instead of laughing inappropriately and couldn't help admiring him.

There then followed an uncomfortable silence as my master retrieved his notebook and pencil from his jacket pocket. I sniffed around under the bed but found nothing of culinary interest.

'How are you feeling, sir?' my master asked, showing a surprising hint of concern. I really could not help groaning, and adjusted my position on the floor as I did so.

His Lordship winced as he also adjusted his position in bed. 'As well as can be expected, Lewis, as well as can be expected under the trying circumstances.'

My master acknowledged the reply with a less than interested, 'good' and then, 'Are you up to a few questions, sir?'

His Lordship winced once again as he sat up a bit straighter, emitted a seemingly manufactured smile and nodded. 'Let's see how it goes, Lewis, shall we? Cannot guarantee anything, but I will try my best.'

'Could we start with what happened two days ago,' my master began dubiously. 'Why were you late for your appointment with Mr Edwards?'

His Lordship hesitated, seemingly puzzled that this should be the opening question. 'Late? What do you mean, Lewis? What do you mean "late"?'

My master cleared his throat and swallowed hard. 'Late for your arranged meeting with Sir Terrance Edwards, sir. What else could I mean, sir?'

His Lordship's sheet-white fat face jiggled with what appeared to be uncontrolled anger at the mention of his assailant, and then, as if by magic, his face emitted a sly grin. 'Let me explain,' he began pompously, 'I had a meeting with an old golf club chum about ten miles away,' he paused, and appeared to wince from the effort, 'and on the way back, my car hit an object on the road which punctured a tyre.' He once again stopped and breathed in heavily. 'It took me a while to change it, wheel nut a hell of a problem, I'm afraid. Bloody inconvenient and nobody around to assist. Bloody nuisance.'

'Most unfortunate,' my master quietly mumbled, with what I suspected was a hint of sarcasm and possible disbelief, while writing in his notebook, 'but how did you know you would be late before you set off to your game of golf and subsequent meeting, sir?'

His Lordship looked surprised at the question (I was just as surprised but also full of admiration at his willingness to challenge the pompous oaf), and for a fleeting moment appeared flustered. 'I didn't Lewis,' he finally responded with a hint of annoyance. 'What do you mean, what are you inferring, man? Spit it out do.'

My master smiled, and without looking up from his notebook, said, 'Mr Ecclestone told me that you gave him instructions to show Sir Terrance into your study if you were late back.' He appeared to read from the notebook while explaining, 'Mr Ecclestone was very clear on this point, very clear indeed. It sounded to me as if you had a feeling you might be late.'

His Lordship chuckled, and then released a hesitant cough. 'Just in case,' he replied with another wince, 'Ecclestone is very efficient, Lewis, but he does need clear instructions on occasions.' And the smug smile had returned.

'But what made you think you might be late?' my master persisted, 'It's not something I would consider.'

His Lordship started and then issued a further smug smile, 'Maybe you should, Lewis. The nineteenth hole, Lewis, can often encourage tardiness in the best of timekeepers.'

My master acknowledged this with a nod of his head and a barely discernible smile.

'Where did you get the puncture, which road, sir?' my master asked.

His Lordship appeared to think for a moment. 'About halfway home, Lewis, most dashed inconvenient, out in the heart of the countryside, not a damned soul around and not my forte car mechanics, I am afraid. Well, to be honest, I can do it but prefer to leave it to somebody else, if you know what I mean. I'm somewhat used to having menial jobs done for me, hey.'

My master inclined his head and wrote something in his notebook, and then without looking up, 'Then you didn't stop near Sir Terrance Edwards' house on that night, sir?'

His Lordship appeared taken aback, and then emitted a laugh, which induced another wince of pain. 'No Lewis, it was definitely halfway home, a good five miles away. And why would I stop by that man's house when I had a meeting arranged with him at my place? That would make no sense at all, man.'

My master once again seemingly ignoring the answer. 'Why were you meeting Sir Terrance Edwards, sir?'

His Lordship appeared to think for a moment.

'To discuss when he was to pay back the money he owed me,' his Lordship replied instantly. 'The bounder reneged on our agreement and I intended to ask for the money back pronto.'

His previously white face had now gained some colour and his fat jowls wobbled with indignation.

My master appeared to ignore the answer. 'And why did he shoot you?' he asked.

His Lordship shifted in his bed and winced again from the effort. 'I was insisting on having my money back, Lewis. Edwards was clearly unable to pay and thought killing me would solve the problem. Seems clear to me and should to you.'

'How much did he owe you? It seems an over-the-top reaction from someone who was considered a reasonable man,' my master replied.

His Lordship's face turned a bright purple and his fat cheeks shook uncontrollably. 'None of your damned business, Lewis,' he hesitated and then firmly continued. 'I should like to rest now. Kindly leave me in peace and go and do your job,' he snapped loudly.

My master appeared not to notice the angry tone. 'I will need a written statement at some point,' he explained calmly while casually getting up from his seat.

'Not now,' his Lordship snapped, 'maybe never, I don't see the bloody point, inspector.'

I crept out of the room while my master strolled out with his head held high, and sporting a grin and a very puzzled look on his face.

Discovering Some Forensic Details (well, sort of)

The next day I followed my master to the surgery from which the learned Dr Gatewood plied his trade, as such. It was foul weather, with the rain spearing down as if the heavens were flooded. My master drove the three or so miles with great caution, and I curled up shivering from the unseasonal cold while trying to close my ears to the deafening noise of the rain bombarding the roof of the car. In the end, I was somewhat relieved to get out and escape for the warmth and dryness of our destination.

The door, when we arrived, was hesitantly opened by an elderly lady, the ever-present (I mean she was rumoured to have served as secretary for numerous previous doctors over an infinite period of time) Miss Crace. She welcomed my master with the greatest of decorum, and sneered in my direction as I entered uninvited and trailed muddy splodges over the floor and carpet.

We were led through an empty waiting room (I wasn't surprised, Gaters was the last person I would seek medical help from) and after a mumbled acknowledgement of the tap on the door, we were shown into a disturbingly plush room. Gaters was sitting behind an ornate mahogany table, and appeared to be reading from a large book placed in front of him.

'Thank you, Miss Crace,' Gaters mumbled officiously and without looking up from the extensive tome.

The secretary nodded her grey head in no particular direction, and then slowly, well, laboriously, crept out of the room, and gently closed the door behind her (and no doubt stayed behind it with her ear to the keyhole. I only wished I could open the door and catch her out).

'Take a seat, Clive,' Gaters addressed my master, and I just lay down uninvited.

'Cheers,' my master oddly replied, as he creakingly lowered himself into the chair opposite the doctor.

There followed the usual human nonsense of asking how each other how we were, whether a drink would be appropriate, and a general moan about the weather. I just yawned and patiently awaited the juicy information on the deaths and the (unfortunately) near death.

'Let's start with Lord Marshall-Atwood, shall we?' Gaters pronounced (let's not, I thought). 'As I said the other day, he was pretty lucky that his assailant was a poor shot. The bullet went through the shoulder, and luckily (here we go again) caused very little damage. He will in all likelihood make a full recovery. I'm pretty sure of that.'

'Thank heaven for that,' my master said, 'And it was the same gun that Sir Terrance Edwards shot himself with?' my master prompted.

I thought of the Poacher's dog and I winced and wanted to let out really detailed details in determination in truth, but kept quiet. (Did that make sense? It certainly did if you read it the correct way, I think!).

'Yes, it was, and his Lordship was shot at very close quarters, which probably means that he charged his assailant in an attempt to arrest the gun from him,' the doctor replied with a disturbing amount of misplaced confidence.

My master remained silent, and looked rather more thoughtful and studious than I usually gave him credit for.

'Now for the first suicide,' Gaters continued. 'The same gun as we have already said and he shot himself through the left temple, gun once again at very close range but almost certainly held right next to the skin when the shot was fired.'

My master kind of held up his hand, almost as if asking for permission to speak. 'You mentioned the other day that there was a bump on his head.'

Gaters paused for a moment. 'Yes, that's right, quite a knock as it happens and quite fresh, I suspect he may have bumped his head when leaving the window in the Hall, but of course that's only a guess.' (Yep, it was!).

My master slowly nodded his head. 'Makes the most sense, I guess, although there are probably other possibilities to consider.'

There was a pause, which allowed me to roll over in exasperation, and to just reach a small piece of biscuit that the good doctor had kindly recently dropped on the floor. It was stale, but who cares, it smelled delicious.

'Now to the second suicide,' Gaters resumed. 'Strange one this,' he hesitated almost showing a sign of intelligence, 'very thin sharp knife plunged very neatly into the lower stomach, and he slowly bled to death,' he paused once again. 'Very strange way to kill yourself, I must say though.'

'Quite,' my master replied.

Pretty much impossible, I thought, but remained silent.

Into Another Day

The next day the three wise crime-busting monkeys sat around my master's office desk, while I lay on my rug listening to their badly informed waffle.

'Perhaps we should just put the whole matter to rest,' I heard the fool Ding-Dong suggest. 'We really would be just wasting our time to continue to look into this case, when it is quite clearly a great tragedy that needs no further explanation or work.' The other two stared at him. 'It was suicide following a desperate action that Sir Terrance Edwards clearly instantly regretted,' Ding-Dong continued dubiously. 'After all, he would have thought he had killed Lordship Marshall-Atwood.'

I just shook my head with contempt and sighed loudly.

Abel then surprisingly interjected. 'I think we need to clear up a few loose ends, sir.'

He plainly had a few more brain cells than Ding-Dong, or was he just trying to ingratiate himself with my master?

'Such as?' Ding-Dong said with a sad scold on his plump face.

Abel cleared his throat and said unconvincingly, 'Well, er, we need to clear up the money angle,' a pause, 'and, er, what about Lord Marshall-Atwood's car being seen where his account says it shouldn't have been? And why did the Poacher kill himself? Makes no sense.'

He looked doubtful and endured a glare from his colleague who wanted no more work than was necessary.

Ding-Dong clasped his face in his hands, and said incredulously, 'The man was found in a locked room and shot with the gun by his body, for God's sake. A clear case of suicide. The witnesses of the supposed whereabouts of the car are less than reliable, so why on earth should we waste time clearing up so-called loose ends, which are not loose ends at all.? Barely, anyway.'

He seemed to ignore the Poacher case, and was certainly becoming passionate when there was a prospect of work to do and a chance of avoiding it.

My master, who had been listening with disinterested silence, took a deep breath. 'Constable Abel, ask a few questions around the village, try to find out if anybody else saw Lord Marshall-Atwood's car on that night, and if so when and where, and also if they have seen it parked in lanes previously, as Old Broadstairs claimed.' He then turned to Ding-Dong. 'And Constable Bell, check up on Lord Marshall-Atwood's meeting at the golf club, and whether anybody saw him changing his tyre,' he hesitated, 'and I will speak to Lord Marshall-Atwood again if he will comply with my request to see him.'

Ding-Dong gave a look of despair, but there was a 'Yes, sir' in unison; one much more enthusiastic than the other.

'Let's tie those loose ends up,' my master almost mocked.

If only he would ask for my help and, for God's sake, stop ignoring the Poacher's death and see what Bell thinks and knows about it.

It was a further two days later when my master was given royal permission to speak to his Lordship again. Yes, it was getting tedious and I knew that none of them, unlike me, had a clue about what had really happened.

Anyway, in the meantime (not so) Abel had found a rather large wad of money hidden away in a small, discreetly placed safe in the office of Sir Terrance Edwards, at which the daughter had displayed distinct astonishment. Abel also seemed rather subdued. I suspected something was worrying him, but, unusually for me, I had no idea what it could be.

Anyway (again), we were eventually shown into his Lordship's luxurious hospital room. I smirked as he seemed mildly affronted when my master once again sat down in the chair next to his bed without requesting permission. I slumped onto the floor, similarly without permission, and joyously found a half-eaten, only slightly mouldy biscuit under the bed, which I joyously gobbled down as rapidly as possible.

'How are you feeling, sir?' my master asked with little sign of sensitivity. 'Thank you for agreeing to see me, by the way,' with even less indication of gratefulness and failing to wait for a reply to his question.

His Lordship, in response, sat up straighter in his bed. 'The least I can do, Lewis, in the circumstances, but can we make it quick; I'm still very much on the sore side of well.' He winced, rather too easily in my opinion but then I had absolutely no sympathy for the posh git. 'Although I cannot imagine why you are wasting your time bothering me about something that is so clearly cut and dried.'

My master smiled meekly. 'We need to be absolutely clear about what happened when we do police work, sir,' was his masterful and somewhat sarcastic reply.

His Lordship smirked. 'Of course, do forgive me for trying to tell you how to do your job, constable.'

My master appeared to ignore the sudden demotion, and fished out his trusty notebook and pencil.

'Perhaps you could tell me in your own words what happened when you arrived home on the night you were shot,' my master prompted with pencil poised and a gentle nod of his head.

His Lordship once again winced with apparent pain. 'Yes, yes, but I am sure Ecclestone would have given you a more than adequate account of that man's actions,' he paused, seemed to think for a moment and then continued. 'Is it from the moment I entered my house that you want, Lewis?'

My master did not look up. 'Yes please, sir. That would be most helpful indeed.'

I shuffled out a fraction from under the bed hoping to clearly hear some more deliciously gross or false details.

'When I arrived home, Ecclestone answered the door and informed me that that man Edwards was waiting for me in my office,' he began confidently. 'I was a little annoyed at being told what was clearly obvious since I was late home and so I dismissed him and rushed to my study to confront the man.'

'Confront'; an odd choice of words, or was it?

'Without removing your coat, sir?' my master quietly interjected, to the clear puzzlement of his Lordship.

'Yes, yes, Lewis, I was late. I did not want that man to be kept waiting any longer.' He paused. 'If only I had known what I had awaiting me, I may not have been so obliging.' He then seemed to reflect with genuine regret.

My master wrote something in his notebook and then said casually, 'Yes, quite so.' Then he asked, 'Did you cut yourself when you changed your tyre, sir?'

He was smarter than I gave him credit for; not in my league but a touch better than the average bobby nonetheless.

His Lordship appeared puzzled but also appeared to be calculating a satisfactory reply.

I just smiled to myself and sniffed under the carpet.

'Not that I can recall,' he finally replied with a minor show of contempt, 'but perhaps it is very possible given the difficulty I had removing one of the nuts.'

My master seemed to let it pass. 'Could you tell me what happened next, sir?'

'Next, Lewis?' His Lordship looked puzzled; it was as if he had lost track of the conversation.

'After you dismissed Mr Ecclestone,' my master replied with admirable patience, 'you entered the study to, as you put it, confront your guest, Sir Terrance Edwards?'

His Lordship winced once again, reddened a touch and then sat up a bit straighter.

I stood up and sniffed around the floor.

'Guest, Lewis,' he barked with disapproval. 'I strode into my study,' he appeared to emphasise the word 'my' for no apparent reason, 'and Edwards was annoyingly sitting behind my desk, which immediately struck me as being odd as well as being more than somewhat bloody rude.' He paused and gave me a glance of malevolence which encouraged me in my search for scraps. 'He had a smirk on his face which fortified me to slam the door shut, and to order him to get out of my chair. The bloody cheek of the bally man!'

He stopped.

I sat down and stared at him.

His Lordship stared at me and grimaced. 'He then stood up, produced the gun and shot me without a word.' A statement that produced the most obvious and perhaps somewhat manufactured wince yet, he really was playing very hard for some sympathy.

My master allowed his Lordship to gather his equilibrium and then, 'He shot you while standing behind your desk, sir?'

(That's what the man had said, although I guess he may have been confused! He wouldn't be the only one, me excepted of course!).

His Lordship nodded unconvincingly with an accompanying wince.

'What happened next, sir?' my master persisted.

His Lordship looked incredulous and shook his head. 'No idea, Lewis, I remember nothing else after the shot being fired. I presume I was unconscious, could have been dead for all that bloody lunatic cared.'

My master failed to mask a self-satisfied smile. 'Odd thing is that Sir Terrance Edwards placed the chair back behind your desk before he fled through the window. He must have been a very tidy person. Would have thought he would have been in a hurry to get out.'

'Damn odd, Lewis,' his Lordship responded with a mild look of concern. 'I guess when madness takes over you do some very strange and unthinking things.'

My master nodded his head slowly and twitched his nose, a habit he had clearly learned from me.

'Are you sure he shot you from behind the desk?' my master persisted.

His Lordship frowned, as if in thought, and clearly with a hint of annoyance. 'That's my remembrance, Lewis, but he may have moved towards me, I just do not have a keen memory of the moment and certainly want to forget it if at all possible. Bloody nightmares don't help.'

My master made a note on his pad and smirked.

'What did you burn on the fire?' my master asked casually as he continued to write.

His Lordship looked confused and his face became quite red as he appeared to be thinking deeply.

'Not sure what you are getting at, Lewis. Ecclestone lights the fires and I had been out all day,' he paused. 'You will need to ask him if you need an answer to that one, I'm afraid, old boy.'

He did not seem to be at all curious about the question, which was rather curious in itself.

'There were some remnants of cardboard that had almost burned to ashes by the time we arrived, I just wondered if you had thrown anything on the fire when you went into the room,' my master explained casually. 'Mr Ecclestone said all he had put on the fire was some coal and wood, and that he had no idea where the cardboard could have come from.'

His Lordship looked unimpressed but gave the impression that he was thinking hard. 'I get shot by a lunatic and you are concerned about what was burnt on the bloody fire, man. Really, Lewis! Your companion lying on the floor here would have more of an idea of the right priorities,' he suddenly and inexplicably shouted.

I couldn't help thinking that the end of the rant was the most astute and truthful comment he had made so far, but remained mute.

'It must have been Edwards who threw something on the fire while he was waiting for me,' his Lordship, suddenly calm, mused. 'Seems to me the only possible explanation for your little manufactured and irrelevant enigma.'

He smirked and my master just inclined his head in a kind of acknowledgement of the suggestion.

'A witness told me that they saw your car parked close to Old Moss House on the night you were shot,' my master deftly changed the subject. 'Did you stop off there at any time prior to going home that evening?'

His Lordship looked puzzled, or was he calculating a response? 'You mentioned this last time we spoke to one another; the answer is categorically no, Lewis. Why on earth would I stop off at that man's house when I knew he was to visit me that evening? It makes no sense at all, man! I have already told you this.'

(A good repost? Maybe.)

'Quite so,' my master replied with a distinct smirk of satisfaction.

There were a few moments of quiet as my master appeared to be writing something down in his notebook. The scratching was very annoying and I shuffled around on the hard floor to try to get comfortable while his Lordship seemed to slowly sink a bit further into his hospital bed.

'Had you spoken to the Poacher in the last few days before the shooting?' my master finally, to my relief, broke the silence.

His Lordship appeared to think for a reply. 'Not that I can remember,' he paused, appeared to think once again. 'I may have told him to keep off my land at some point, but I am dashed if I can remember when that was.'

A politician's reply, he seemed to be hedging his bets, and I wondered why. (Well, to be honest, I knew why!).

'One last thing,' my master said, 'we found a great deal of money in Sir Terrance Edwards' safe.'

He left it at that.

His Lordship screwed up his face and then winced again (The wimp!) as he attempted to sit up straighter.

'Most odd, Lewis, most odd indeed. Pity he had not given it to me, hey, what do you say, man?'

'Quite so,' my master replied dubiously and was about to speak when the nurse reappeared with a crashing opening of the door.

'I think it is time to leave now, sir,' she barked at my master. I almost barked back, but instead followed him out of the room as he exchanged pleasantries with his Lordship and the surly nurse.

I was left wondering why he bothered.

Later that day we were sitting in the local pub. Abel was downing his second pint while my master, deep in thought, sipped at his first. I just sniffed around the floor for scraps of pork scratchings or crisps, and lived in hope for a few splashes of the amber liquid.

'Any progress on the Poacher's death?' my master finally asked.

Abel gulped down his pint and signalled to the barmaid for a top-up.

He shook his head. 'It's a mystery, sir,' he began with a slight drunken slur of his words (I wondered how many pints he really had downed throughout the day), 'nobody appears to have seen him after he left Old Moss House that night, and I cannot for the life of me work out why he should kill himself in such a strange and stupid way.'

My master was thinking, and failed to acknowledge a word that was said while Abel, used to such behaviour, just gulped through the froth of his newly poured drink.

'It seems a damned coincidence that we have an attempted murder and two suicides all in one night,' Abel continued, and then tailed off, his eyes betraying his inebriation and a lack of sleep.

Quite so, I thought, and was tempted to scream out the answer to the puzzle.

'There was no way in or out of that room,' my master either asked or stated.

'No, that's right,' Abel replied almost thoughtfully (quite an achievement for him).

'What about the knife, any idea where he got it from?' my master asked.

Abel took another gulp of his ale and appeared to hesitate for a moment. 'No idea, sir,' he took another sip, 'the odd thing is that it looks like something that the Poacher would never waste his meagre funds on; he was more into practical knives, not something fancy like that.'

'Yes,' my master replied while staring into his still almost full glass of beer. 'Could he have stolen it at some time?'

Abel inclined his head. 'Could be, wouldn't put it past the tea leaf.'

My master rifled through his notes for a moment. 'Damned funny business,' he almost whispered to himself.

They both took a gulp of beer. 'Any clue as to why he should want to kill himself?' my master finally asked, I guessed more in hope than anticipation.

Abel dumbly shook his head slowly. 'Not a thing. He seemed to be okay earlier, although shook up a bit like the rest of us were.'

Not me, I thought, but decided not to correct him.

My master once again looked through his notes and then screwed up his forehead. 'It is all such a bizarre coincidence that the Poacher should be close to Old Moss House just when Sir Terrance Edwards killed himself, generously and rapidly helped out the girl, and then he should go home and inexplicably kill himself.'

Quite so, I thought.

Two Days Later

Abel came rushing into my master's office without knocking on the door.

'Sir,' he loudly pronounced, 'I know where the killing knife came from.'

It was an announcement that impelled my master to drop his pencil, and one that held me in a state of anticipation.

'You do?' was my master's open-mouthed reply.

Abel vigorously nodded his head and slumped down in the chair opposite my master. 'I spoke to Ecclestone,' he paused as if for dramatic effect but only achieved a look of frustration and a mild cough form my master. 'It was stolen from the manor house a couple of days before the Poacher killed himself.'

I could have guessed that this was to be the answer a few days earlier, but had to hand it to the (less than) Abel that for once he had done a reasonably good job, although he would clearly never be able to join the dots and start to get the truth from the whole cryptic puzzle.

My master appeared to contemplate the new-found information. He then recovered his pencil from the floor and wrote an unknown scrawl in his notebook.

'Was the Poacher seen at the manor at that time?' my master finally managed to ask.

Abel broke out in a sickly smile. 'Funnily enough, sir, he was seen by Ecclestone in deep conversation out in the gardens with his Lordship on the very day Ecclestone discovered that the knife had gone missing.'

My master elicited a moan of some sort and appeared to jot some irrelevance in his notebook. 'Was he seen in the house at any time?'

Abel shook his head with a look of disappointment. 'No, sir. I asked Ecclestone to think hard, but he was sure that he had not seen him in the house, but of course that does not mean that a character like the Poacher would not have been able to get into the house unnoticed.'

'Yes, I see,' my master quietly mumbled. 'I guess that solves the problem of how the knife came into the possession of the Poacher.'

I could have screamed with frustration but instead nudged my master with my nose.

We were off to the Hall again, to where his Lordship had the previous day been returned after his sojourn at the hospital. My master had a look of puzzlement mixed with anger on his face, and had to brake rapidly on more than one occasion to avoid ploughing into a plodding citizen or oblivious pheasant.

On leaving the car he slammed the door and strode purposefully to the crusty old ornate door. I trotted unobtrusively behind him, juggling the facts with the very likely reality, which I suspected none of my imbecilic colleagues (if you could call them that) would guess in a universe's lifetime.

The obese Penguin answered the door, and I suspected he would be in for an upper crust scolding once my master had left his muddy footprints on proceedings.

The Penguin had a look of surprise on his face, and when my master asked to see his Lordship, his neck began to wobble like a jelly.

'I will need to see if he is up for visitors,' Ecclestone stuttered, and I wondered whether he suspected his discussion with (less than) Abel had prompted our visit.

'Do that,' my master replied, and then entered without invite (he was clearly learning from me).

The Penguin looked back angrily and then waddled off upstairs. I sat in the hallway, smirking to myself, while my master trod up and down in clear frustration.

The wait seemed to go on for an eternity, which prompted me to have a good sniff around. The carpet stank of some awful perfume, and I concluded that it must have been cleaned very recently; no doubt to erase the blood spots of a few days before.

Finally, I sniffed the sweat of the fat Penguin, and, as if by magic, a few seconds later he was wobbling down the staircase. My master looked up and emitted an exasperated intake of breath.

'Lord Marshal-Atwood is not well enough to speak to you at present,' the Penguin gasped asthmatically, as he finally managed to reach the bottom of the staircase. 'He expressed his regret, but asks you not to trouble him while he is in recovery from the terrible, traumatic experience he has had the misfortune to endure.'

My master sighed loudly with undisguised frustration. 'This is not good enough, Ecclestone,' he shouted with surprising anger. 'I will ask for a warrant if this continues.' He paused almost for dramatic effect, and then appeared to think twice about continuing.

The Penguin's face, which was already red from the exertion of mounting and descending the stairs, wobbled and turned a light shade of purple. 'I would like, and politely ask you to kindly leave the house, sir,' he babbled through desperate gasps for air. 'We have no further business at this time.'

'I will be returning soon, Mr Ecclestone,' my master replied loudly, 'and I will also be getting one of my constables to take a formal statement from you about that knife. Do not for one moment think this is the end of it.'

Ecclestone looked rattled, and I suspect was more worried that his Lordship had overheard my master's comment, than by the prospect of having to give any statement.

It was no more than an hour later when my master was summoned to the office of Chief Constable Henry Ambrose Crockford.

It was no more than a further thirty minutes before my master was sitting in a chair opposite the desk of the chief constable, while I had unobtrusively, I think, crept under the said chair.

Crockford was a white-haired, tall, thin, public school-educated, ex-army major, and knew nothing much about police work.

'Lewis,' he pronounced without prior chat, and with a quintessential Etonian accent, and an amusingly very red face, 'Lord Marshall-Atwood is most annoyed, and as a consequence so am I.'

I stifled a loud laugh, while my master remained sitting upright and silent.

'Your pestering of a sick man must stop, Lewis,' he mumbled, almost as if he did not believe what he was saying. 'As far as I know, there really is no further point in wasting valuable police time on this case.'

My master shifted in the clearly uncomfortable chair and cleared his throat. 'Sir, there are a few points in this case that really do not make sense and are in need of clarification,' he began dubiously and somewhat bravely.

Crockford waved his hand in front of his face and shook his head. 'Such as?' he asked with a large dose of mockery and lack of interest.

I felt like biting his bony leg or ankle but did not want to get my master in any more trouble.

'I have serious doubts about the truthfulness of Lord Marshall-Atwood's overall account of the matter,' my master replied, with far less than the required confidence or forcefulness.

Crockford's face began to turn a troubling brighter scarlet, and for a moment I was convinced he was going to explode, but then the colour seemed to slowly recede. 'Such as, Lewis?' he said with a sarcasm beyond necessity. 'Tell me what you are getting at. Do humour me before I totally lose patience and ask you to vacate my office.'

My master demurred and fetched his notebook from his pocket. 'Small things, but not insignificant,' he began, 'the chair under the desk, Lord Marshall-Atwood being shot closer than he described to us, his car being seen where it should not have been, the changing of the tyre, blood on the hallway carpet—'

He was not allowed to continue as Crockford interrupted. 'Explain yourself, man, before I lose all interest, and you lose any of the credibility with me that you may have left,' he mockingly interjected. 'What do you mean "the chair under the desk" anyway? What is that supposed to mean, man?'

My master smiled and bravely, or maybe foolishly, asked, 'Have you not read my report, sir?'

Crockford shook his head. 'Indulge me,' he replied. (I suspected he hadn't.)

'According to Lord Marshall-Atwood's account, Sir Terrance Edwards was sitting behind the desk when he entered the room. He then stood up and shot Lord Marshall-Atwood, and then swiftly fled through the window.'

My master paused, clearly expecting some kind of response from his superior.

After an awkward pause. 'Yes,' Crockford finally prompted with a slow shake of his head. It was going to be a torturous and very long afternoon.

My master appeared to calm himself for a moment. 'Sir, if you had just shot somebody in his study and were in a hurry to get away, would you return to the desk and place the chair underneath it before you left?'

Crockford appeared to think for a moment. 'People do strange things when under stress, Lewis. You of all people should know that.'

(Reasonable point, but wrong of course!)

'Lord Marshall-Atwood was shot at close quarters, his account indicates that he was shot when he entered the room, and Sir Terrance Edwards did this from behind the desk,' my master continued with a dreadful lack of confidence.

I really wished I could help him out.

Crockford thought for a further moment. 'Lord Marshall-Atwood was clearly mistaken, Edwards must have been closer than he remembered,' he once again countered with a distinct lack of patience or imagination, 'and to be completely honest, I am not surprised considering the shock he must be suffering, as well as the pain.'

(Possible and probable, but wrong!)

'Is Lord Marshall-Atwood really capable of changing a tyre on his car?' my master interjected.

Crockford smiled broadly. 'I would think so, Lewis. As a young man, he was a bit of a car enthusiast, raced cars a bit as far as I recall. Just because he is rich, it doesn't mean he is incapable of getting his hands dirty on occasion, you know.'

My master winced. He really should have known this but seemed undeterred. 'Why was there fresh blood on the hall wall and carpet?'

Crockford smirked and shook his head. 'Lewis, the blood could have come from anywhere; the cook, a cut finger, a dead chicken, who knows, and how do you know it was fresh anyway?'

My master appeared to think for a moment.

'The car, Lord Marshall-Atwood's car, was seen by witnesses in places that clearly contradicted Lord Marshall-Atwood's statement,' my master persisted with a fast-diminishing ounce of confidence.

'I do not think the so-called witnesses could be called, in any way, reliable. Do you, Lewis?' Crockford asked with more than a hint of impatience.

My master was very quickly losing the argument, and to be honest it was nobody's fault but his.

'Where did the money come from?' my master then asked.

'I take it you are referring to the money in Sir Terrance Edwards' safe?' Crockford asked

My master nodded in response. 'Yes, sir.'

'Then that is for you to discover, Lewis. But I do not think its presence has any bearing on changing the obvious explanation as to the events we are discussing, Lewis. Do you?'

My master did not respond for a moment then said, 'The cardboard burnt in the fire in the study, where did it come from? There is no reasonable explanation for its presence.'

'No idea, Lewis, no idea at all,' Crockford exasperatingly sighed. 'Probably thrown in there by Sir Terrance Edwards while he was waiting to carry out his heinous crime. Who knows and who cares to be honest. It is totally irrelevant, man.'

My master winced.

'Sir Terrance was shot through his right temple,' my master admiringly, and probably foolishly, persisted.

Crockford slammed his fist down on the desk, I winced in response, but I couldn't help pricking up my ears in admiration for my master's bravery. 'Close this case now, Lewis. It is clear to me that Edwards shot Lord Marshall-Atwood, then killed himself in a fit of remorse, or more likely to avoid the hangman, the coward. Now get out of my office and take that scruffy and stinking companion of yours with you. Go now before I really lose my temper and contemplate firing you to hell and high water.'

Crockford's face was now almost purple, and spittle sprayed in all directions from his mouth, while my master's face had drained of all colour and was as white as virgin snow. I just lay by the desk and shook my head in disgust at the total and untrue disrespect Crockford had shown me.

My master, after a moment of reflection, pushed back his chair and with the politest 'sir', left the room. I trotted behind him, felt a hard stare penetrating my back and sadly wondered why my master was so incapable of gathering and pointing out the basic facts in support of whatever he believed to be the true events of the past few days.

Oh well, the end of the road I guess, case concluded (Well, sort of!).

When we arrived back at the office, with my master in the foulest of moods that I had ever had the displeasure to witness, we were confronted in the waiting room by, of all people, crazy Miss Hemmingway. Her timing, as usual, was impeccable!

'Sergeant,' she squeaked.

'Inspector,' my master barked back loudly.

Miss Hemmingway blinked rapidly and let out a whine, but then, as if my master had not spoken, 'Sergeant, I must show you something immediately, it is so, so important.'

My master sighed loudly, while I smugly smiled broadly.

'Yes, Miss Hemmingway, how can I help you this time?' he asked with an amazing restraint but an obvious sign of impatience.

'He is in the newspaper, *The Times*, that man, that man I saw,' she enthusiastically and loudly shouted, while holding up what I presumed was the said copy of the newspaper. 'He was arrested for painting on the walls of the Houses of Parliament.' She paused and then demurely said, 'There is a picture of him. It is definitely the man I saw in my back garden. It is him; I am sure it is him.'

She handed over the newspaper to my master who gave it a perfunctory glance, and then, with admirable control while walking to his office door said, 'You were so lucky he did not daub your house with paint, Miss Hemmingway. So very, very lucky.'

Miss Hemmingway looked offended, gave me a filthy glare, and then turned tail to leave the building.

My master, without looking back, entered the office, mumbled something like, 'Fuck off to the lot of you ignorant fuckers' and then violently slammed the door closed behind him, just before I could enter in his wake.

'Shit,' I mumbled and proceeded to sniff the floor, found nothing of any interest, and then lay down, wondering if anybody would ever get to the truth of the matter.

I somehow doubted it, but who knows, it's a total dog's dinner.

'Look out, right down, dig it down in time', I heard Abel shout. Or I think that's what he said, but I was half- asleep and he is unlikely to have worked it out.

'It's a cross and tick, I think,' the fool Bell responded.

It certainly is, I thought, as my eyes closed to the world and I dreamt of chapter titles for my forthcoming book.

Chapter Seven

In Search of Chudleigh Knighton

After receiving the manuscript from the mysterious Alan Corbett-Hemingway, I had spent two consecutive evenings reading through it, making notes, and speculating as to its authenticity.

On the third evening I began to search the web to see if there was any basis to the story, and it took me almost the whole evening to find not even a brief mention of some suicides or attempted murders in Chudleigh Knighton.

The manuscript obliquely hinted that, if the events were real, then they were in the South West of England, and so I widened my search to the whole of Devon, but once again, with no success. I gave up at this point and instead attempted to complete a crossword in a tax-avoiding billionaire's right-wing propaganda broadsheet.

The next evening, I telephoned Alan Corbett-Hemingway and after waiting an age for a reply, was met with a squeaky public school-intoned, 'Hello, may I assist you, Mr Brookes?'

I had no idea how he knew it was me, but let it pass.

There followed a tiresome exchange consisting of pointless introductions, and, from me, superfluous kind remarks about his uncle, who for the life of me I did not recall.

'What did you make of the papers, the manuscript?' Alan finally, and thankfully, asked.

I paused and explained that it was a puzzle of some interest, but I was more than curious to find out whether it was just a strangely written attempt at a mystery novel, or whether there was any truth to the events.

'I presumed it was just a story,' Alan replied dubiously, 'but then I remembered my great-aunt mentioning that she had known a friend who worked for a Lord Marshall-Atwood in the early 1950s. I am not sure why and when she said this, but it may well have been in connection with me telling her I wanted to be a writer of mystery stories. But it may not have been, I just do not recall with any clarity.'

'I get the impression that you have more to tell me, and this is why you have decided to pique my curiosity.' I then prompted him in frustration, 'Get on with it, man.'

He hesitated, and for a moment seemed put out by my directness, but then proceeded to update me with his findings.

'Lord Marshall-Atwood had very much existed, and had lived in a place called Bovey Tracey, which happens to be a stone's throw from Chudleigh Knighton,' he began to explain, 'and he lived a somewhat privileged life.'

Alan then paused, and as I was about to prompt him, added, 'And that's as much as I know,' he hesitated, 'and I wondered if you might have the time and contacts to see if you could put this to bed.'

It was now my time to hesitate, wondering what he meant by "putting it to bed". It was as if he wanted it all to go away, which did not make sense since he was the one pursuing the matter. I dismissed it as a public school thing, and yes, I know, I'm an inverted snob!

'You want me to investigate this on your behalf?' I mused aloud.

I awaited a reply and heard some whispering in the background, and then, 'If it has truly piqued your curiosity, I would be perfectly willing to pay your expenses, and of course a little retainer on top,' he hesitantly confirmed.

I coughed, as I do, but not so much from my filthy tobacco addiction, but from surprise; it appeared that I was to start a new career as a private investigator.

Two days later I received some open return tickets to Devon in the post, along with a sizable bundle of His Majesty's notes of various denomination. There was also a note explaining that I had been booked into The Cromwell Arms inn for three nights starting the next day. I grinned at the prospect of a free holiday and, although still very doubtful as to the authenticity of the manuscript, I was curious to, as Alan said, 'put it to bed', with the added bonus of making some much-needed dosh in the process.

So, it is the next day and I have the great privilege of tasting the delights of riding on a South-Western Railway train to Newton Abbot. The train is, of course, expensive, late, stuffy, smelly and filthy, but that is part of the pleasure of the great British privatised railways. I take comfort that, at least, I did not have to cough up the extortionate fare.

The day is, of course, one of constant pouring rain (another delight of the post-Brexit isolated island that we have the non-existing choice to live in, unless of course if we happen to be a high-value worker or fortunate enough to have a second passport), and rather than staring through the grimy window, I resort to reading a Murdoch marvel, while sweating profusely in the somewhat, well, grossly inadequately air-conditioned carriage.

The rain has fortunately desisted when we finally, twenty-five minutes late and five minutes too early to claim any compensation, arrive in the South Devon station of Newton Abbot to no announcement and, of course, no apology for the lateness.

I grab my Union Jack-emblazoned backpack (A gift, of sorts, from my ex-wife!) and push my way onto the rubbish-strewn platform. I look around for some help with finding my way out of the surprisingly unpleasant-looking station, but eventually discover that the main entrance is on the west side of the station through South Devon House, and I finally, after a few false starts, decide to take the step-free route to the taxi rank on the south side of the building.

The taxis are queued up with an air of boredom and hopelessness, and the front taxi driver, similarly built to me but a younger man, seems so shocked at getting a fare, that for a moment he remains in his cab while I stand by the back door awaiting help with my bag.

I cough loudly and he seems to awake from his fugue, and with an air of reluctance steps out of the taxi, and slowly shuffles to the back of the car to open the boot. He makes no attempt to assist me with depositing my bag in the car boot, and leaves me to struggle breathlessly, before slamming the boot shut without a word.

The five or so miles to Bovey Tracey are conducted in an awkward total silence (Except for the drone of some brain-numbing local radio station playing in the background!), which at least gives me the opportunity to soak in the delights, or not, of the very damp South Devon countryside.

Fore Street turns out to be the home of The Cromwell Arms inn, and I am deposited on the pavement with little ceremony, and reluctantly hand over an extortionate amount of money, for which I insist on receiving a receipt.

The inn itself is a surprisingly charming seventeenth-century white building with an odd unidentifiable flag hanging from its roof.

Since it has once again begun to rain, I dither no longer, pick up my bag and crash through the sky-blue painted doors to find the inside of the inn. I am met by a plump smiling (reluctantly, I guess) pleasant-looking middle-aged woman, who proceeds to tell me that there is free Wi-Fi and free parking available (both of which are of no particular interest), and that guests can enjoy fresh home-cooked food, a selection of daily specials, and a wide range of cask ales and wines (all of which are of great interest). She then, while handing over the key to room number 11, unnecessarily informs me that there are fourteen rooms at the inn which are all traditionally furnished with en-suite facilities, and that there is a flat-screen TV and a refreshments tray waiting for me in my room. She does, however, fail to help me with finding my room, or with carrying my bag up the narrow staircase.

After struggling up the stairs, it is late afternoon when I finally slump my less-than-athletic frame onto the bed, which proves to be surprisingly comfortable. The window is rattling with the intensity of the pouring rain and the hypnotic beat slowly pushes down my heavy eyelids.

I wake to an insistent knocking on the door to my room.

I stagger to the door and I am met with a very pleasant smile from a young prettyish plump lady, who I immediately guess is the daughter of the receptionist/owner.

'Sir, Mr Brookes,' she stutters with a broad West Country brogue, 'did you still want to eat at half past seven tonight?'

I shake my head to chase away the aftershock of a rude but pleasant-to-the-eye awakening, and glance at my watch which efficiently confirms the time to be somewhat north of half past seven.

I fake a smile and express a great keenness to sample the food, to which she sexily blushes and explains that my table is available post-haste, or something to that effect.

To cut a long story short, the food proves to be surprisingly good, although a bit fancy for my liking, and I wash it down with some West Country cider of the most excellent quality. I then, after breaking the strict non-smoking rule in my room, enjoy a long night's sleep, dreaming of the inn keeper's ravishingly plump red-faced daughter.

I awake to bright sunlight lasering through the slightly opened curtains, and then, after showering and dressing, enjoy a satisfying full English breakfast elegantly served by the dreamlike inn keeper's daughter.

After sneaking another criminal smoke in my room, I prepare for a trip to the cemetery.

It is a mild day with the sun sneaking a glimpse occasionally from behind white clouds. Some would say it was a nice day for walking, but not me. I'm a few-steps-a-day man myself!

I have been given directions by the receptionist/owner of the inn, and been told it is an approximate fifteen minutes' walk, but for me it proves to be a dangerously out-of-breath and sweaty twenty minutes.

The cemetery is on Coombe Lane, next to a surprisingly grand church, and turns out to be a very neatly kept affair.

I am looking for the graves of any of the characters mentioned in the manuscript, and so after gathering my breath and sneaking a quick drag on my latest cigarette, I begin an inspection of the gravestones.

It doesn't take me long to find the large marble stone commemorating the life of the Marshall-Atwood family, well, to be precise, Lord Irvine Marshall-Atwood (died 11th September 1958), who appears to be buried alongside 'His Loving Wife' Lady Evelyn Marshall-Atwood (died 4th March 1950). This seems to work with the manuscript, and a few hairs stand up on the back of my neck.

After another smoke and sharing a piece of toast that I had squirrelled away in my coat pocket after breakfast with a nosy pigeon, I shuffle around a bit more and eventually find a less elaborate affair of a gravestone with the names of Sir Terrance Edwards (died 10th March 1953 and Eleanor Edwards (died 9th September 1949), which once again works with the manuscript, and puts the date of the events described as early March 1953.

I wander around a bit more and at the end of the cemetery notice an elderly woman placing some flowers on a grave. She looks up as I approach, and I notice a tear falling from her right eye.

'Good morning,' I cheekily broach, 'nice and warm.'

She looks up at me as I walk to the grave, and I am shocked to see the name, Clive Lewis peeking through the green moss.

The woman seems to notice my look of surprise.

'Are you alright, dear?' she asks.

I clear my throat, and unobtrusively discard my cigarette. 'Yes, yes, I was just surprised to see the grave of Inspector Clive Lewis,' I venture, for it could have been any old Clive Lewis, and I could be following a very long and false trail.

'Sergeant,' she replies with a hint of a sniffle, 'you have given my father a posthumous promotion,' there is sudden smile and a sparkle appears in her eyes, 'and not before time.'

I smile in what I hope is a comforting way and then ask if I could buy her a cup of tea and a cake.

'That would be nice,' she replies, 'just let me say goodbye to Dad first though.'

We take a five-minute stroll to The Copper Kettle, a quaint little restaurant providing snacks, teas and lunch. I buy Norma Bradley, née Lewis, a weak tea, and myself a strong coffee, along with, for me, a large slice of chocolate cake.

We sit in the corner of the small room and appear to be the only customers.

'October is a quiet time of the year in these parts,' she explains. 'The summer season is well and truly finished. Not that there is much of a summer season these days. Dead as a dormouse most of the time in these enlightened times, I'm afraid.'

I nod and take a large bite out of a surprisingly moist and delicious ginger slice.

'Did your father die recently?' I ask somewhat stupidly, since I guessed she was probably in her middle to late seventies and the gravestone looked very old.

She picks up her cup with her right hand and sips her tea gingerly and then shakes her head with a demure smile. 'No, Mr Brookes, he died many years ago, the 11th of May, 1953, to be precise.' She pauses and another tiny tear appears. 'I was ten years old; my birthday was the following day.'

I am stunned. I want to feel pity for this old woman, but the revelation of the date of her father's death has stumped the old compassion card.

'It was an accident. His car came off the road while he was driving to buy my birthday card and present in Newton Abbot,' she continues, and then begins to lightly sob.

I really do not know what to say, I cannot quite understand why she should be so upset after so many years (Maybe underlining the validity of my ex-wife's view of me as an unfeeling fucking miserable psychopath!), and so I remain diplomatically and falsely sympathetically mute.

'Our dog died as well. He was a black standard poodle, and followed Dad everywhere.' She is now visibly upset. 'I suppose it was fitting that they both went to heaven at the same time.'

Fucking hell, I think, as I plan an exit strategy.

I buy Norma Bradley another drink, but she seems unaware of any cases that her father had been involved with at the time, and says she knew of nobody else who would be able to help.

'Too much time has passed, they have all died,' she sadly, but I am guessing wrongly or untruthfully, pronounces.

Realising I have little more to gain from any further chat, I thank her for her company and make my way back to the local church, which has the rather over-greedy name of Bovey

Tracey Church of St Peter, St Paul and St Thomas of Canterbury, and think that surely one apostle would have sufficed in such a small village.

The church is unfortunately locked, and there is no sign of any religious officialdom in residence, so I decide to walk back to The Cromwell Arms to get myself a well-earned hearty lunch.

The owner, whose name I discover is Mrs Cooper, she is reluctant to elicit her Christian name, but with a wink adds, 'Only to close friends, love, and you are certainly not that at the moment,' invites me to sit down at my table and takes my food and drink order.

Upon delivery from the daughter, and as I chomp into my beef and ale pie, the delightfully buxom Mrs Cooper wanders over to my table and sits down opposite me.

'Do you know if there is anybody around here who was an adult and lived here in 1953?' I ask without any attempt at preamble and with a large dollop of hope.

She leans close to me and places her right hand on my left hand. 'Now why would you be asking such a question, Mr Brookes?' she asks conspiratorially, with a wink of her right eye and a smirk.

I gulp and nearly choke on an unusually large chunk of fatty beef, or is it gristle, and grab a glass of water with my right hand just in time to save my life and dignity.

'Just heard that there were a few unfortunate deaths here in the early 1950s,' I breathlessly reply, with an accelerating heart rate and a sniff of a seductive whiff of perfume.

Mrs Cooper rapidly pulls her hand away as if I had elicited an electric shock, and leans back in her chair.

'Well, where did you hear that, Mr Brookes?' she asks, with what appears to be genuine puzzlement. 'And there was I thinking that you were here on a late, leisurely pleasure-seeking holiday.'

I grin innocence and shrug my shoulders. 'A late holiday it is, Mrs Cooper, leisurely we will see, as we will with the promise of pleasure, but the kind gentleman who paid for it asked me to look into a thing or two while I was here. A win-win, situation, Mrs Cooper.'

She leans forward conspiratorially. 'Is that right, Mr Brookes? Well, maybe if you offer to buy me a drink tonight, I might well be able to give you the name of somebody who could possibly help you with your "looking into a thing or two" and I am sure we could discuss your seeking of pleasure. There are, after all, lots of things you could find to do in this neck of the woods.'

I smile and wink. 'Sounds good to me. It's a deal, Mrs Cooper.'

'Call me Joan,' Mrs Cooper tells me as we sit down before an ancient wooden table in the corner of the rather grubby and almost deserted Bell Inn.

It is around half past nine and I take a large swig from my pint of Doom Bar, which proves to be not at all bad. Mrs Cooper, Joan, has in front of her a, 'pint of good old South West scrumpy,' and wears an elaborate ample figure-hugging red dress and a permanent salacious smile.

I had been served an adequate, and surprisingly filling steak and kidney pudding at The Cromwell Arms before Joan dragged me (not unwillingly) in the direction of the town square, and then into the welcoming doorway of The Bell Inn.

I smack my lips and place the pint glass onto the table in front of me and then witness Joan doing the exact same thing. She has a broad smile on her face and licks her lips provocatively.

'Well, Mrs Cooper,' I say, 'you said you could help me with a thing or two.'

I take out my packet of cigarettes and jiggle it in my right hand while hopefully wondering how far 'a thing or two' could lead.

'Funny how my daughter could have sworn she smelt smoke in your room when she cleaned it this morning,' she replies with a smirk, quite clearly not answering my question. 'I pointed out to her that it was strictly against the rules of The Cromwell Arms, and that a fine upstanding gentleman like Mr Brookes would in no way break such strict regulations.'

She has a devious smile on her face and swigs another mouthful of her cider.

'Not the only thing she found in your room either,' she continues with a wink, 'some scruffy pieces of A4 paper were scattered over the desk she'd intended to polish.'

I gulp a mouthful of beer and elicit the most fake smile I could ever remember manufacturing.

'Caught red-handed,' I reply with a chuckle. 'I wondered why it was so neatly stacked when I got back. For the life of me I could not remember doing it. Guess you read it?'

She laughs noisily, revealing some dazzlingly white capped teeth, which strike me as far too large for her mouth.

'Also caught red-handed,' she replies. 'Skim-read it. Where did you get it from, or did you write it yourself?'

I spread my arms wide and then shrug. 'Just an attempt at that mystery novel I never got round to writing,' I lie with no conviction, and well aware that she does not believe me.

'Where did you get it from?' she asks.

'I wrote it,' I reply.

'No, you didn't.'

I drink some more ale and smack my lips in appreciation.

'A sort of a friend of a sort of friend gave it to me,' I tell her.

'You being an ex-copper and all that?'

She smiles broadly.

'Are you sure you're not a copper?' I ask, and then fake a laugh to accompany her sudden outburst of jollity.

There is a pause, and she seems to be thinking deeply, or is it sadly?

'My dad was,' she finally replies rather quietly. 'He was Constable Abel in your story.'

'Fuck,' I whisper under my breath, this village certainly seems to be rather incestuous. There is a mutual lull in conversion as I weather the shock. I imagine she must think me an absolute prick (Which of course I probably am!) if she thinks I wrote the fucking stupid story.

'And he was nothing like he was portrayed in that stupid travesty of a story of yours,' she scolds with more than a tinge of anger. 'He would have been much younger, and he was far from unintelligent. In fact, he made it to inspector before retiring from the force.'

She breathes heavily, and grabs what is now an empty glass.

'My dad died last year, made the grand old age of eighty-five,' she begins to explain, 'he became the sergeant after Clive Lewis had the fatal accident.'

I leave it a moment and offer to buy some more drinks. She nods agreement and I skulk off to the bar with my tail between my legs and my brain calculating a swirl of possibilities.

'I wasn't born then so I only know what my dad told me about that time. It was, and is, a time that local people do not want to talk about very much, and I guess most by now know nothing about it,' she explains when I return to the table with my best sympathetic face fixed on.

'So, the manuscript was based on true events,' I prompt, on the probably accurate presumption she has skim-read it in full.

She looks down at her fresh cloudy drink, and appears to think deeply before replying, 'I only know what my dad told me, and he was very clear that it was a very unfortunate affair from start to finish. Sir Terrance Edwards tried to kill Lord Marshall-Atwood, felt remorse at his actions, and killed himself.'

I nod and quietly ask, 'And what did Clive Lewis think, do you know?'

She chuckles and shakes her head. 'Dad said Clive was always trying to play the Hercule Poirot and trying to find conspiracies and mysteries where there were none.'

I wait for her to continue, but she just sips at her pint.

I concede. 'What did Clive Lewis think? Did your father happen to say?'

'Mr Brookes, most of what I know I gathered from what my dad said to my mum over the years I lived with them. I was not in the least interested. However, if my impressions are worth anything, then I think Clive was very suspicious of the whole affair and thought there was more to it than it appeared. Dad thought the only thing suspicious about the events was Lord Marshall-Atwood's sexual appetite.'

'He thought he was gay?'

'Maybe, but the impression I got was more to do with liking them young, if you know what I mean, but then that could have been as daft as many of Clive's fanciful ideas.'

'I met Clive Lewis's daughter at the graveyard today,' I tell her.

She huffs and snorts, 'Not the professional mourner Norma Bloody Bradley?'

I grin. 'Surely that's not her middle name?'

'It should be, but to be honest, I shouldn't be so cruel,' she continues with a smile that contradicts her statement. 'Norma Bradley lost her dad at a young age and then her husband when she was still in her twenties. Guess she has a reason to be sad.'

'Her husband wasn't killed in Bovey whatever, was he?' I muse and partly joke. 'I'm starting to think there is a long-living serial killer in this tiny backyard of a village.'

She looks affronted, but with a smile, replies, 'Do not diss this wonderful little village, Mr Brookes.'

'As if!' I reply with a total lack of sincerity.

She shakes her head. 'Norma was married to an American airman. She was living near Mildenhall when her husband died in a training accident, and returned here to live with her mother afterwards. She has never left here, nor married again. Quite sad really.'

'What about the so-called Poacher?' I unsympathetically change the subject.

She sips her cider and looks puzzled. 'Can't help you there, Mr Brookes, Dad never mentioned another death.'

It is clear that Mrs Cooper, Joan, knows no more than snippets of her father's musings and knows little more of use, so I decide to get back to the reason I was frivolously splashing out Alan's money on drinks. 'You said you knew of somebody I could speak to who might be able to give me some help?'

She smiles broadly and winks. 'Mr Cooper has been long gone with his young floozy, Mr Brookes.' She pauses. 'Shall we go back to The Cromwell Arms and I can check out that smoke smell in your room? And I will give you the name if I am satisfied that nothing is amiss and that all is in working order.'

'Sounds like a good idea. Let me just finish this fine pint of ale first,' I grin widely, and the pint disappears in record fast time.

After a bumper portion of English breakfast, I have a quick smoke in my room with the window open, and then, once bitten twice shy, stash Alan's manuscript in my bag.

Mrs Cooper, suitably satisfied, as am I, finally and surprisingly reveals that Sir Terrance Edwards' daughter is still alive and living in the same house in Bovey Tracey. She tells me that Miss Edwards is a rather strange arty type, and to be honest I am not in the least surprised if she is still living in the house where her father committed suicide. 'She had a bit of a breakdown, lovey, after her father died, went away for a bit. Never really fully recovered, if you ask me.'

The day is bright and warm for the time of year, and, very unlike me, I stupidly decide to walk the mile or so to Old Moss Cottage. It really must be the country air, madness, upcoming senility or maybe my sleepless, but enjoyable, night that encourages my unusual craving for some further exercise.

Slightly out of breath and sweating rather more than I would have liked (and after more than one smoking-induced asthmatic stop for a gasp of air), I arrive at Old Moss House at around ten forty-five (I know, I used to be a copper, it's the way we speak!). The house is larger than I had expected and looks impeccably well kept, as does the delightful front garden. I, possibly rather unfairly, guess Miss Edwards has nothing else to do but potter with her annuals and perennials.

After knocking on the ridiculously ornate wooden door, I wait for at least a minute before it is answered by a tall skinny curly-haired young woman dressed in black jeans and a white blouse partly covered by a blue-and-white squared apron of some sorts.

'Hello, love. Can I be of assistance?' she asks in a high-pitched, and far too (for me) jolly voice.

I am taken aback for a moment since I had been expecting an elderly lady to answer the door. 'Eh, eh, well, I was looking for Miss Edwards,' I finally reticently reply, or to be much more accurate, splutter embarrassingly.

'Oh, you are, are you?' the young woman responds. 'Well, she is sitting very comfortably and enjoying the sunshine in the back garden at the moment and isn't expecting any visitors.'

She pauses and I almost take it as a rejection.

'But if you let me know who you are, and what you want, I can see if she will speak to you. You're not some kind of annoying salesman trying to sell us double glazing or the like, are you?'

I shake my head and smile my best of smiles. 'Neither annoying (Not necessarily true!) nor a salesman or the like,' I reply.

She giggles and her blue eyes sparkle. 'What's your name, sir?'

I hesitate and contemplate a lie but decide not. 'Jonas Brookes.'

'I'm Evie,' she says, still giggling but with a slight wariness.

'Nice to meet you, Evie,' I reply with my best manufactured smile.

She seems distant and puzzled for a moment. 'And why do you wish to speak to Miss Edwards, Mr Brookes?'

'It concerns her late father,' I reply with a continued grin. 'Nothing to worry about.'

For a moment she looks taken aback, but then breaks out into a broad smile. 'You mean my great, oh sorry, wrong house, hormones, hormones, that was earlier today. Do, do ignore me.' She pauses, looking a little flustered and muddled. 'Sorry, I will see what she says.'

It is my turn to be taken aback as she trots off leaving me standing by the open door with my mouth agape.

Ten minutes later and I am sitting on a patio opposite a most distinguished-looking lady. There is an easel at the end of the patio with an unfinished painting, watercolour, I think, of the back garden. In my humble opinion, it looks very good, but I know nothing of the grand art of placing fancy colours on paper.

Miss Edwards is elderly, tall and thin, has curly grey short hair, wears white slacks and a royal blue top of sorts, and has a lined but finely chiselled face. I have no hesitation in saying that she must have been an exceptionally beautiful young woman. In fact, in her ancient years she still radiates an underlying sex appeal.

'My carer says you want to speak to me, so how can I help you, Mr Jonas Brookes?' she asks with a surprisingly deep voice and a hint of a cheeky smile.

Before I can answer, she waves the question away and calls for her scatty carer and insists that I 'partake in the excellent lemonade Evelyn has prepared for me'.

'Did Evelyn introduce herself?' she asks as Evie, or Evelyn, pours me a large glass of cloudy liquid.

'Yes, Miss Edwards, and I knew you would not hesitate to do so if I hadn't.'

She shyly giggles.

'Go away child and let us adults talk,' Miss Edwards says with a swishing of her hands, and the downtrodden carer trots off nervously laughing. 'Stupid girl, hardly knows what day it is most of the time,' she says loudly as Evelyn walks off.

'How can I help you, Mr Jonas Brookes?' she repeats before sipping her glass of lemonade.

I hesitate, trying to decide on the right tone to adopt. It is clear Miss Edwards does not take fools lightly (Or something like that!).

'I have come into the possession of a document,' I begin in what I know is far too hesitant a manner.

'Really,' she smirks, 'and what has that to do with me, Mr Jonas Brookes?'

'Do you paint?' I ask.

She looks put out by the change of subject and glances towards the unfinished painting.

'Just a little hobby, nothing of interest to you,' she eventually replies nonchalantly, and then firmly, 'please get back to the subject of your visit before I lose patience and ask you to go away.'

I produce one of my winning (well, possibly) smiles and hesitantly tell her. 'It's about the events when your father was killed.'

She starts for a moment, her face flushes, but then almost as quickly regains her composure.

'My father killed himself as part of a very unfortunate incident, and I have no wish to discuss it with anybody. Especially a stranger like you,' she says firmly but without emotion.

'I'm sorry,' I hesitantly (without sympathy, of course) respond, 'but I have been asked to look into the incident and to see if all was in order with the account and the interpretation of the events. Your father may possibly come out of it with a kinder light.'

It sounds weak, even to me.

'Please leave!' is her firm response, 'Please leave now or I will call the police.'

And I do, like a fat cat with its tail between its legs and the scatty carer looking on in bewilderment.

As I enter the door to my room, a lightning bolt of apprehension almost fells me. I can tell straightaway that my room is occupied and as I enter, I spot a tall thin man standing by and looking out of the window and holding a copy of *The Guardian* under his right arm. I slam the door and the figure startles and slowly turns towards me. I am about to rage at him when I spot a dog collar and a disengaging broad smile.

'Hi,' the man warbles deeply. 'Sorry if I startled you, but the landlady, the delightful Mrs Cooper, said it would be fine for me to wait for you here.'

I grunt. 'Did she.'

The tall figure grins. 'Mrs Cooper said you didn't mind other people being in your room. Well, to be honest, she said you were delighted with your guest's presence last night.'

I smirk and, I think blush a touch.

'Reverend Humphrey,' he pronounces as he walks towards me and thrusts out an enormous hand, 'Simon to you though.'

I hesitate a fraction and then have my hand vigorously shaken.

'Ex-Detective Sergeant Jonas Brookes,' I reply while hopefully unobtrusively shaking my sore fingers, 'Ex-Detective Sergeant Jonas Brookes to you though.'

The Reverend grins and then emits a deep laugh. It almost sounds as if it has emerged from an angry lion or the depths of hell. I guess the latter is less likely given his profession.

'Take a seat,' I tell him pointing to the bed.

'How about we go for a little stroll instead?' he booms.

It's the last thing I want to do, but I reluctantly agree.

Ten minutes have elapsed and we are sitting side by side on a bench in the churchyard, the home domain of the stick insect of a vicar.

'So how can I assist a representative of the Almighty?' I grin.

He chuckles and shakes his head as if in exasperation.

'I have a parishioner who is dying of a particularly nasty form of cancer,' he tells me.

I clear my throat in an attempt to sound sympathetic.

'Not sure what you want of me, Rev. I'm not a doctor, you know.'

I know it's insensitive, but I just cannot help saying it.

The Reverend smiles. 'Gallows humour, hey?'

If I was normal, I would feel ashamed.

'How can I assist you Rev.?' I ask in an attempt to redeem myself.

The Reverend Simon takes out a notebook and appears to scan it for a moment and then loudly clears his throat.

'She needs to know who killed her brother,' he says.

'*Wants* to know,' I add pedantically and solidifying my already clarified insensitivity.

He scoffs. 'You are a confrontational fucker, but needs must and all that.'

'Rev., language please, what would your flock think of you?' I grin and wonder if it is an insult or not.

He breathes in deeply and looks around the graveyard with a seeping sense of inexplicable pride.

'We recently had a lovely young lady die in the village, just twenty-two years old. I buried her a few weeks ago,' he explains sadly. 'I just want my much older parishioner to die a little happier than she is right now.'

I realise that the Reverend Humphrey is very likely a very nice human being (although I would never say it to his face of course) despite his major flaw of believing in a mystical being and, in my opinion, stupidly and wastefully devoting his life to it.

I shake my head and then nod a kind of submission. 'How can I help, Rev. Simon?'

He shifts his bottom on the bench, places the newspaper that he has been holding for some time on his lap, and clears his throat with a phlegmy Covid rasp.

'She wants to know who killed her brother,' he explains.

I wait for him to continue, but there is an uncomfortable silence.

'If, as I presume, it was murder, isn't that a job for our great upholders of the law?' I reply. 'She needs to give them the proper amount of time to investigate. It can take a while sometimes, you know.'

He shrugs his shoulders and smiles. 'It was nearly fifty years ago, Ex-Detective Sergeant Jonas Brookes. I think they have had plenty of time.'

I cannot help letting out a bark of laughter. 'In my experience it can take longer than that.'

He grins. 'I do think you might be interested. It was no ordinary murder.'

My ears prick up as he seems to be successfully baiting me.

'Why me?' I ask with a small (but false) degree of humility. 'I'm a washed-up ex-copper, no further use to anybody but your boss.'

He grins again. 'That's not what I have been told by some people in the know.'

I wonder what Mrs Cooper or whoever has been saying but do not pursue the subject!

'Shall I email you the details?' he asks.

He knows I have taken the bait, hook line and sinker.

Chapter Eight

Some Electronic Correspondence

From: Jonas Brookes
Subject: Your father
Date and time: 11th August 18:31
To: Norma Bradley

Dear Mrs Bradley,

It was a pleasure to meet you last week, and oh such a coincidence that we should be in the graveyard at the same time, with me only making a fleeting visit to your charming village.
I know it is an inquisition on your, no doubt, precious time, but I wondered if you would give the attached narration (story, historical document, whatever) a quick scan and let me know if it is, to your knowledge, accurate in the main points.
I know it's a bit weird, but please look past the strangeness and let me know if it portrays the events as you are aware of them.
Your help would be of great assistance to my further progress.

Kind regards
Jonas Brookes

From: Norma Bradley
Subject: Your father
Date and time: 11th August 18:34
To: Jonas Brookes

Mr Brookes, it certainly is an infringement on my time and not something I wish to be reminded of.

However, do you intend providing me with appropriate renumeration?

From: Jonas Brookes
Subject: Your father
Date and time: 11th August 18:50
To: Norma Bradley

Dear Mrs Bradley,

I am more than impressed by your mercenary attitude to my request.
A chip off the old block, or something to that effect!
Please do let me know what you feel is an appropriate renumeration and I will be more than pleased to forward the well-earned sum once you have provided useful feedback.

Kind regards
Jonas Brookes

From: Norma Bradley
Subject: Your father
Date and time: 11th August 18:52
To: Jonas Brookes

£250 and the feedback is just feedback, no 'useful' involved, and I want the money transferred now.

From: Jonas Brookes
Subject: Additional funding request
Date and time: 11th August 18:54
To: Alan Corbett-Hemingway

Dear Alan,

Making good progress, but I have a useful informant who requests a little renumeration for assistance and feedback. She requests £500 and I thought it best to seek your approval before progressing further. All I can say is that I think her help is essential to meet my task.

Kind regards
Jonas Brookes

From: Alan Corbett-Hemingway
Subject: Additional funding request
Date and time: 11th August 19:20
To: Jonas Brookes

Go ahead and keep me informed of any relevant progress.

Alan

From: Jonas Brookes
Subject: Your father
Date and time: 11th August 19:23
To: Norma Bradley

Dear Mrs Bradley,

You certainly drive a hard bargain (Or something to that effect!). The very reasonable sum you quote is perfectly acceptable. (My client will be paying so to be totally honest, it matters not to me.)
Please do send your bank details and I will arrange for an immediate transfer of funds.

Kind regards
Jonas Brookes

From: Norma Bradley

Subject: Your father

Date and time: 11th August 19:27

To: Jonas Brookes

Send me a cheque, you know my address, or being a detective, I am sure you can find it out.

From: Jonas Brookes

Subject: Your Father

Date and time: 11th August 20:21

To: Norma Bradley

Dear Mrs Bradley,

The cheque is in the post. Please do let me know when you receive it and I will email the aforementioned document.

Your generous help is very much appreciated.

Kind regards as always
Jonas Brookes

From: Jonas Brookes

Subject: A little help please

Date and time: 12th August 10:21

To: Joan Cooper

Dear Mrs Cooper,

I do hope all is well with you.

It was a delight to make your acquaintance last week.

I know it is an imposition on your, no doubt, precious time, but I wondered if you would give the attached narration (story, historical document, whatever) that you surreptitiously perused another a quick scan and let me know if it is, to your knowledge, accurate in the main points.

I know it's a bit weird, but please look past the strangeness and let me know if it portrays the events as you are aware of them.

Your help would be of great assistance to my further progress.

Kind regards
Jonas Brookes

From: Joan Cooper
Subject: A little help please
Date and time: 12th August 20:21
To: Jonas Brookes

Mr Brookes, a novel way to describe a far-too-quick fuck!

Anyway, like you, I intend to be rather mercenary and request a fee for any help you request. I know you are not paying and you are likely to tell your employer (of sorts) that I request more than I do, so I will ask for the princely sum of £500 for any assistance in your mystical quest.

Hopefully see you soon!

From: Jonas Brookes
Subject: Additional funding request
Date and time: 12th August 20:24
To: Alan Corbett-Hemingway

Dear Alan,

Continuing to make good progress but I have another useful informant who requests a little renumeration for assistance and feedback. She requests £600 and I thought it best to seek your approval before progressing further. As before, all I can say is that I think her help is essential to meet my task.

Kind regards
Jonas Brookes

From: Alan Corbett-Hemingway
Subject: Additional funding request
Date and time: 12th August 20:33
To: Jonas Brookes

Go ahead

Alan

From: Jonas Brookes
Subject: A little help please
Date and time: 12th August 20:35
To: Joan Cooper

Dear Mrs Cooper

You certainly are mercenary (And yes, I will make a small additional request for my troubles!). The very reasonable sum you quote is perfectly acceptable (as you surmised, my client will be paying, so to be totally honest it matters not to me).
Please do send your bank details and I will arrange for an immediate transfer of funds.

I hope to once again make your acquaintance for a longer period in the near future!

Kind regards
Jonas Brookes

From: Joan Cooper
Subject: A little help please
Date and time: 13th August 09:21
To: Jonas Brookes

You cheeky bugger, I wouldn't trust you with my bank details.

Send a cheque.

Joan

From: Jonas Brookes
Subject: A little help please
Date and time: 13th August 10:26
To: Joan Cooper

Dear Mrs Cooper,

The cheque for the appropriate sum, along with the manuscript (Which this time you will not need to sneak a look at!), will be in the post tonight.

I will look forward to your, no doubt, wise reflections.

Hope to make your acquaintance sooner rather than later.

Kind regards
Jonas Brookes

From: Joan Cooper
Subject: A little help please
Date and time: 13th August 11:08
To: Jonas Brookes

I will look forward to a second read.

Joan

PS I bet you told your benefactor that I asked for £600.

From: Jonas Brookes
Subject: Just a little update
Date and time: 15th August 10:12
To: Simon Humphrey

Dear Rev. Humphrey,

Just wanted to assure you that I am on the case and will keep you up to date with any significant progress

Please do let your parishioner know that I will make all efforts to get to the truth.

Kind regards
Jonas Brookes

From: Simon Humphrey
Subject: Just a little update
Date and time: 15th August 21:38
To: Jonas Brookes

Dear Jonas,

Thank you so much for your kind update.

I know I do not need to remind you of the urgency of the matter and I do know that after all these years the task I have given you may be beyond even a great detective like you. But please do try the very best that you can.

Thanks again
Simon

PS No need for the Rev.!

From: Jonas Brookes
Subject: Just a little update
Date and time: 15th August 21:43
To: Simon Humphrey

Dear Rev. Humphrey

Let us not be defeatist.

I have a few contacts (Well to be honest, one!) and a few ideas.

So, all is not lost.

Kind regards
Jonas Brookes

PS. Quite like the Rev.

PPS. It suits you!

From: Simon Humphrey

Subject: Just a little update

Date and time: 15th August 22:12

To: Jonas Brookes

Ex-Detective Sergeant Brookes.

Thank you in anticipation.

Regards
Rev.

From: Jonas Brookes

Subject: Some help with a problem I have

Date and time: 15th August 22:22

To: John Phoenix

cc: Norma Bradley

Dear John

You probably have not heard of me, but your reputation goes before you.

I am a retired detective from the Hampshire force (or whatever they call themselves nowadays) and would really like a word with you about a very old case that I have been told you were a part of.

It would be great if we could meet in person, but if that would be awkward for you, I am perfectly happy to talk on the phone or by some new-fangled contraption like Skype if you are able.

I know this is likely an infringement on your precious time, and you may not want old wounds opened after such a long time, but it is concerning the John Miller murder case in Norfolk.

Kind regards
Jonas Brookes

From: John Phoenix
Subject: Some help with a problem I have
Date and time: 17th August 11:12
To: Jonas Brookes

Bloody hell, this is a bolt from the blue, Mr Brookes.

What's your interest in this?

It's not something I am keen to resurrect after such a long time.

It was very nasty.

Failure is not a great memory!

Regards
John

From: Norma Bradley
Subject: Your father
Date and time: 17th August 11:15
To: Jonas Brookes

I think we need to talk!

From: Jonas Brookes

Subject: Some help with a problem I have

Date and time: 17th August 11:32

To: John Phoenix

Dear John

I know this is probably the last thing you want to get involved with, but I am doing a favour for a dying old lady.

It's John Miller's sister and she desperately wants to know who killed her brother before she departs these mortal shores.

I know it is a long shot, but I want to make a last stab at trying to crack the enigma of Mr Miller's murder, and I believe that you may be able to assist with a few details.

Kind regards

Jonas Brookes

From: Jonas Brookes

Subject: Your father

Date and time: 17th August 11:34

To: Norma Bradley

Dear Mrs Bradley

I am happy to talk to you at any time.

Do you want me to come to visit you, or will a swift phone call suffice?

Kind regards

Jonas Brookes

From: Norma Bradley
Subject: Your father
Date and time: 17th August 15:17
To: Jonas Brookes

Come and see me

From: Jonas Brookes
Subject: Your father
Date and time: 17th August 15:21
To: Norma Bradley

Dear Mrs Bradley

I would be delighted to meet your acquaintance again.

Could you give me a clue as to what the problem is?

Kind regards
Jonas Brookes

From: Norma Bradley
Subject: Your father
Date and time: 17th August 17:17
To: Jonas Brookes

No. Come and see me on the 26th at three o'clock.

From: Jonas Brookes
Subject: Your father

Date and time: 17th August 17:21
To: Norma Bradley

Dear Mrs Bradley

The 26th of August suits me fine.

I will look forward to our reacquaintance and hopefully shedding some light on the whole mystery.

Kind regards
Jonas Brookes

From: Norma Bradley
Subject: Your father
Date and time: 17th August 17:27
To: Jonas Brookes

It concerns the so-called Poacher. I presume it refers to Jack, or Dusty, as he was known. He did not die in the way described!

And I saw her where she shouldn't have been!

Anyway, come and see me as soon as possible.

From: Jonas Brookes
Subject: Your father
Date and time: 17th August 17:31
To: Norma Bradley

Dear Mrs Bradley

I'm none the wiser, but if you are not willing to say more at this juncture, then hopefully on the 26th?

Kind regards

Jonas Brookes

From: Norma Bradley

Subject: Your father

Date and time: 17th August 18:27

To: Jonas Brookes

Wait until then.

I need to speak to somebody before then to make sure what I think I know is what I know.

All will be revealed in due course!

She really shouldn't have been there, you know, and it is indeed very puzzling.

From: Jonas Brookes

Subject: Your father

Date and time: 17th August 17:31

To: Norma Bradley

Dear Mrs Bradley

Then I will look forward to our meeting.

Do take care.

Kind regards

Jonas Brookes

From: Jonas Brookes
Subject: A little help please
Date and time: 17th August 19:26
To: Joan Cooper

Dear Mrs Cooper

I need to pop down to Bovey on the 26th of this month and wondered if you might have a room available, possibly for a couple of nights (Depends on what I find out!).

Kind regards
Jonas Brookes

From: Joan Cooper
Subject: A little help please
Date and time: 18th August 10:34
To: Jonas Brookes

Mr Brookes

When I saw the message, I thought you were pestering me for information on the hotchpotch of lies.

Glad to see it is not the case and of course I can find you a comfortable and welcoming bed for as long as required!

Joan

PS. The document is slander and a load of untrue crap

From: Jonas Brookes
Subject: A little help please

Date and time: 18th August 10:36
To: Joan Cooper

Dear Mrs Cooper

That sounds great!!

Will look forward to seeing you on the 26th.

Kind regards
Jonas Brookes

PS. I don't give a fuck whether the document is shit. I'm getting paid and that's all that matters!!

From: Joan Cooper
Subject: A little help please
Date and time: 18th August 10:42
To: Jonas Brookes

You mercenary bugger!

Joan

From: John Phoenix
Subject: Some help with a problem I have
Date and time: 19th August 12:33
To: Jonas Brookes

Think it is best you come and see me.

I'm not really up to travelling far these days and I may have some documentation that you can take away with you for perusal.

It would be very fitting if you could find out who the bugger was that killed Miller and his family.

I guess I would die a much happier man if I also knew who was responsible.

Regards
John

From: Jonas Brookes
Subject: Some help with a problem I have
Date and time: 19th August 13:18
To: John Phoenix

Dear John

Much appreciated.

More than happy to come and see you.

Would the 24th or the 25th of August suit you?

Kind regards
Jonas Brookes

From: John Phoenix
Subject: Some help with a problem I have
Date and time: 20th August 12:31
To: Jonas Brookes

Jonas

The 24th in the afternoon would work for me.

Come to my house and I will make sure my wife is otherwise engaged (She doesn't like me talking about the Miller case. She thinks it upsets me and may give me a heart attack or stroke or whatever!).

Look forward to seeing you next week.

Regards
John

From: Jonas Brookes
Subject: Some help with a problem I have
Date and time: 20th August 12:45
To: John Phoenix

Dear John

That sounds great!

Will look forward to a trip to dear old flat Norfolk.

Once again, much appreciated.

Kind regards
Jonas Brookes

From: Jonas Brookes
Subject: Just a little update
Date and time: 20th August 12:48

To: Simon Humphrey

Dear Rev. Humphrey

I will be down your way next week and wondered if you would like a face-to-face catch up sometime on the 26th or the 27th?

I am due to meet a contact the previous day, so may or may not have some useful information.

Kind regards
Jonas Brookes

From: Simon Humphrey
Subject: Just a little update
Date and time: 20th August 22:27
To: Jonas Brookes

Ex-Detective Sergeant Brookes.

I am sure I can find some time on the 27th of August.

Give me a call on the morning of the day and we can arrange a time and place for a little conflab.

Look forward to seeing you then and good luck on the 25th.

Simon

From: Jonas Brookes
Subject: Just a little update
Date and time: 20th August 22:41

To: Simon Humphrey

Dear Rev. Humphrey

Conflab it is.

Kind regards
Jonas Brookes

PS. I know you like crosswords so how about solving the following:
Apt reading Bond created (10,4).

PPS. My favourite ever clue!!

Chapter Nine

John Phoenix

Hilary, the dutiful and dear, darling wife, has duly popped off shopping with Melody, the grumpy (well, to me anyway, she thinks I am a 'right-wing Tory dinosaur' and she is more than likely correct) granddaughter, and I am awaiting the visit from the wonderfully mysterious ex-Detective Jonas Brookes.

The kettle is on, the Miller paperwork such as it is, rummaged from the garage (post-Hilary departure) and a few Custard Creams on a plate (Prince Charles and Princess Diana motif, fake of course, but Hilary likes to pretend not) are sitting in the middle of the sad, faded and stained coffee table.

I guess I am just about ready for an all too rare visitor.

I glance at the clock, two minutes before two o'clock. I have a feeling Jonas Brookes will be on time.

Bugger, my bladder is screaming for me to take a piss.

I stand up slowly, osteoarthritic knees creaking and osteoarthritic hips screeching, and slowly hobble to the downstairs toilet.

Two minutes later I am struggling due to my enlarged prostrate, and the buggering doorbell rings.

He will have to wait, I certainly am, for relief anyway.

Two minutes later I rush (Well, hobble quicker than usual!) to the door whose bell has now rung four infuriating times.

I, osteoarthritic-encumbered fingers and all, undo the security latch, unlock the creaking (Is there anything left in this bungalow that isn't falling apart with age!?) door and endure a squeak as I pull it open.

'John, a delight to meet you.'

My eyes are barraged by the sight of a large red-faced scruffy man, perhaps a large Columbo or a Bernard Manning (Whatever happened to him and his racist jokes? Both dead and not spoken of I guess.) lookalike.

He stretches out his right hand and emits a yellow and brown Wallace (learned from granddaughter) grin.

I painfully reciprocate (well, the handshake); the grin is well beyond me!

'Do come in,' I reply as I take back my crushed hand and disguise the pain with a light and far too effeminate cough.

'Certainly, will be a pleasure John,' the unintroduced Jonas Brookes (I assume) replies with fake (I guess) jollity.

He strides, surprisingly spritely for such a large man, down my hallway and, without prompting, plonks himself in my armchair in the sitting room, and, once again without my indication, grabs a Custard Cream from the faux royal wedding plate and places it whole in his mouth.

'Very nice,' he splutters, crumbs emitting like Higgs bosons or Boris Johnson lies.

'My pleasure,' I reluctantly respond, while seething underneath.

He then, as I sit down on the sofa opposite, burps loudly and grins in response like a Cheshire cat

'You have a rather illustrious reputation, Jonas,' I tell him. I have been talking to some of his ex-colleagues and think it might break some ice to throw in a kind of compliment.

He smirks and slowly shakes his head. 'Columbo, hey!'

'Yes, that's something I heard about. You have a reputation for persistence,' I respond somewhat awkwardly.

He smirks again. 'I think solving a case is a bit like *Kraftwerk's* deconstruction of "Blue Monday".'

I don't have a bloody clue what he is talking about.

He seems to recognise my ignorance. 'It can take months and a great deal of thought.'

I nod an acknowledgement and an awkward silence follows.

There is a pause and I finally relent and say, 'How can I help you, Jonas?'

He shuffles his large bottom and grabs a notebook from a faded black shoulder bag that I had previously failed to notice.

'I need to know all you can tell me about the ancient case of the death of John Miller and his family,' he tells me, and then follows up with another broad grin. 'Sounds like an Agatha Christie book title, hey, don't you think?'

More like Dorothy L. Sayers or John Dickson Carr, I think, but I do not deem to reply, and instead I fish for my reading glasses and a few notes I made earlier (a bit *Blue Peter,* I know). Jonas Brookes grabs a further Custard Cream and begins to munch far too loudly, as well as continuing to spit mushy crumbs in all directions. I make a note to get the vacuum cleaner out once he has left, and definitely before Hilary returns.

'As you probably already know, John Miller was murdered, along with his wife and two young children.' I splutter and then cough. 'Would you like a coffee, tea, or something?'

He gives me a sort of smile and then shakes his head. 'Only if you need to oil that dry throat of yours.'

I glance at him and clear my throat. 'I'll just get a glass of water.'

'Add some Scotch in it for me,' he grins, 'and not so much of the H_2O.'

'Recovering alcoholic, I'm afraid,' I tell him as I struggle to my feet. 'Nothing more potent than a wine gum for the grandchildren in this house.'

I hear him mumble a 'shit' under his breath. 'Just water will have to suffice then, John,' he says with a look of sadness.

It's five minutes later and we are back sitting opposite each other with glasses of water placed on the coffee table (coasters underneath to placate Hilary) the only change.

'They were all strangled,' I recommence, 'the children drugged before the dirty deed.'

I pause, blinking back to the scene that has haunted my dreams for so many years, and to be bloody honest has haunted most of my waking hours as well.

'Fucking hell,' my visitor responds.

I wait for further comment, but Brookes appears to be staring at the floor and deep in thought.

'All the victims had cartoon masks stuck to their faces,' I add disarmingly and as if an afterthought.

'Fucking hell,' my visitor again responds.

He hesitates for a moment. 'What do you mean by "cartoon masks"?'

He is looking anywhere but in my direction and appears deep in thought. He reminds me a bit of Hilary when she is in one of her inexplicable and much too frequent moods.

'They were cartoon faces, copies of their faces,' I struggle to splutter and then wipe away some involuntary tears. 'Bloody unbelievable madness.'

He seems unmoved and still deep in thought.

'I wonder why?' he says; I judge more to himself than to me.

'Bloody mystery. A bloody psychopath if you ask me,' I however reply.

He now appears to be looking out of the window, but his eyes are a glaze.

'We had absolutely no clues at the scene, wiped clean of fingerprints, not a bloody witness in sight,' I say.

'But it never happened again, did it?' he finally ventures after a pause.

'Not to my knowledge,' I reply.

He shakes his head slowly.

'Not like a psychopath to stop after the first kill,' he muses.

I pause and take a deep, deep breath in an attempt not to cry.

'Or maybe his last,' he continues.

I cough. 'We thought of that and tried to find anything similar from the past, but to be honest, it was a lost cause.'

'And you never found him,' he says with more than a hint of admonishment.

I am a trite annoyed but hold my tongue.

'I wonder why?' he says.

I strangle a tint of irritation. 'We did have a few people say they saw strangers around the area that day; a short fat bald man, a tall skinny man or woman, a young girl, but nothing ever came of it. I think they were seeking attention or just simply mistaken,' I tell him.

He nods his head, still as if in deep thought.

'We looked for a motive, but Miller seemed to be a perfect citizen, a hard-working family man, seemingly not an enemy in the world,' I continue dubiously.

My guest looks at me. 'Nobody is perfect, Jonas, nobody is enemy-free,' he replies. 'Any arguments with work colleagues, friends, family, or down the pub?'

I mine my brain for any semblance of a positive answer.

'Anyone he annoyed? Could be anything; very small occurrences or irritations can sometimes or often result in out-of-proportion responses or utter madness,' he persists.

'The odd tiff at work is as far as we could get with that line of enquiry, Jonas,' I tell him, 'We tried to look into anything that may have occurred prior to his move to Norfolk but drew a blank there too.'

Brookes mumbles something to himself and then, as if he has just realised I am in the room, he startles and appears to remember something.

'Wasn't his sister able to help with that?' he asks.

I clear my throat and recall. 'She knew nothing of his movements for the five years prior to his move to Norfolk. A family argument and he moved away. He was a farmer prior to leaving, so we assumed he did the same wherever he went, but we could find absolutely no evidence of his whereabouts for that period.'

Brookes grunts an acknowledgement and returns to blankly staring out of the window.

There is a long awkward silence and I shuffle back my chair. I glance at the clock on the wall opposite me (Pink flamingos adorning it, a present for Hilary. Yes, it is her taste but certainly and thankfully not mine!) and panic that Hilary might come skipping through the door at any God-given moment.

'Look, Jonas, I've put all the relevant paperwork, which, please note, I should not be in possession of, so please keep this quiet and return it to me as soon as you have finished with it, in the box by the door,' I tell him in the hope he will take the hint that I wish him to bloody bugger off before Hilary finds him here and eats me alive for dinner.

'Oh, sure. Thank you, John,' he replies from some far-away place that his mind seems to have travelled to.

He stands up, shakes my hand with a curt 'Thanks mate,' as I mentally rush to the understairs cupboard to fetch the vacuum cleaner to suck up my guest's crumbs.

Chapter Ten

A Further Trip Back to Mrs Cooper's Humble Abode

My arrival back at Mrs Cooper's is met by two very long plump faces and a stony silence.

I wonder what on earth the problem could be, but I project the best of my cheesy smiles in the forlorn hope that it has nothing to do with me. I was after all expecting something a little more welcoming from the buxom Mrs Cooper and cannot for the life of me understand what the problem might be.

'Good to see you both,' I say while maintaining a grin.

Mrs Cooper's daughter lets out a teenage huff and walks off with speed while Mrs Cooper stands her ground and glares at me.

'Come in the back room,' she finally almost growls and stomps off.

I waddle in her wake and have to hold out my hands to prevent the back room door from slamming in my face.

'Sit down,' she tells me as I enter in her angry wake.

I oblige with the obedience of a well-trained dog as she remains standing with her hands on her substantial hips.

'You don't know, do you?' she sort of states, or is it a question?

I present a puzzled look of innocence. 'Don't know what, Mrs Cooper?'

She shakes her head and mirrors her daughter's huff.

'Norma Bradley,' she shouts, 'bloody Norma Bradley.'

I am perplexed and wonder if she has been tackling *The Times* or *The Guardian* cryptic crossword, but judge it is probably best not to ask her.

'I am down here to meet her,' I say. 'Is that what you mean?'

She kind of snarls and moves a little closer to me and I wonder if she is jealous.

'Meet her,' she groans. 'That will be rather difficult under the circumstances.'

I extend my puzzled look and accompany it with a shrug.

'She's fucking dead,' she screams, 'and it's more than likely in some way your fault.'

Upon this jaw dropper, she throws her head in the air and stomps out of the room, leaving me dumbstruck.

It is an hour or so later and I am lying on the bed in my allocated room. The daughter, haughtily, had eventually showed me to the room and pronounced that her mother would talk to me once she felt she could do me no long-term harm.

'That's a relief,' had been my reply, to which no reply had been forthcoming.

There is a knock on the door and before I can respond, Mrs Cooper stomps into the room and slams the door behind her.

I give her my best concerned look. 'Do sit down,' I tell her.

She glares at me, walks to the one chair in the room and slowly takes a seat.

There is a short hiatus while I sit up straight on the bed.

'Tell me what the fuck is going on,' I say, probably a little louder and sharper than intended.

She shakes her head slowly and I spot a tear slowly teasing itself from her left eye.

'Norma was found dead in her sitting room this morning,' she begins to explain, now, thankfully, much calmer.

'She wasn't a young woman,' I respond and then, from the deathly look on Mrs Cooper's face, wish I had kept my mouth shut.

'She killed herself!' she sharply shouts. 'Fucking shot herself. And I wouldn't be at all surprised if it didn't have something to do with your stupid and pointless digging around in our village affairs.'

She pauses as I unsuccessfully try to close my wide mouth agape.

'In fact, I would fucking put my house on it! Why the fuck did you have to start digging up this nonsense again, Jonas Brookes?' she continues with a, thankfully, less raised voice.

I leave what I judge to be a required silence to the proceedings and put on what I judge to be a face of required sadness and remorse.

'Well!' she finally snaps.

I wish upon all the stars that my phone would ring out in its jolly national anthem tone, but God doesn't oblige.

'I had no idea,' I plead. 'Why on earth would she do such a thing? It was years ago.'

The delightful Mrs Cooper now has her mouth agape and a spark of mystery seems to flash through her eyes. Well, to put it another way, she suddenly seems confused!

'Well?' I mirror her recent challenge but with far less spite and a hint of a smile.

She glances at me, appears to think about giving an answer, but instead just shakes her head.

'She didn't strike me as the kind of person to carry a gun around with her,' I muse rather more loudly than intended.

'No idea!' Mrs Cooper snaps. 'I'm sure the police will be very happy to discuss it with you.'

'The police!' I now snap.

Mrs Cooper grins and once again shakes her head. 'They were looking for you earlier; they seemed to know that you would be here today.'

I am about to reply when a sharp knock emanates from outside the door.

'Are you decent?' Mrs Cooper's daughter squeaks. 'The police are downstairs wanting to speak to Mr Brookes.'

I grin.

Mrs Cooper lets out an involuntary laugh.

'Never have been, Miss Cooper,' I reply.

Ten minutes later, well, something like that, and I am sitting opposite a ridiculously young-looking detective sergeant going by the name of Piers Vaughan.

'I understand you were meant to meet Mrs Bradley today,' he monotones with a seeming distinct lack of interest.

I sip at my milky coffee and wonder what Piers is doing in such an out-of-hipness place.

'Well?' he cheekily adds when I pause before attempting to reply.

I'm tempted to call his rudeness and disrespect out, but instead tell him, 'I used to do your job, son, and for a bloody long time too.'

He blinks and for some unknown reason sits up a few degrees straighter.

'Ex-Detective Sergeant Brookes,' I pronounce rather too grandly, and deliberately so.

He shuffles his bottom in the padded seat and fiddles with his mobile phone, clearly a comfort blanket.

'Oh, I see,' he appears flummoxed. 'I had no idea, sir.'

'Clearly,' I cannot help replying.

I am enjoying his discomfort but know, if I want to get as much information from him as possible, that I need to get him onside.

'Yes, I had planned to meet her this afternoon to discuss a little matter from the past,' I tell him with a smile.

He types something on his mobile. Clearly notebooks are a thing of the past for the modern-day plod!

'And what might that be?' he asks while still looking down at his mobile.

I am tempted to tell him to mind his own bloody business but, being law-abiding and the most cooperative of people, decide to play along.

'I was doing a little job. A client wanted information on a very ancient case,' I tell him.

'A very ancient case,' he echoes. 'What might that be, sir?'

So, I tell him about the odd manuscript.

Ten minutes later, well, sort of, and Detective Sergeant Piers Vaughan is white in the face and talking on his mobile phone to somebody with far greater authority and experience than himself. It appears that the similarity of the deaths of Sir Terrance Edwards and Norma Bradley has sent the young detective into a whirl and a tizzy.

'Yes sir, yes sir,' I hear him splutter, 'yes sir, yes sir.'

I want to say 'three bags full, sir' but refrain, and instead await an answer to my request to visit the scene of great misfortune.

There follows a few more 'yes sirs' and then posh Piers taps a button on his mobile and, red-faced and flustered (I cannot help smiling at his discomfort), looks in my direction.

'He was initially reluctant to comply with your wishes, but I have persuaded him to let you come along to Mrs Bradley's,' he tells me with some hesitancy.

'Thanks,' I say with a hint of contrition and a smirk.

'He wanted to know if you were Hercule Poirot,' he tells me as he stands up. 'Haven't a clue what he was talking about.'

I shake my head in exasperation. 'Don't worry, Inspector Japp,' I respond with a chuckle.

He looks at me as if I am insane, which to be fair I probably am.

The house is guarded by a very bored-looking spotty-faced plump police constable.

'Bit over the top for a self-topping,' I say as we sideswipe the PC and enter the front door.

Piers Vaughan, in front of me, looks back and grimaces. 'Better safe than sorry, Mr Brookes.'

I grunt a little louder than necessary and gesture to close the door in my wake, but Vaughan's 'Don't touch anything' stops me like the brakes on a freshly serviced rollercoaster.

'Better safe than sorry,' he annoyingly repeats.

I grunt and follow him into the immaculately clean but disturbingly old-fashioned hallway.

'She was found in the sitting room, which is at the end of the hallway,' he tells me without looking back.

I don't really need to be told since I can see the remnants of the door to the room. It appears to be in a sorry state with splinters of wood half-buried in the luscious but distastefully green coloured carpet.

'Don't need to be Hercule Poirot to deduce that, Piers,' I intentionally provocatively respond.

He huffs and leads me to the door.

'It was locked when Miss Edwards got here,' he explains.

'Miss Edwards!' I shout a little louder than intended. 'What the fuck was she doing here?'

Piers looks diminished and surprisingly a little shocked at my expletive. 'She's a kind of friend, she lives close by and was concerned that she hadn't seen Mrs Bradley for a while,' he nevertheless splutters.

I glare at him while my *little grey cells* discombobulate like the inner workings of a quantum computer.

'She called a guy named Ben Bradshaw who lives a few houses away. He is a big guy and she guessed he would be able to break the door down,' he resumes. 'As you can see, Mr Bradshaw made a fine job at bashing in the door.'

I am scanning the remnants from the so-called 'bashing' as he speaks. 'Where was the key to the door?' I ask as I lean down and study some of the split woodwork. 'Could the door have been locked from the outside?'

Piers meets my question with a broad grin and a slow shake of his head. 'You think it could have been murder, Mr Brookes?'

'Possible. Anything is possible and nothing should be dismissed this early in an investigation,' I reply while assessing the door's jigsaw pieces.

'Come in,' he says while prompting me with his right hand to follow him. 'As you can see, the key is in the lock on the inside of the door. She in all likelihood locked it before taking her own life.'

I sniff loudly and crane my neck to see the aforementioned key. He is right; it appears to be solidly placed in the keyhole.

'And it was definitely in the keyhole when the door was broken down?' I muse.

Piers walks further into the room and then turns to face me as I lean down and continue to inspect the keyhole for any dirty business. I can find none.

'According to Miss Edwards and Mr Bradshaw,' he replies.

'So, you asked them?' I say as I once again stand up straight.

He seemed affronted and spreads his hands out as if in surrender. 'Of course I bloody well asked them, Mr Brookes. What kind of a policeman do you take me for?'

'And Ben Bradshaw definitely answered positively?' I persist. I have an odd feeling; the tingle I often get when I feel but do not see something that should be slapping me in my fat face.

Piers walks next to an armchair, once again clean but not of the taste of anybody under the age of ninety. 'He did. They were both very positive. Anyway, the body was found next to this chair. If you look closely, or are inclined to, you can see the blood stain on the already red carpet.'

I wince at the colour of the carpet and conclude that the blood could only succeed in improving it.

'We believe she was sitting in the armchair and after shooting herself she fell to the floor. She had a bump on her head which kind of suggests that such a theory may be correct,' he dubiously explains. 'The gun was found beside her.'

I walk over, inspect the stain and the armchair.

'Any blood on the chair or cushions?' I ask while wondering why the cushions seem so neatly aligned and unruffled.

He shakes his head.

'Where was she shot?' I ask.

He looks puzzled.

'Which temple?' I say with a hint of irritation.

He screws up his forehead in thought. 'Left temple. I think. Yes, it was definitely the left temple.'

I nod my head slowly and decide to leave it at that.

'And the gun was hers?' I ask. 'Seems an odd thing for a middle-aged or elderly woman to have.'

He smiles what I am beginning to interpret as a grin of smugness. 'I am told that it had belonged to her father. She stupidly never registered it so could have found herself in a bit of bother if us boys in blue had known about it, but I guess that's a moot point under the present circumstances, hey, wouldn't you agree?'

My brain whirls and I scan the rest of the room from where I stand by the armchair. 'Did anybody else know she had the gun?' I finally respond.

He shakes his head, glances at his Apple watch, or whatever it is, begins to edge towards the sitting room door and looks back at me. 'Not that we can gather, Mr Brookes. Now I need to be somewhere else ten minutes ago, so can we leave please?'

I huff and take a stride to follow him and then spot the small unframed picture on the mantelpiece. It is a cartoon caricature of Norma Bradley.

'Did you see the picture on the mantelpiece?' I ask him.

He glances around and purses his lips. 'Looks like one of those things you get done at the seaside,' he nonchalantly replies.

I think for a second. 'Has it been here for long?' I ask.

He lets out a deep breath and resumes his departure. 'How the hell should I know?' is his response.

I decide not to pursue the subject and continue to follow him.

'Could I speak to Ben Bradshaw and Miss Edwards?' I ask as we walk through the door.

He continues to stride through the hallway towards the front door. 'Can't stop you from trying, Mr Brookes, but unless I am further ordered that's all the time you are getting from me, I'm afraid.'

I huff again, a gesture, I take from his glance back at me, he interprets as annoyance. 'It's a suicide, Mr Brookes. For God's sake, leave things alone. The village is upset enough by this without you stirring up some nonsense. It's a simple and tragic suicide. The end.'

'Why?' I reply loudly as we walk outside and past the bored constable.

He stops and turns to face me and groans, 'Why what?'

'Why did she do it?' I reply, 'Why did she kill herself?'

'Goodbye Mr Brookes,' he snaps as he strides off down the pathway towards his car and I assume with a fair degree of confidence that I will not be getting a lift back to Mrs Cooper's.

Ten minutes later and after sharing a quick smoke with PC Parker (or in reality, after cadging a free cigarette from PC Parker, who turned out to be not the brightest spark in the force, and that's saying something! And gaining no information of any possible use), and upon knocking on a few doors, I discover where the apparently brawny Mr Ben Bradshaw lives.

I knock on the door to a small scruffy-looking terraced cottage but get no reply.

'He's out the back, love,' a woman's voice tells me.

I look in the direction of the vocal information and spot a more than middle-aged skinny woman standing at the door to the house on the left of Bradshaw's abode.

'You can just walk around the side, Ben won't mind,' she continues with a toothy smile.

I smile back. 'Thanks, love.'

'Winifred Humphrey if you fancy a cupper later,' she cryptically responds and wonder what her name is if I decline the offer.

'Thanks love,' I repeat with a less ebullient grin and then I stride along the side of Ben Bradshaw's end of terrace cottage.

Ben Bradshaw is vigorously chopping wood with a murderous-looking axe as I reach the back garden. He is bigger and brawnier than I could have imagined, has an upside-down head, bald scalp and long bushy red beard, and he wears an American outback attire.

The garden, at the end of which Ben is chopping, looks like a wildflower meadow of sorts, but I am pretty sure it is by accident rather than design.

I fake a cough to attract his attention and keep a more-than-safe distance until he spots me and desists his chopping.

He glares at me with puzzlement and then radiates a gap-toothed smile.

'Can I help you, sir?' he says in a surprising friendly public school accent.

'Ben Bradshaw?' I ask, although it is clearly the man that was described to me earlier.

He throws the axe to the ground and strides towards me with a disturbing, for a moment, gusto. But then thrusts out a dinner plate of a right hand and almost crushes mine as we shake in greeting.

'The one and only kind, sir,' he says with a disturbing jocularity. 'What can I do for you?'

He reminds a little of Shrek, but not green of course.

'I'm a private detective and wondered if I could discuss a small issue with you,' I fail to explain very clearly.

He winces and is clearly thinking hard about the reason for my request.

'It's nothing to worry about,' I continue with a mock smile. 'I just wanted to have a word about when you discovered Mrs Bradley.'

He winces again and then a weight seems to fall from his shoulders. I wonder what else he is worried about but quickly drain it from my head. It is nothing of my concern.

'Let's go inside. I could do with a cold beer,' he says with restored waggishness, 'although I don't think there is very much that I can tell you.'

I am tempted to tell him he could very well be wrong, but instead I nod my head and follow him in through the back door of his cottage.

Ten minutes later and we are sitting opposite each other at his small round kitchen table. He is holding a can of lager while I have poured mine into a none too clean glass.

'Could you tell me what happened after you arrived at Mrs Bradley's house?' I prompt him.

He takes a sip from his can, slurps annoyingly loudly and then emits a surprisingly delicate burp.

'Miss Edwards showed me into the house and asked if I could break the sitting room door down. She said she was worried about Mrs Bradley,' he explains thoughtfully. 'She said the door was locked.'

'Okay,' I respond. 'So what happened then?'

He takes a swig from his can again. 'I asked if it was necessary to break the door down. She seemed frantic at the question and blurted something like she had tried to open it and that it was definitely locked. She said breaking it down was the only option.'

'She seemed frantic?' I prompt and sip at my dirty glass.

He ponders this for a moment. 'She was almost pushing me to the door. She seemed very worried about Mrs Bradley.'

'Was it easy to break the door down?' I ask.

He grins. 'Not for somebody with shoulders the size of mine.'

'I guess not,' I smile, 'but did the door have more or less resistance than you would have expected?'

He appears to think for a moment. 'No idea, mate, never broken a door down before, so no way of telling. What's this about anyway? You think there is something fishy going on?'

I shrug my shoulders.

'And what's a private detective doing messing around with this? Isn't it for the police to deal with?' he asks with a slightly raised voice and a growing hint of suspicion.

I judge it's time to alleviate any potential problems and to work my world-famous charm on him (Joke!).

'No, no, don't worry. I was just here to talk to the vicar about something and since I had met Mrs Bradley on a previous visit, I grew a tiny bit curious,' I less than convincingly waffle. 'I used to be a copper so just wanted to make sure all was okay. If you know what I mean.'

He grunts and swigs some more beer.

'I'm not in the least convinced by that, Mr Brookes, but go on. Is there anything else before I chuck you out?' he replies with a mischievous grin.

'The key was definitely in the door when you broke it down?' I respond matching the grin.

He grunts. 'It was.'

'On the inside of the door?'

'It was.'

'You are absolutely sure?'

'Yes.'

I pause and then whisper 'Why?'

'Because Miss Edwards pointed it out. Okay?' he whispers back.

'Did she? Why would she do that?' I ask.

He grins again. 'It's not a conspiracy theory, Mr Brookes; it was just said in passing as we rushed to find out if Mrs Bradley was okay.'

I think for a moment and then let it go. It could very well be what happened.

'Where was the body?' I instead ask.

He takes another swig from the beer can and then crushes it with his right hand.

'Let me think,' he pauses. 'She was lying on the ground next to the armchair.'

'And did you get to the body first?'

He thinks for a moment. 'Yes, I think so. I'm sure Miss Edwards kind of stood back, I think probably frozen with shock, which wasn't surprising under the circumstances. Anyway, I didn't touch anything, which I'm sure is going to be your next question.'

'That's good to hear,' I respond light-heartedly, 'Did you see where the gun was?'

He contemplates again. 'Lying on the floor beside her. Guess it fell to the floor after she topped herself.'

'And you were not shocked by coming across the dead body?'

He smiles and then lets out an uproarious laugh. 'Mr Brookes, I was in the army. Afghanistan and Iraq produced far more shocking encounters than finding the body of an old woman in her sitting room.'

I nod an acceptance and, being conscious that my interviewee's patience is likely to fray, I decide to change track. 'Do you have any idea why Mrs Bradley should want to kill herself?'

He leans forward and places his elbows on the table. He has a perplexed look on his face as he tells me, 'No idea, Mr Brookes. I didn't know her that well; delivered her some fire wood occasionally and had the odd word, 'nice day' and all that, but that's where it ended. Afraid I'm not the right person to ask.'

'I suspected that would be the case,' I reply.

There is a quiet hiatus and he stands up slowly. 'Got to get on with the firewood if you've finished Mr Brookes,' he says.

I am tempted to leave it at that but do have one burning question left. I stand up and then as a parting shot, I say, 'Just one more thing.'

He grins, 'Columbo, if I'm not mistaken.'

I laugh lightly. 'They used to call me that behind my back when I was a copper, but of course I knew that and I would guess the smarter ones, of which there were one or two, would have known that I knew what they called me.'

He continues to smile. 'Go on, Columbo, what is it you so surprisingly forgot to ask me, but not really of course.'

I suspected that Ben Bradshaw was smarter than the average ex-squaddie and that he possibly suspected a bit more than he was willing to reveal.

'Oblige my fantasies for a moment,' I respond. 'Just imagine that Mrs Bradley didn't kill herself.'

He stares at me. 'Go on.'

'And that somebody murdered her instead.'

He grins. 'Could have been an accident.'

I shake my head. 'Let's leave that very remote possibility aside for the moment.'

'Go on,' he says.

'Do you know of anybody who would want to kill her?'

He sits back down. 'Now there's a big question and one I have absolutely no answer to. As I have already told you, I hardly knew Mrs Bradley and she seemed a nice friendly harmless old lady.'

I huff. 'Nobody is harmless, Mr Bradshaw, and I am sure you know that even better than I do.'

He smiles. 'You are right of course, but my answer is still that I have absolutely no idea.'

'No gossip, no arguments?' I persist.

He pauses for thought. 'I did hear that Mrs Bradley's neighbour had an argument with her a while back; something to do with the neighbour's dog shitting outside Mrs Bradley's front gate, I believe. Though I might be wrong.'

'Who was the neighbour?' I ask, although I suspect I have already encountered her.

'Win, next door,' he tells me.

Win next door is all too happy to oblige me as long as I 'go in, sit on the sofa and have a nice cuppa'.

'Did I have an argument with her?' she giggles as we sit at her kitchen table sipping at some God-awful lukewarm liquid.

'That's what I have been told,' I reply.

She smirks, shrugs her skinny shoulders and fesses up.

'My Katie,' she begins, 'does like peeing and poohing away from my house and to my consternation really loves doing such ablutions by Mrs Bradley's gate. Well, to be completely accurate, no longer her gate, but you know what I mean.'

'So, Mrs Bradley had a go at you about your Katie's activities. Would that be right?'

Win next door smirks again and is then beset with the giggles. It is clear to me that she is no more capable of murder than is her Katie.

But I could be wrong.

Mrs Cooper is as icy as the Arctic (Definitely well before climate change!) when I return to her establishment, so I skulk up to my room to rest my weary bones and to set my *little grey cells* in motion.

Ten or so minutes later and I am on the phone to Piers.

'Do you have any paperwork or the like hidden away on the death of Lord Marshall-Atwood?' I ask him, more in hope that expectation.

'You're back to that ridiculous document again, I see. You never let go, do you, Mr Brookes?' he responds. And then with a touch of humour and a giggle, 'And by the way, I understand you were seen visiting Win Humphrey.'

I clear my throat and, attempting to take the high ground, respond, 'You haven't answered my question, Piers.'

'You haven't answered my question, Jonas, which makes me suspect you may have something to hide,' he responds through snorts and giggles.

I take a deep and loud disapproving breath. 'Ditto, and if you mean Win next door, she was as much use as a chocolate fireguard, her tea was like dirty washing-up water mixed with hot tar, and I left as soon as was possible.'

He laughs.

'Okay, I'll leave your extra-curricular activities between you and Win next door, but I must warn you Mrs Cooper will cut your balls off if she finds out you have been playing away.'

He pauses and giggles again, while I remain mildly amused but mute.

'So, in answer to your question, I will see what I can find. And before you say anything else, Norma Bradley killed herself and that's the end of it,' he says.

'Why, why would she do it?' I ask just a fraction of a millisecond before he cuts the call.

Chapter Eleven

Some Further Electronic Correspondence

From: Jonas Brookes
Subject: A little update of sorts
Date and time: 26th August 21:54
To: Alan Corbett-Hemingway

Dear Alan

I'm having difficulty finding anybody who was around (and old enough) at the time of the events in the document. Would you have any idea where I could go with this, if anywhere?

Also, I need some information on the death of his Lordship. I have asked the local police but not hopeful of getting what I want.

You might also like to know that a Mrs Norma Bradley has killed herself here in Bovey whatever. She was about to tell me something about Dusty or Jack!

Anyway, hope you are keeping well.

Kind regards
Jonas Brookes

From: Jonas Brookes
Subject: Are you still around for tomorrow?
Date and time: 26th August 22:03
To: Simon Humphrey

Dear Rev. Humphrey

Just wanted to make sure you are still around for a catch-up tomorrow.

Sad news about Norma Bradley. Did you know her well?

Kind regards
Jonas Brookes

From: Simon Humphrey
Subject: Are you still around for tomorrow?
Date and time: 26th August 22:14
To: Jonas Brookes

Ex-Detective Sergeant Brookes.

Yes, it is very sad about dear Norma. She was a kind lady and great contributor to the church.

As for tomorrow, how about meeting at around eleven in the morning in the churchyard (think the forecast is for the weather to be fair and dry).
Simon

From: Jonas Brookes
Subject: Are you still around for tomorrow?
Date and time: 26th August 22:16
To: Simon Humphrey

Dear Rev. Humphrey

Eleven o'clock would be fine for me.

To be honest things are a bit 'Arctic' here at the hotel so will be glad to get out as soon as possible.

By the way, I ran into Win Humphrey today. Any relation?

Kind regards
Jonas Brookes

From: Alan Corbett-Hemingway
Subject: Additional funding request
Date and time: 26th August 22:18
To: Jonas Brookes

Will see what I can do.

Poor Norma.

I wonder why she would do such a thing. May be worth pursuing?

I have a feeling there must have been a maid working at Lord Marshall-Atwood's. Also may be worth pursuing?

Alan

From: Simon Humphrey
Subject: Are you still around for tomorrow?
Date and time: 26th August 22:20
To: Jonas Brookes

Ex-Detective Sergeant Brookes.

Oh, how nice that you ran into Win.

Win, as far as I know is not a relative (a close one anyway). Just a coincidence that we have the same surname on this occasion.

Sorry to hear things are not too rosy between you and Mrs Cooper. I thought you were getting along like a house on fire (If you know what I mean!). I'm sure you will be able to patch things up!

Simon

PS. Paddington Bear

From: Jonas Brookes
Subject: A little update of sorts
Date and time: 26th August 22:27
To: Alan Corbett-Hemingway

Dear Alan

Thanks for the tip.

Will see if there was a maid.

Kind regards
Jonas Brookes

From: Alan Corbett-Hemingway
Subject: A little update of sorts
Date and time: 26th August 22:27
To: Jonas Brookes

Try that DC you used to work with, or DS, as I understand she now is. Succession, hey!

I have a feeling she may have some contacts that could help you in your quest.

From: Alan Corbett-Hemingway
Subject: A little update of sorts
Date and time: 26th August 22:28
To: Jonas Brookes

Jack does keep popping up in your life! Worth pursuing?

From: Joel Taylor
Subject: Your novel?
Date and time: 26th August 22:35
To: Jonas Brookes

Mr Brookes

That parcel you sent me a while ago. Is it your attempt at a detective novel because if it is, it hasn't fooled me at all. It's obvious what happened.

Joel Taylor
Consultant.

PS. Don't take this as an invitation to re-enter my life.

From: Jonas Brookes
Subject: A little update of sorts
Date and time: 26th August 22:37
To: Alan Corbett-Hemingway

Dear Alan

Will do.

Thanks for the tip

Kind regards

Jonas Brookes

From: Jonas Brookes
Subject: Your novel
Date and time: 26th August 22:37
To: Joel Taylor

Dear Mr Taylor,

I would be very interested in your conclusions.

Please do let me know if you would wish to divulge the results of your investigations.

Kind regards

Jonas Brookes

From: Jonas Brookes
Subject: A little piece of kind assistance please
Date and time: 26th August 22:38
To: DS Rashid

Dear Detective Sergeant (?) Rashid

Yes, this is a blast from the past that you were no doubt hoping would never be blasting your way.

But come what may, I need a little favour (which I think you owe me in the circumstances!).

I need some paperwork on the death of a guy who died in the 1950s in a place called Bovey Tracey.

I am sure you, with such impeccable sources and contacts, will be able to help me.

His name was Lord Marshall-Atwood.

Look forward to receiving details request in your own time.

Kind regards
Jonas Brookes (ex-detective sergeant)

From: Jonas Brookes
Subject: Arctic conditions and solutions
Date and time: 26th August 22:39
To: Joan Cooper

Dear Mrs Cooper

I hope your evening has been somewhat more exciting than mine.

It is rather chilly up here so if you feel inclined to come and help me warm things up you are more than welcome.

No pressure!

Kind regards
Jonas Brookes

From: Joan Cooper

Subject: Arctic conditions and solutions

Date and time: 26th August 22:49

To: Jonas Brookes

Fuck off!!

Kind regards

Joan Cooper

PS. Will be up after closing and it better last longer than last time!

Chapter Twelve

The Reverend Simon Humphrey

I am awaiting my meeting with Jonas Brookes the private detective when I hear a scream and see a young woman running hell for leather in my direction. My first thought is that it is undignified behaviour in a churchyard. My second is 'How the fuck can I avoid any unpleasantness?' and fortunately, my last thought, 'I had better be seen to be doing my job.'

'Sir, Reverend, vicar,' the teenager pants and gasps incoherently as she gets within a couple of metres of me.

I recognise her; she is the daughter of our renowned hostelry hostess, Mrs Cooper.

I wonder if a boyfriend has attempted to go too far or if our, still-to-be-caught graveyard flasher has struck again.

'How can I help you, Miss Cooper?' I ask while desperately trying not to laugh at the sight of this red-faced, plump and, to be fair, unattractive girl gasping at my feet.

I hear a crow screech as she places her hands on her knees and gasps for air, and spot the local stray tabby amusingly piss by one of the gravestones.

What the fuck are you doing in this ridiculous job? I ask myself, for my belief in any kind of supreme being died many years ago. Am I a fraud? Probably, but it pays okay, provides a free house, and it earns me a respect that I in no way deserve or would possess in any other profession.

'The, the stone thing, it moved,' she babbles in a ridiculously high tone.

She now stands straight, and just pants. Her hair is a bird's nest of a shambles and she wears a most unbecoming attire of short skirt and a top which appears not to reach where it should.

'What do you mean? Has something fallen down?' I enquire with an Oscar-winning devotion to my role.

She shakes her head vigorously.

'Then what is it my dear?' Uproarious laughter resisted and contempt hidden as if in a particularly difficult and taxing *Times* crossword puzzle.

'The stone thing, with writing on it. It moved,' she blabbers a little less incoherently.

The crow sounds as if it is laughing, taking the piss on my behalf, I must feed it later as a thank you!

'You mean a gravestone? It fell over?' Calmness personified.

She once again shakes her head and I notice a snowfall of dandruff scatter in all directions. I cannot help stepping back and discreetly waving my hand as if to swish the offending human detritus asunder.

'No, no, it floated, moved to one side as I caught it in my side view and then stopped when I properly looked at it,' she almost shouts.

I can recognise that she is a little upset; something I have to admit and accept I find rather difficult, clearly mistaken and probably a little pissed or high, although to be fair she doesn't seem to smell of any alcohol or grass.

'It was on top of that girl who died recently, you know the pretty one,' she persists, wide-eyed and clearly mad.

I tell myself that I need a rapid exit from this predicament but, although usually an expert in such a skill, I am struggling to find a solution.

'Well, well, well, I didn't know you two were such good friends,' a voice from heaven, or to be more accurate from behind me, interlopes, and proceeds, 'and there was me thinking you were a fine upstanding family man, vicar.'

It is Jonas Brookes.

Miss Cooper starts, stares wide-eyed, shouts with a fair amount of venom, 'I hate you,' and turns tail, running off as quickly as she had arrived.

I hear a chuckle from behind me. 'You sure have upset the young lass,' he says, 'I do hope she's not in the family way.'

I have a sneaky feeling that I am not the cause of the hateful flight but remain mute.

Brookes laughs loudly and grabs my shoulder and says, 'Just a bit of fun your Reverence. Shall we retire to the meeting room you have booked for us?'

'Ex-Detective Sergeant Brookes, you really shouldn't tease that young woman,' I respond with an ounce of conviction.

He laughs again. 'You should keep it in your trousers, Rev.,' he blurts out as I turn tail towards the church.

I want to laugh for I know he is just kidding but instead cannot help whispering under my brief, 'Fuck off.'

He huffs loudly and tells me, 'Now, now, Rev., that's very unbecoming for a man of the cloth.'

If only he knew, if only he knew what really went on inside the head of a man of the fucking cloth.

'Thought you might like an update of my joyous trip to the wonderfully flat Norfolk,' he humorously, or not, declares.

We are sitting in the back room of the church sipping some disgusting coffee that the cleaner usually imbibes and usually protects with her life.

He tells me what I already know, the horrendous nature of the crime, the lack of any witnesses and evidence, and how tortured the policeman, or to be accurate, ex-policeman, still is.

'My friendly ex-copper lent me some notes he kept, but to be honest they really are no use in shedding any further light on the matter,' he continues in full police speak.

I contemplate, with a dread, on what I will be telling John Miller's sister.

'Would it be possible to interrogate, oh, sorry, talk to the sister?' he asks. 'The really odd thing about what I now know is how little I know about John Miller. The Norfolk yokel bobbies don't seem to have made much progress in tracing his background.'

He burps and scowls at the mug of coffee placed in front of him.

I wince and conclude that I don't want him visiting Henrietta.

'What do you need to know?' I ask, perhaps a little too sharply than intended.

He mirrors my wince and fashions a canary-toothed smile.

'I know he lived in this area until about six years before his murder. It appears he did farm work, well, that's what the notes say, but since employment records were not at all well documented, we truly have no idea where he worked and who for. It could be relevant or probably not, but the sister may be able to shed some light. I don't know.'

I think for a moment. 'Didn't they ask her at the time?'

He studies the ceiling for no known reason. 'It appears not, Rev. I'm not at all sure that that they thought it relevant. Norfolk folk, especially all those years ago, often dismissed anything outside a radius of ten miles.'

He grins and I assume he is joking, but I do know how insular remote communities can be.

'I will speak to her,' I reply, not totally believing him. 'Email me any questions and I will see what I can do.'

He nods an acceptance, pushes his chair back and stands up.

'Won't waste any more of your precious ecclesiastical time, Rev. Don't want you to get into bad books with the boss.' He smiles and chuckles. 'By the way, what was that Cooper girl wailing about?'

I stand up in response. 'She says that she witnessed a miracle in the churchyard,' I joke. 'To be totally accurate, she said she saw a gravestone move of its own volition. Apparently, it floated when she wasn't looking.'

'A Weeping Angel,' he grunts as he leaves the room and walks down the aisle of the church.

I don't have a clue what he is talking about.

'Think she is still upset that such a young woman should die,' I explain to his back. 'It was poor dear Olivia's grave, after all.'

He stops as if the brakes of a train have exerted their full force upon him.

'Olivia!' He seems shocked, his face is as white as a ghost (Forgive the pun!).

'Olivia Bartholomew,' I clarify.

And almost before I can utter the words, he collapses to the ground like a dynamited chimney stack.

For God's sake; the second in six months!

Chapter Thirteen

Mrs Joan Cooper

That great fat lying lump Jonas Brookes is as white as a glacier when he stumbles into the reception area. He looks dishevelled and his hair mirrors that of the 'great' Boris Johnson, our one-time pretend comedy prime minister.

'What the fuck has happened to you?' I ask with not a modicum of sympathy, or to be honest, concern. 'You look like you've been dragged through a hedge backwards by a vampire.'

It is becoming a morning habit. My useless daughter came running (well, as far as that is possible given her lack of noticeable exercise in the past) through reception earlier, looking as if she had seen a ghost. Or had she been in the aforementioned hedge with Jonas Brookes? Surely not, although I wouldn't put it past him, but I am sure she has far better taste!

Now red, well, scarlet-faced, he gasps for a breath and emits a pitiful tobacco-stinking wheeze.

'Sit down for fuck's sake,' I loudly whisper, since our only other current resident has deemed this moment to be the one in which he decides to stomp obliviously into reception. Fortunately, he gives us a fleeting glance, appears startled and furtively slips out of the door to the much saner outside world.

Anyway, Brookes stumbles to the frayed sofa (I really must open my piggy bank and get it replaced. If only the piggy bank existed!) in the corner of reception and places his dishevelled rapidly balding head between his knees. To be totally fair, which I am loathe to be, he does look disturbingly shook up.

Fearing he may be in the process of having a heart attack, and calculating the possible damage to my business (as it is), I shuffle off to get him a glass of water. I choose the dirtiest and most chipped option and make sure I fill it with warm rather than cold water, and, to my disgust, I accidently rinse my not too clean right forefinger in the selfsame water.

I shuffle back and hold out the glass to my now giddily sitting upright guest of sorts.

'Here, drink this before you go and collapse on my freshly vacuumed carpet,' I tell him with about as much mock concern of a Tory health minister. 'The last thing I need is sick, snot and blood to fucking clean up.'

He holds out a fat yellow-stained hand, grabs the glass and gulps the water down quicker than he came last night.

'Mrs Cooper, you are a lifesaver,' he smirks annoyingly and smiles with crooked teeth the colour of piss-stained snow.

'Forget the meaningless gratitude and tell me what the fuck happened to you,' I snap with a touch more venom than intended, but with a resulting satisfying removal of his Aardman animation cartoon smile.

He shrugs his shoulders and with a mocking manner says, 'Now, now, Mrs Cooper, do be polite to your paying guests. You don't want me looking elsewhere next time I visit this delightful part of the country, do you?'

I grunt more than an ounce of derision. 'You know you are not paying. It's some fool of a client of yours who is no doubt paying you well over what I am charging you for the privilege to stay in my humble but welcoming abode.'

He winces and acts mock innocence, for he knows I know I am right.

'I collapsed, fainted, in the church,' he tells me with a wince and grin.

'God rightly and sensibly struck you down, no doubt,' I snap back. 'Not a great idea for somebody like you to frequent the Almighty's mortal home.'

He laughs, ruffles his hair and asks, 'Do you speak from experience, Mrs Cooper?'

I feel that I should slap him but instead am interrupted by the phone on the reception desk beginning to ring an annoying chirp.

'You had better answer that, Mrs Cooper,' he says. 'It could be a prospective customer and I guess you could do with one or two of them at this time of the year.'

'Cheeky sod,' I huff, glare at him, think of administering the delayed slap, decide to leave it until later, and then turn around and stomp off to the reception desk.

'I will hopefully see you later, Mrs Cooper,' I hear him say to my back as I walk off, and as I glance back, notice him surprisingly swiftly and furtively creeping up the stairs with a schoolboy grin on his fat face.

It is two o'clock and I am reminded by text that I had agreed to talk to Brookes about the ridiculous cartoon story travesty of history that he sent me a few days ago. I am part convinced he wrote it to wind me up, but know that he in all probability didn't. Who did write it and why, is the mystery that compels me to even consider talking to him about it.

I text back to the effect that I will meet him in the hopefully empty bar in five minutes, and vow to make him wait at least another ten.

He is slumped back in one of the tired but comfy chairs munching on a packet of cheese and onion crisps as I finally deem to make his unedifying acquaintance.

'Mrs Cooper,' he splutters whilst spraying half-chewed crisp crumbs asunder.

I ignore his greeting and take a seat a safe distance away from his continuing snowfall of munched snack.

'I don't have much time, so can we get on with it,' I say with a genuine but amplified annoyance and disgust.

He smirks, licks his greasy fingers and swallows hard, his Adam's apple, although well camouflaged by his fat neck, appearing to bob in protest.

'Have it your way, Mrs Cooper. Any which way you wish will suit me,' he replies with a generous amount of a *Carry On* film double entendre.

'Get on with it, you fat fool,' I snap back with the venom of a black mamba.

He feigns mock hurt.

'You gave me some invaluable insight into the document a few weeks ago,' he begins with an annoying, and no doubt deliberate, officiousness, 'although, of course, your interjection resulted from the dubious acquisition of something that was clearly not yours to see at the time of perusal.'

He sounds like a copper and I cross my legs and pout in synthetic injury.

'I really, honestly have nothing to add to what I already told you,' I reply.

He blinks and sniffs with what appears to be a combination of frustration and disappointment. 'Do tell me about Norma Bradley. Where does she fit into the proceedings?' he says.

I huff with annoyance. 'She killed herself. What the fuck else is there to say?'

'Has she always lived here in this delightful village?' he sarcastically asks without a hint of regret.

I think of walking off for a moment, or even for good.

'I can see a knowing smile in those gorgeous hazel, well, brown eyes of yours, Mrs Cooper,' he smirks. 'Do please tell me what you are thinking, out of spite, of not telling me.'

I think of walking off again but decide there is no harm in answering him.

'No, Norma married an American airman, went to live in Norfolk when they got married and returned when he sadly died a couple of years later,' I tell him.

He pauses, appears to think for a moment and then he beams a broad smile. 'Is that so? In which case my fiddling around might well be a touch to blame for the unfortunate happenings.'

'Fuck off, you insensitive fuck,' I scream back and walk away without a glance back in his direction.

'Thank you for your help, Mrs Cooper,' I hear him say as I close, well, slam, the door behind me.

Chapter Fourteen

Even More Electronic Correspondence

From: Jonas Brookes

Subject: A few questions for the bereaved sister

Date and time: 27th August 22:15

To: Simon Humphrey

Dear Rev. Humphrey

Firstly, may I assure you that I am in rude health and that it was likely a very light breakfast that contributed to my little fainting fit.

Can I also thank you for your swift action in facilitating my swift recovery? (Too many swifts. I know!!).

Anyway, if I recall with any accuracy, you, on my behalf, very kindly agreed to put one or two, possibly pertinent questions to John Miller's sister.

Could you therefore please enquire as to the answers to the following:

1. Why did she fall out with her brother?

2. Does she know where he lived for the five unaccounted years after their little fall out?

3. If she does know where he was living, does she know what work he was doing and who he worked for?

4. Does she know if he had any enemies?

5. Besides herself, does she know if he fell out with anybody else when he lived in Dorset?

6. Has she any clue as to why somebody or somebodies should want to kill John Miller and his family?

7. Why wait until now to pursue the issue?

8. Could her brother shoot a gun?

9. Did her brother have any hobbies?

10. Was her brother likely to take a bribe? (You might want to word this a bit more diplomatically than I could ever muster!)

11. Does she know if her brother did any painting? I do not mean painting and decorating, but was he in any way an artist?

12. Do tell her I am doing my best to solve this case and ask her if there is any other information that she may have that could further assist my extensive investigations.

Hope this is alright with you, Rev.

Kind regards
Jonas Brookes.

PS. How did Olivia Bartholomew die?

From: Simon Humphrey
Subject: A few questions for the bereaved sister
Date and time: 27th August 22:25
To: Jonas Brookes

Ex-Detective Sergeant Brookes

I am so glad that you are well, you did give me a little scare for a few moments.

I will try my best with the questions, but John Miller's sister is rather ill and I am not sure whether her medication may impair her memory. I shall see.

Why your interest in dear departed Olivia?

Simon

From: Jonas Brookes
Subject: A few questions for the bereaved sister
Date and time: 27th August 22:33
To: Simon Humphrey

Dear Rev. Humphrey

Your assistance will no doubt be of great assistance with my investigations, but please do not overstress the sister.

My interest in Olivia Bartholomew, well, it's a long and complicated story, but the gist is that I met her about six months ago in Winchester and she seemed hale and hearty in health on that occasion.

Kind regards
Jonas Brookes

From: Simon Humphrey
Subject: A few questions for the bereaved sister
Date and time: 27th August 22:42

To: Jonas Brookes

Ex-Detective Sergeant Brookes

The mention of Olivia did seem to have a devastating effect on you. The meeting in Winchester (She was certainly far afield for a Bartholomew!) must have had a deep impact on you, although, of course, she was amazingly attractive, wasn't she?

Anyway, your aged hormones aside, if they exist at your age!

Olivia killed herself.

It was quite bizarre to be honest. Locked her bedroom door and stabbed herself with a letter opener and left a note saying that she wished she had painted her room yellow and to reverse the note at school.
Whatever that was supposed to mean!

Very, very sad and her parents are absolutely inconsolable. Particularly bad for her father. You will not know this, but when he was nine years old, his fourteen-year-old sister disappeared. Apparently left her friend's house and was never seen again.

Simon

From: Jonas Brookes
Subject: A few questions for the bereaved sister
Date and time: 27th August 22:44
To: Simon Humphrey

Dear Rev. Humphrey

Thanks for that. It was certainly a tragedy for all involved.

Anyway, Mrs Cooper has promised me a nightcap once she has cleared up.

Kind regards

Jonas Brookes

From: Jonas Brookes

Subject: A little piece of kind assistance please

Date and time: 27th August 22:50

To: DS Rashid

Dear Detective Sergeant (?) Rashid

Just a little supplementary request.

Could I please have as many details as you are able to gather on the death of Sir Terrance Edwards about four or five years prior to that of his Lordship and also (I know I am asking a lot!), the death of a policeman called Oliver Lewis. They both occurred around Bovey whatever and at about the same time, give or take a few months.

As always, your help is of great assistance and appreciation.

Kind regards

Jonas Brookes (ex-DS and, sort of, colleague)

PS. I have attached a rather strange story (and before you ask, no, I did not write it) that covers the death of the Edwards guy. You may or may not find it useful to help with your investigations and feedback.

From: Simon Humphrey

Subject: A few questions for the bereaved sister

Date and time: 27th August 22:51

To: Jonas Brookes

Ex-Detective Sergeant Brookes

Do enjoy your nightcap!

And don't go fainting on Mrs Cooper!

Simon

From: Winifred Humphrey
Subject: Something I forgot to mention
Date and time: 27th August 22:52
To: Jonas Brookes

Dear Sir,

I forgot, or failed to mention, might be a more accurate portrayal of the circumstances, to say that I witnessed the Edwards woman's carer visiting Mrs Bradley on the day that she unfortunately died.
Well, I think it was her. I was wearing my reading glasses at the time. Yes, I know I should get some varifocals and I keep meaning to make an appointment, but you know how it is, and so it was all a bit fuzzy, as a lot of things are nowadays.
Oh, and George Hampton popped around with what looked like some vegetables the previous day (yes, I was wearing my proper specs on that occasion).
Please do come round and see me if you require anything else, if you know what I mean. An old lady can get very lonely!

Wishing you success in your quest, or whatever.

Win xx

From: John Phoenix
Subject: Something I forgot to tell you

Date and time: 27th August 23:12

To: Jonas Brookes

My wife is asleep and I have crept downstairs to send this message since it is keeping me awake.

I forgot to tell you something about the John Miller case and it has been eating away at me since. What I am about to tell you was kept from the press and public and, as interest waned over time, there seemed no point in bringing it up.

So please keep it to yourself!

The fact is that John Miller was found with a key in his mouth. It was the key to the front door to his house, a door which was locked when we arrived on the scene. We always presumed that the killer locked it with a second key, but some of my colleagues thought that the lock had been interfered with; in other words, locked with other means, which led us to think, for a while, that it was a burglar, but, of course, nothing was taken.

Well, I've got it off my chest and hopefully now I can get some peace and sleep.

I do hope you are able to shed some light on this, Jonas, I really do.

John

From: Simon Humphrey

Subject: A few questions for the bereaved sister

Date and time: 28th August 08:34

To: Jonas Brookes

Ex-Detective Sergeant Brookes

I do hope you had a good night's sleep!

I thought you might like to know that I have arranged to meet John Miller's sister on the 30th of August.

Will you still be around after this date?

Simon

From: DS Rashid
Subject: A little piece of kind assistance please
Date and time: 28th August 09:13
To: Jonas Brookes

Mr Brookes

You really do have the cheek of the devil!

You claim that I owe you something. For the life of me, I have no idea why!

You should have left Joel Taylor alone. You were warned. It's not my fault that you were so fucking stubborn.

Anyway, I have searched my conscience and decided to help you out in your new career, if that's what it is.

Give me a few days and I will get back to you with any details I can dredge up. No promises about the quality of the information, and, to be honest, I do not want to know what the fuck you are up to investigating such ancient events.

So, leave me out of any of this if you take any of this further as no doubt it will lead to trouble!

From: Jonas Brookes
Subject: A few questions for the bereaved sister
Date and time: 28th August 09:33
To: Simon Humphrey

Dear Rev. Humphrey

I had an excellent night's sleep thank you!

Appreciate you arranging the meeting with John Miller's sister.

Unfortunately, I will not be in Bovey whatever beyond today's date, so could we possibly arrange a phone call or is it Zoom or Sky or something that you youngsters use to see and talk to each other from afar.

Kind regards
Jonas Brookes

From: Jonas Brookes
Subject: Something I forgot to mention
Date and time: 28th August 09:35
To: Winifred Humphrey

Dear Ms Humphrey,

Thank you kindly for the update on your remembrances.

Much appreciated.

Kind regards
Jonas Brookes

From: Winifred Humphrey
Subject: Something I forgot to mention
Date and time: 28th August 09:45
To: Jonas Brookes

Dear Jonas,

You are very welcome.

Once again, best wishes in your noble search for the truth.

Win xx

From: Simon Humphrey
Subject: A few questions for the bereaved sister
Date and time: 27th August 09:46
To: Jonas Brookes

Ex-Detective Sergeant Brookes

I am sure we can arrange something once I have spoken to John Miller's sister.

Not for me to interfere, but it might be an idea to speak to your doctor when you get back to sunny Winchester tomorrow, fainting fits at your age could be a sign of high blood pressure or something or other.

Simon

PS. It's Skype, although I prefer FaceTime myself!

From: Jonas Brookes
Subject: A few questions for the bereaved sister

Date and time: 28th August 09:48
To: Simon Humphrey

Dear Rev. Humphrey

FaceTime it is!

Kind regards
Jonas Brookes

From: Jonas Brookes
Subject: A few questions for the bereaved sister
Date and time: 28th August 10:18
To: John Phoenix

Dear John

Fuck, that's some detail to forget to tell me.

It could be the key to the whole puzzle!

Kind regards
Jonas Brookes

From: Jonas Brookes
Subject: A little piece of kind assistance please
Date and time: 28th August 10:26
To: DS Rashid

Dear Detective Sergeant (?) Rashid

Your help will, as always, be greatly appreciated.

Do take care juggling your many roles (Well, at least the two I know of!).

Kind regards

Jonas Brookes (ex-DS and, sort of, colleague)

From: Jonas Brookes

Subject: A little piece of kind assistance please

Date and time: 28th August 10:27

To: DS Rashid

Dear Detective Sergeant (?) Rashid

Sorry just one more thing!

There was a maid working at his Lordship's when he supposedly topped himself. No idea if she is still with us on this mortal hellhole of an island, but would you please be kind enough to find out her name and to search out whether she is still breathing, and if so, where I can find her.

Once again, your help will, as always, be greatly appreciated.

Kind regards

Jonas Brookes

From: DS Rashid

Subject: A little piece of kind assistance please

Date and time: 28th August 09:13

To: Jonas Brookes

Mr Brookes

Once again, you really do have the cheek of the devil!

I will see what I can do

From: Jonas Brookes
Subject: Thank you so, so much for your delightful accommodation
Date and time: 28th August 18:26
To: Joan Cooper

Dear Mrs Cooper

Just to let you know that I have arrived home safely.

Also, just to let you know I appreciated your warm and welcoming hosting of my most enjoyable stay.

Give my regards to your daughter who I hope has fully recovered from her earlier scare. I do hope she doesn't encounter any more Weeping Angels in the churchyard, although stranger things have happened!

Did she know Olivia Bartholomew?

Kind regards
Jonas Brookes

From: John Phoenix
Subject: Something I forgot to tell you
Date and time: 28th August 18:37
To: Jonas Brookes

Keep me informed and if you have any further queries, please initiate by email.

Don't want to wife involved, if you know what I mean. My life would be hell if she knew I was digging this up again.

From: Jonas Brookes
Subject: A few questions for the bereaved sister
Date and time: 28th August 18:39
To: John Phoenix

Dear John

Of course, wouldn't dream of causing your dear wife any distress.

Kind regards
Jonas

PS. I assume you checked out local locksmiths?

From: John Phoenix
Subject: Something I forgot to tell you
Date and time: 28th August 18:37
To: Jonas Brookes

No locksmiths remember a stranger asking for the key to be duplicated.

A locksmith did say there were scratches inside the lock, which could have indicated messing around with it, but more likely due to many years of wear and tear.

All a touch of John Dickson Carr, Ellery Queen or Agatha Christie?

I don't think so!

John

From: Joan Cooper
Subject: Thank you so, so much for your delightful accommodation
Date and time: 28th August 19:13
To: Jonas Brookes

You sarcastic fucker.

PS. I'm still not sure of the real reason you were so interested in Olivia Bartholomew, but I am sure it is nothing above board! She was far too young and pretty for a fat ugly old fuck like you!

PPS. What the fuck is a fucking Weeping Angel?

From: Jonas Brookes
Subject: Thank you so, so much for your delightful accommodation
Date and time: 28th August 19:26
To: Joan Cooper

Dear Mrs Cooper

As you have possibly already gathered (being a very smart young woman), everything I ever do is more than above board!

I do hope to see you in the near future.

Kind regards
Jonas Brookes

PS Check out *Doctor Who*. It isn't all walking, talking, killer tin dustbins, you know!

From: Joan Cooper

Subject: Thank you so, so much for your delightful accommodation

Date and time: 28th August 19:33

To: Jonas Brookes

I repeat, you are a sarcastic fucker.

From: Simon Humphrey

Subject: A few questions for the bereaved sister

Date and time: 1st September 11:41

To: Jonas Brookes

Ex-Detective Sergeant Brookes

I now have John Miller's sister's responses to your questions.

I have listed the questions as you asked them in the attachment and inserted the replies in red underneath each. I do hope this is okay with you.

As for the answers, I will leave it for you to assess, interpret, and possibly conclude.

John Miller's sister is very poorly, so quick action on this would be extremely appreciated.

Simon

Attachment:

Questions and, hopefully, answers that make some sense and are of some use to the investigation.

1. Why did she fall out with her brother?

She says that he was not the most honest of people when she knew him and that she was convinced that he had stolen some money from her and her husband. She said that he strongly denied it and accused the husband of taking it. She did not believe him and the row that followed led to John leaving and cutting off any communication. She said that she later discovered that her husband had been responsible, but since she had no way of contacting her brother, they never had the opportunity to reconcile.

2. Does she know where he lived for the five unaccounted years after their little falling out?

She says she has no idea but suspects he did not go far. But clearly, as she pointed out, she really has no idea.

3. If she does know where he was living, does she know what work he was doing and who he worked for?

Ditto as above. He generally did farm work or some kind of manual work, so the presumption is that this was what he was doing in the missing years.

4. Does she know if he had any enemies?

She says he was often getting into fights as a young man, but at the time he left he was a much calmer person. Enemies, nobody she could ever imagine who would commit such a dreadful crime.

5. Besides herself, does she know if he fell out with anybody else when he lived in Dorset?

Ditto above.

6. Has she any clue as to why somebody should want to kill John Miller and his family?

She has no idea. She did suggest that maybe, and this is because she had no idea who his wife was, the target could have been his wife, but the police were pretty certain this was not the case. But who knows?

7. Why wait until now to pursue the issue?

She repeated what she had already told me. She is dying and wants answers before she dies. She said she has spent many years trying to drive the tragedy out of her head but now is the time to confront it. She said she thought John Phoenix was a kind and helpful policeman but could have done more.

8. Could her brother shoot a gun?

Yes, she says he was quite proficient with a gun.

9. Did her brother have any hobbies?

She said that he was obsessed with countryside sports: shooting, hunting, point-to-point (whatever that is!), trapping animals. He used to walk for miles and, as a boy, liked to play football and cricket.

10. Was her brother likely to take a bribe? (You might want to word this a bit more diplomatically than I could ever muster!).

She thinks it unlikely but she said it depends on the reward, after all we are all tempted by something we truly want or need are we not?

11. Does she know if her brother did any painting? I do not mean painting and decorating but was he in any way an artist?

She laughed at this. She said he could hardly draw a stick man, unless, of course, he had lessons after they lost contact and she thought that most unlikely.

12. Do tell her I am doing my best to solve this case and ask her if there is any other information that she may have that could further assist my extensive investigations.

She said she appreciated your 'attempts' and that she would be very grateful if you could get to the truth as soon as possible.

From: Jonas Brookes
Subject: A few questions for the bereaved sister
Date and time: 2nd September 17:32
To: Simon Humphrey

Dear Rev. Humphrey

Kind thanks for your reply and attachment.

Hopefully the replies are helpful, so please do thank your client for her willingness to accommodate my whims and fancies (or 'attempts', or such).

I do not wish to get your hopes up, but I can see some glimpse of light at the end of the long dark tunnel of death.

Do take care.

Kind regards
Jonas Brookes.

From: Simon Humphrey
Subject: A few questions for the bereaved sister
Date and time: 2nd September 18:45
To: Jonas Brookes

Ex-Detective Sergeant Brookes

In which case I do so hope to hear from you soon with further instruction.

Simon

From: DS Rashid
Subject: A little piece of kind assistance please
Date and time: 4th September 09:23
To: Jonas Brookes

Mr Brookes

Firstly, you need to understand that this is a one-off and I will not be conversing with you in any possible way after this communication.

I do hope this is clear, because despite everything, I really truly wouldn't want any unpleasantness to befall you.

Secondly, the maid is Joyce Worthing and she lives in Norfolk. I think you are capable of finding out her whereabouts, so will leave it at that.

Thirdly, I have attached some brief information on the cases you mentioned. To be honest, I have no idea what you are doing and what has got you to have a bee in the bonnet about these cases. They are clearly two suicides and a tragic accident, but it is your prerogative to waste your own time and, presumedly, your client's money.

What a sordid profession you seem to have taken up!

Finally, as I have already said but I feel it is necessary to reiterate, leave Joel Taylor alone. It is in your best interest. Okay?

Oh, and I am not sure if you are aware, but Jason Leach recently lost his appeal. Well, a few days ago he, talking of suicides, took his own life. Hung himself apparently. Thought you might like to know that there was no hint of mourning at this station.

I do not hope to hear from you again.

Goodbye.

Attachment 1 – The death of Sir Terrance Edwards and the Poacher

As the manuscript indicated, Sir Terrance Edwards was found dead in his sitting room, shot through the head with the door locked. A shot was heard by his daughter and another man (the Poacher in the manuscript, but I am unable to get a name for him). The information in the manuscript is roughly accurate, Edwards did try to kill Lord Marshall-Atwood and then fled and subsequently killed himself. There really is nothing to question here.

As you are probably aware, there was no second death (the Poacher) and it is not clear who it may refer to, although Jack (surname unknown) did assist the girl with entering the sitting room at the time, but as far as can be gathered disappeared shortly afterwards.

Attachment 2 – The death of Clive Lewis

Clive Lewis was tragically killed in a car accident. The brakes on the car were found to be worn and this was assumed to be the cause of the accident. The police found no evidence to pursue the matter.

Attachment 3 – The death of Lord Marshall-Atwood

Lord Marshall-Atwood was found dead in his bedroom, shot through the head with the door locked. The gun belonged to him and it is understood that he had been very depressed at the time. Nobody else was in the house at the time and it was considered a tragic case of suicide. There really is nothing else to add or say.

> From: Jonas Brookes
> Subject: A little piece of kind assistance please
> Date and time: 4th September 22:21
> To: DS Rashid
>
> Dear Detective Sergeant (?) Rashid
>
> Thank you so much for your undoubted in-depth assistance. Not sure why you made those attachments, such detailed but succinct information would surely have fitted adequately within the body of the email. But hey, that's my opinion, for what it's worth!
>
> I for one believe it is sad news that Jason Leach has taken his own life, if that is what happened (Oh yes, you can probably anticipate a conspiracy theory coming on, but I bet the CCTV was out of commission at the time (Bit Epstein, hey?!)).
>
> Kind regards

Jonas Brookes

PS I believe you are wrong on all three counts!!

Chapter Fifteen

The Hunt for a Maid

I wake sitting up and gasping for breath. I am awash with sweat and my heart is beating faster than Lewis Hamilton's racing car.

'Fuck,' my inner voice screams. 'Fuck.'

It was the dream again. Olivia fucking Bartholomew is haunting me!

It is pitch dark, the middle of the night, I surmise, my chest burns with pain and I pray that I do not die to a God I do not believe in.

I cough, phlegm in my chest rattling like balls in a lottery draw and my eyes threatening to eject into orbit.

My unconscious is being haunted.

I reach over to grab the glass of water perched on the bedside table. I spill a sizable splosh as my hands shake like someone with Parkinson's but manage to take a gulp of the remnants. As usual it tastes of metal, an unkind metal, and is an excruciating lukewarm.

Yes, I am being haunted by a now dead girl, or such.

I wake sitting up and gasping for breath.

It's the fucking mobile phone, God save the fucking Queen again, and I am standing to attention.

I take a deep intake of air and then grab for the phone on the bedside table. Not surprisingly it falls to the floor and I have to lean precariously out of the bed to retrieve it, muscles in my neck shooting pain and my arm seemingly nearly vacating its socket.

'Fuck it,' I mumble as I miraculously press the required answer button.

'That's a fine way to greet an old colleague,' I hear a public school posh woman's voice admonish me.

I grunt and sit up straight.

'DS Rashid, or whoever, or whatever you are,' I respond with a distaste mixed with anticipation. 'Whatever do you find to talk to me about at this ungodly hour?'

I hear a giggle and voices in the background.

'It's nine thirty-five in the morning, Mr Brookes, certainly not ungodly for us worker ants,' she replies to the further accompaniment of giggling.

Somebody is listening in on the call, and it is fucking annoying.

'How fortunate it is that I am no longer part of your colony,' I reply through gritted teeth and a cough. 'Not that I was ever truly and exactly any such thing.'

She giggles along with her anonymous companion on this occasion.

'Let's get down to business, shall we?' she says.

'Let's,' I grumpily respond, 'although I have no idea what 'business' is.'

'Cantankerous old git,' I hear in the background.

'I have the maid's whereabouts,' DS Rashid tells me.

I grit my teeth and ignore the first comment, although they are only responding to my well-worn fake persona. 'Well, spit it out.'

'Told you so,' I hear in the background.

'Get a pen and paper and I will tell you,' DS Rashid tells me.

Another trip to Norfolk. It is becoming a nasty habit!

This time it is to a dreadfully dilapidated seaside town called Great Yarmouth. I understand from my brief search on the internet thing that it was a fashionable place to frequent in the 1950s, but upon first sight I am finding it hard to fathom, since the tackiness is almost ironic.

It reeks poverty, and like many such areas thinks voting Tory will solve the degradation. Hey ho, maybe they are right! Every day is like Sunday. Wasn't that *The Smiths* or maybe *Morrisey*? Whatever happened to him?

Joyce Worthing, the maid, well, she was a long time ago, lives or possibly exists in a care home and has managed to survive the influx of unrestrained coronavirus-riddled fellow inmates. Poor thing!

Anyway, I have booked into the Close Wood Guest House in Great Yarmouth, sixty-five quid, free Wi-Fi and, most importantly, a free full English breakfast.

It's clean and the welcome is warm. What more could I ask for? And, of course, Alan has given me far more than sixty-five pounds sterling for my overnight stay! A win-win situation.

Anyway, again, I am walking (Yes, it's becoming a bad habit!) to Park House Care Home, which, according to the internet thing is, 'Care accommodation offering en-suite facilities to twenty-five residents with elderly care needs, while respecting their individuality and personal choice', which sounds good to me. I might ask if they will take me on if the food is up to standard!

The walk is fume-choking, the streets are in need of a severe spring clean and as I arrive to witness the not-so-amazing vista of Park House, a seagull shits on my head.

Fuck!

I fiddle in my coat pocket for a tissue and discover I have tragically failed to re-stock.

Fuck! Again.

My mobile phone rings. Fucking 'God Save the Queen', or 'King', pollutes the car noise, and I stupidly, bird shit creeping slowly and relentlessly towards my forehead, answer it.

'Mr Brookes?' a man's voice asks with the utmost civility.

'Yes,' I snap with the welcome of an angry pit bull.

'I wonder if you might have a few moments,' the voice continues, clearly ignoring my none too welcoming response.

'No,' I once again snap back.

'I notice you recently retired and I wondered if we could discuss some excellent investment opportunities,' the voice persists.

I press the end call button and shout 'fuck off' to the consternation of an elderly woman who is amazingly rapidly Zimmer-framing towards Park House.

I smile at her and she stick her curly white-haired head in the air, huffs, and shakes her head with the disgust of an old school headmistress, which she may well have been.

'Do you have a handkerchief or tissue?' I ask her with an outward jocularity that really doesn't exist within me.

She shakes her head and trots off with a speed that should be impossible if she is not faking her infirmity.

'Thanks love,' I sarcastically continue while wiping the bird shit from my forehead with my right hand.

'Don't call me love,' she croaks with a raised fist as she reaches the entrance to Park House.

Suitably admonished, I wipe my hand on the garden wall outside the care home and wait for her to enter the selfsame place before dubiously following in her footsteps.

The reception is small and reminds me of my dear departed mother's house. It is almost designed to look like a stage set from the 1950s.

'Can I help you, love?' a voice from afar percolates my probably highly inaccurate historic musings.

A woman, probably in her forties, bleached short curly hair, a fake smile and as thin as a stick insect bounces towards me.

I clear my throat. 'Before I ask anything else would it be okay to wash this bird sh… eh, mess, off my head?' I ask with a finely tuned degree of bashfulness and charm.

Her eyes grow to the size of tennis balls (Well, appear to!) and her sunken cheeks blush blood red.

She stutters. 'Yes, yes, yes, of course. The bathroom is just to the left halfway down the corridor. How, how, unfortunate, the sea gulls are rather numerous in this part of town, I am afraid. Oh dear, dear, dear me. Dear me.'

I raise my right hand and perform a limp wave of appreciation and trundle off to the bathroom.

If I am not mistaken, I hear a mocking giggle in the background, but I must be mistaken. I'm sure the lady is far too polite and professional to deride her customers (or whatever I am)!

Ten minutes later, with far too fine, damp hair plastered down on my scalp, and I am being shown to the room of the mysterious maid, or let's start calling her Joyce Worthing, shall we?

Anyway, the giggling stick insect turns out to be called Sharon and proves to be accommodating enough to show me to room 9, Joyce's last residence in this mortal land, so I presume!

'Joyce is somewhat unusual,' she tells me as we reach the door and probably in a loud enough voice for Joyce to hear her.

'Oh, really?' I respond while, hopefully, surreptitiously tidying my humid hair and covering the all-too-large bald patch.

'She's a bit of a handful, love,' Sharon smilingly persists. 'Knows her own mind if you know what I mean, lovey.'

I don't know what she means but nod an acknowledgement anyway.

Sharon knocks on the door and turns towards me with a surprisingly cute smile.

I have to admit that I think our Sharon is possibly quite kind to her aged residents and likely cares for them in her way.

Oh fuck, I'm betraying a hint of kindness. It really must stop!

Sharon knocks a second time and then opens the door a crack. 'She's a touch hard of hearing,' she whispers with a recognisable giggle.

I smile back and slowly nod my head.

'It's Sharon, lovey.' Sharon almost bursts my eardrums. 'We have a visitor for you.'

She turns to me, screws up her face and quietly giggles. 'You have to talk loudly; she doesn't like wearing her hearing aids.'

Again, I smile and nod my head in acknowledgement.

'Is it the detective chap?' a loud croaky familiar voice replies. 'If it is him, then tell him to come in. If it's my money-grabbing son, then tell him to piss off.'

I have a feeling I'm going to enjoy the company of Joyce Worthing!

Sharon is briskly despatched by Joyce Worthing and I am sitting in a frayed armchair opposite the very same lady I met, well, kind of, at the entrance earlier.

Joyce has a permanent toothless grin on her face and her artful cheeky eyes are surveying me with the intensity of a hunting barn owl.

'Well, what do you want?' she croaks. 'Come on, spit it out. At my age, I don't have all bloody day to waste on false civility.'

I suspect she does have all day, but I wouldn't dare contradict her.

'And none of that foul language, mind you,' she giggles, and reaching for a water jug on the small table next to her. 'Do you want some water? I'm afraid it's horribly tepid and tastes of gnat's piss, but at least it's wet.'

I huff a laugh.

'You worked for a Lord Marshall-Attwood many years ago,' I say before nearly choking to death after a sip of what turns out to be neat vanilla vodka.

'They are easily deceived,' she tells me with a wink. 'And yes, I was unfortunate enough to work for his Lordship when I was an innocent young slip of a girl.'

I have a feeling she was never innocent but hold my counsel.

'You were there when he died,' I respond.

She grimaces, her toothless face screwing up implausibly. 'I didn't kill him, you know,' she says. 'Although I would have been tempted on more than one occasion.'

I sip the vodka. 'He killed himself,' I reply before choking once again in response to the potency of the drink.

She giggles again and takes a large swig from her glass. 'So he did,' she says. 'So he certainly did.'

I nod and feign looking at my notebook. 'How long did you work for him?'

'Too fucking long,' she growls and then re-adopts a smile of innocence.

'But how long?' I ask. 'Were you there when Sir Terrance Edwards died?'

She shakes her head slowly. 'Oh, I see, it's not just about my one-time employer, is it? Anyway, I was not there for more than six months before he died, but that doesn't mean that I didn't hear a thing or two about past goings-on in the quiet little village of Bovey Tracey.'

She now has a broad smile and a knowing look on her face.

'Do tell,' I smile back.

'Now why should I do that, Mr Brookes?' she responds mischievously.

'Well, the thing is, I am being paid handsomely by a client who is also willing to pay my informers very handsomely indeed, Mrs Worthing,' I reply.

She giggles again and I get the impression that she was once a charismatic beauty.

'Well, the thing is, I am very happy to assist you, Mr Brookes, as long as the amount of generous renumeration is sufficiently large.'

'Oh, it will be,' I reply. 'It will be, Mrs Worthing.'

And so, she apparently tells me all she knows…

Chapter Sixteen

Joyce Worthing Tells a Tall (Well, Who Knows?) Tale

The job at his Lordship's grand house didn't prove too difficult to obtain, and I certainly found out why after a few days!

The butler, Mr Brady, or whatever his job title may have been, a fat old man who constantly smelt of sweat and mothballs, blind as a bat, death as a post, without further explanation, discreetly and respectfully advised me, 'for my own good', to keep well clear of 'sir's wandering hands'.

'He's very touchy-feely,' the ancient cook (Mrs Honour) told me. 'With the young pretty ones, the younger the better. I'm certainly safe,' she disarmingly chuckled.

Well, to cut a long story short, I heeded their warnings and, in the process, his touchy Lordship must have thought I was a cat on hot bricks every time he got within a yard or two of me.

It was a month or two after I started my job of working in the house and avoiding my arse being pinched by the aristocracy, that I discovered his Lordship was a little more than 'very touchy-feely'.

But, before that, I made a friend.

One day I was taking a walk through the village when a pretty girl almost knocked me over. She was running hell for leather to who knows where.

Well, it turns out it was Carillon Edwards and despite our rather inauspicious introduction, we became good, but distant, friends.

Why distant?

Well, she was very secretive about herself but, nonetheless, we spent some enjoyable times together.

'Miss Edwards,' Mrs Honour scolded, 'for heaven's sake do not mention that girl's name in this house. Sir would kick you out without ceremony.'

I was taken aback and didn't pursue the matter.

So, the gardener's apprentice (Matty, no idea of his surname), who conveniently happened to be 'sweet on me' (Mrs Honour tells me), proves a deep mine of information. To cut a long story short (since you likely already know it), I discover that Carillon's now dead father had tried to slay his Lordship (reason apparently unknown, but Matty reckoned it was a land dispute, while Mrs Honour in a moment of partly inebriated indiscretion claimed it was because his Lordship had tried to assault my new-found friend, Miss Edwards). Donny (the fantasist butcher's assistant) said his Lordship had killed Mrs Edwards (presumedly the wife), and Mr Brady (also slightly inebriated) told me that they had been sworn enemies for many years and it was because his Lordship had had an affair with Mrs Edwards.

Take your pick, who knows the truth!

Carillon lived alone in the very same house in which her father had committed suicide. As far as I could gather, she was 'very wealthy and had no need to work for a living, it will be the ruin of the girl' (Mrs Honour again).

'She disappeared for a year or two after her father's' death,' Mrs Honour tells me.
'Rumoured she went to stay with an aunt of some sorts.'
   'Up the duff,' the fantasist Donny informs me.
   'Went to the loony bin,' Matty tells me.
   'Went to stay with a relative,' Mr Brady says.

   'What do you do all day?' I ask her.
   'This and that,' she replies.
   'Do you read books?' I ask her.
   She shakes her head.
   'I paint pictures sometimes,' she tells me.
   'Oh, you must show me some of your pictures,' I say.
   'Maybe,' she tells me.

I lend her an Agatha Christie novel.
I lend her a John Dickson Carr novel.
Then another.

Ellery Queen, Margery Allingham, Cyril Hare, Sir Arthur Conan Doyle, Dorothy L. Sayers, Christianna Brand, and they are all devoured with a twinkle in her eye.

'I love locked room mysteries,' I tell her.

'So do I,' she replies with a sly grin.

'I like the way Agatha Christie uses poisons,' I tell her.

'So do I,' she replies with another sly grin.

'Do you have any other friends?' I ask her.

She shakes her head.

'No need, I have you.'

I sadly realise she is my only friend too.

'Would you like to meet up on Wednesday?' she asks me.

'I would love to.' She already knows it is my afternoon off.

'I'll see you outside The Cromwell Arms at two o'clock,' she tells me.

'That Miss Edwards gave me a delicious cake for my birthday today,' Mrs Honour tells me.

It is Tuesday and I wonder when they met.

I shake the thought away and feel guilty for not remembering Mrs Honour's birthday.

'Happy birthday,' I say.

Mr Brady bought her some mangy half-dead flowers.

His Lordship offered her a fleeting birthday greeting.

It is Wednesday and Mrs Honour has one of her 'funny turns' and has to go home.

Mr Brady has an afternoon off (friend's funeral apparently).

I leave his Lordship on his own.

I am relieved it is my afternoon off.

It is half past two and Carillon rushes to my side.

'Sorry I'm late, Joyce,' she splutters.

'Is there a problem?' I ask.

Her face, red with exertion, is blank.

'Clock stopped,' she explains.

'No problem,' I tell her.

She has brought some lemonade with her and we sit in a nearby field taking turns swigging from the bottle.

'What time do you need to be back?' she asks.

'Mr Brady will be back at around six o'clock,' I tell her.

'Go back after then,' she says with a knowing wink. 'The old letch will keep his hands off you if Mr Brady is around.'

I laugh and so does she.

I get back to the house at seven o'clock.

Sergeant Abel is standing at the entrance.

'Best you don't go in, miss,' he tells me. 'Not at the moment, love.'

Chapter Seventeen

A Chat About a Killer, 1

We are gathered in the dining room of The Cromwell Arms.

Mrs Cooper, looking as buxom and sexy as ever; Mrs Cooper's sulky daughter, buxom and disinterested (as ever); Carillon Edwards, lean and watchful; Evie, younger, lean, watchful and smiling; Joel Taylor, reactive, twitching, blinking and acting out his usual discomfort with the world; Alan Corbett-Hemingway, a blur in the distance; John Phoenix, perplexed and fearful that his lie to escape the clutches of his loving wife will be imminently discovered; Win next door, like an underfed rabbit in headlights; George Hampton; frail and involuntarily shaking, and Piers, the almost local young detective looking distinctly awkward and plainly puzzled by the proceedings.

'So, this is the Hercule Poirot dénouement,' I chuckle in the most ludicrous Belgium accent, as the assembled cast look on in wonder as I prepare to impart my unrivalled wisdom upon the proceedings.

In your dreams, Jonas Brookes!

There's another fucking pandemic and the consequential fucking full, fucking lockdown again, so much for the wonderfully truthful Boris's insistence that it was all over.

I am stuck alone in my twee bungalow with nothing left to clean, so I compose an email and explanation to my first 'client', the mysterious Mr Alan Corbett-Hemingway:

From: Jonas Brookes
Subject: My conclusions on the manuscript, for what they are worth!
Date and time: 26th September 11:29
To: Alan Corbett-Hemingway

Dear Alan

Since we once again find ourselves chained to our homes with nowhere to go, I would like to feed back my conclusions on the manuscript you supplied me with a few long months ago.

We can do this by telephone, FaceTime or whatever electronic wonder exists, or I can write the conclusions down for you.

Please do let me know your preferences.

Kind regards
Jonas Brookes.

From: Alan Corbett-Hemingway
Subject: My conclusions on the manuscript, for what they are worth!
Date and time: 26th September 11:32
To: Jonas Brookes

What wonderful news! I am of course talking about your reaching of conclusions and not the ongoing pandemic.
Do please initially send your conclusions in the form of writing. After reading your conclusions, we can speak if I feel it is necessary.

With the kindest regards
Alan

From: Jonas Brookes
Subject: My conclusions on the manuscript, for what they are worth!
Date and time: 26th September 11:35
To: Alan Corbett-Hemingway

Dear Alan

I will endeavour to get something to you tomorrow or at the latest, the day after.

Kind regards
Jonas Brookes

From: Jonas Brookes
Subject: My conclusions on the manuscript, for what they are worth!
Date and time: 27th September 10:47
To: Alan Corbett-Hemingway

Dear Alan

I have attached my conclusions to this email.

You must appreciate that I have no actual evidence to support my findings and that I may be totally wrong (Although, for me, this is very rarely the case!).

Do please respond with your impressions once you have had the opportunity to suitably ingest the information.

Kind regards
Jonas Brookes

Attachment – The conclusions of Jonas Brookes upon the attempted murder of Lord Marshall-Atwood, the suicide of Sir Terrance Edwards, and the death of the, so-called, Poacher.

It is the usual tradition in the case of murder mysteries for the culprit to be unmasked at the very last moment; well, let us see.

So where do I start?

I discovered, from a reliable source, that the manuscript, although a little eccentric, is pretty much accurate as to the facts of the case.

Yes, the events did happen as described with one notable exception; the so-called Poacher did not die at this point of proceedings but did play a vital part nonetheless.

Okay, our presumption, the facts and the conclusion of the police at the time, is that Sir Terrance Edwards attempted to kill Lord Marshall-Atwood and, in a state of remorse, and presuming that he had succeeded in the murder, took his own life.

Case closed?

No. No way.

Let me tell you a story; fact or fiction. You make up your mind…

X finds himself in a bit of a fix in that Y has threatened to tell the police that X has committed a nasty crime involving his daughter, which could, at the very least, destroy X's reputation and at worst result in a prison sentence.

X is not willing to accept these scenarios and so decides to take matters into his own hands and remove any possibility of Y divulging his misdemeanour. In his mind, his only feasible action is to eliminate Y and to do so as soon as possible but without suspicion falling upon himself.

So, a few days before (I am guessing, of course, as to the timing) his planned action, X discreetly and anonymously buys a handgun (or maybe he already had one), some fireworks, a wig and a false beard. Also, at some point prior to the day of action, he bribes a gullible accomplice, let us call him Z, to assist in the execution of the plan.

He decides the planned action has to be on a day when the daughter of Y has dinner with a friend and returns at a given time, which fortunately is a regular occurrence, and also luckily is also the day when his housekeeper has her night off and stays with a family friend.

So, the day of action arrives. X has planned a game of golf, tells his butler that he has arranged a meeting with Y who will be arriving early evening and if he is not home, for Y to be shown into X's study and asked to wait and not to disturb him.

X goes to play a game of golf with a convenient respected witness. He leaves his fellow golfer late afternoon and drives to the home of Y. Y is shocked, but upon hearing that X wishes to discuss the delicate matter, reluctantly shows X into his sitting room. With little ado, X bashes Y on the head with a poker, drags him to the armchair, shoots him through the temple.

Next, X locks the door (just in case somebody should enter the house), takes Y's distinctive jacket, leaps back into his car and drives home, parking out of sight of the house. He then, still in his car, puts on the beard, wig and jacket (his Y disguise) and walks to the house. He rings the bell and plays the part of Y with aplomb and allows the half-blind butler to show him into his study 'to wait for his Lordship, sir.'

Once in his study, X rapidly leaves by the window, drives back to Y's house, returns the jacket, returns to the sitting room, removes the wig and beard and throws them into the fire, making sure they will burn by placing some more wood in the fire. With a chisel he breaks away the part of the doorframe where the lock fits and places it near the door. Then, gritting his teeth, he shoots himself in the shoulder and fakes the suicide of Y by placing the gun in Y's right hand. After that, he closes the sitting room door, making sure the broken piece of doorframe is behind it and drives back to his house.

In a lot of pain and losing a little blood, he enters the house (possibly shedding a little blood in the process), is told by the butler that Y is in the study and he, as quickly as is feasible, walks to the study and dismisses the butler. Once in the study, he loudly greets the non-existent Y, opens the window, lights the firework that he has hidden in his jacket pocket and throws it into the open fire, collapses to the floor and waits for it to explode. The butler, duly upon hearing the explosion, rushes to the room to find X sprawled on the floor, presumedly just shot by Y who has escaped by the open window.

Ten minutes or so after these events, Y's daughter arrives home and as she does, she hears a shot and rushes inside. As she gets to the door, she is met by Z who says he also heard the shot (In fact, he is responsible for the shot which he let off behind the house when he spotted Y's daughter arriving). They both enter and, with great concern, Z rushes to the sitting room door, says it is locked (which it isn't) and duly breaks it open with his shoulder, to discover the dead body of Y.

There are, of course, clues to support this little ditty within the manuscript.

Chapter Eighteen

A Chat with a Killer, 1

Lockdown over and as a few weeks before, the skinny but engaging carer Evie answers the door.

She glares at me. 'Not you again. What do you want this time?' she surprisingly barks.

I smile and exude innocence. 'Wondered if I could have a word with Miss Edwards, if that's alright with you?'

She grimaces and slightly closes the door. 'You upset her last time you know, Mr Brookes.'

I continue to smile. 'Sorry about that, but I really do need to speak to her. I can assure you it is in her very best interest.'

She screws up her pointed nose. 'Although it is against my better judgment, I will see what she says,' she says and then briskly closes the door with an unnecessary avidity.

Two minutes later the door reopens.

I am met with a scowl. 'She says she will meet you in her sitting room and that I need to leave the house for a while.'

'That's very kind of her,' I reply with a sickly sarcasm.

The carer, or whatever, huffs loudly, grabs her blue puffer jacket from the coat-rack by the door, pushes past me and stomps up the path and out of the gate, which she closes with a bang.

I grin, step into the house, close the door behind me and cautiously walk towards what I presume is the sitting room.

Miss Edwards is sitting in an armchair and staring into space. I approach the door and tap lightly on it.

'Come in, Mr Brookes,' she calmly says without looking in my direction.

I hesitate for a moment and then walk into the room and slowly, with a wince, sit on the sofa opposite her.

There is a silence as she continues to fail to look in my direction.

'I know why you are here and I have the key,' she finally utters in a monotone drone as she switches her attention to me.

Her stare is disquieting and despite my obvious physical advantage, I begin to fear for my safety.

'You do,' I reply.

She clears her throat and slowly blinks.

'I loved Daddy,' she says as a tear trickles from her left eye. 'He was the kindest person I have ever met.'

I remain silent and am partially blinded as the sun spears through a tiny crack in the clouds and lasers through the glass in the sitting room window straight into my eyes.

I notice her smirk as I screw up my eyes and then turn away from her for a fraction of a second.

'The fuckers deserved what they got,' she growls and sends a shiver of disquiet down my spine.

'The wife and children?' I reply.

She remains silent.

'And why did you wait so long to get your revenge?' I ask.

She smirks. 'Switch your mobile phone off, hand it to me and let me tell you a story, Mr Brookes.'

And so, I do as she asks and I sit back and listen to what she has to say.

Chapter Nineteen

Carillon Edwards

Lord Marshall Edwards was an evil perverted fucker.

Three months before he killed Daddy, his fucking Lordship raped me.

I had been offered a 'bit of work' at the hall, helping out with a dinner party, 'you can earn a little bit of pocket money', the big fat butler guy had told me. I do not blame him; he had no idea what his employer was like; he was blinkered by his admiration.

His Lordship, the pervert, grabbed me as I was leaving to walk home. I will not go into the details of the assault; they are best forgotten and not for repeating out loud; only in my mind, every and all days.

I said nothing. I felt ashamed and mused over whether it had been my fault. I told nobody at the time.

Three months later, I told Daddy I was pregnant and I told him how it had happened. Daddy cried, hugged me and angrily confronted Lord Marshall-Atwood. His Lordship denied it, of course. His Lordship called me a slag, saying it was likely any of the young men in the village. Daddy said he was going to speak to the police. The day after that, Daddy was dead. He supposedly killed himself.

I had a kind of mental breakdown. I was taken away by a distant aunt and my baby was taken away from me and given to somebody else once she was born. I remember very little of that time but for desperately wanting to go back home. I finally returned to Old Moss House on my eighteenth birthday. They could no longer prevent it.

I had worked out what had happened to Daddy long before my return.

I would never have contemplated revenge if I had not killed the girl. I was driving home one evening. I'm afraid I was driving a little too fast for the narrow country lane. The girl seemed to appear from nowhere and I hit her with a glancing blow. I stopped, of course. I was shaking as I approached the girl. She was alive but looked in a bad way. I panicked, spotted a largish log and struck her on the head. Yes, I killed her to save me from getting into trouble. I buried her in the field by the road and nobody ever found her. Her name was Rita Bartholomew and she was fourteen years old, the same age I had been when I was raped.

The incident turned a switch in my head, social norms suddenly seemed pointless and I knew I wanted to get my revenge.

The planning was fun. I befriended the silly girl working at the Hall. I gave the cook a little whiff of poison, knew the butler guy would be out for the afternoon and distracted the silly girl away so that I was free to finally fuck over his Lordship. I made it look like a suicide. Why wouldn't I? It was revenge for Daddy after all and to ape, in part, the way he had slaughtered my daddy was delicious irony. I particularly enjoyed copying the mistake he had made of placing the gun in the wrong hand! And, of course, nobody noticed.

It took me a while to find John Miller. I knew what he had done because I knew the shot that I heard was that of a hunting rifle and not a pistol. It took me a while to realise, but once I did, I just knew that the fucker Miller had been involved. He helped kill Daddy for money. I, in a way, hated him more than his Lordship.

You know the rest!

Revenge is a dish served cold.

The revenge forgotten I lived off my inheritance and from an art income for a few years.

It was a chance encounter that led me on the path to finding my child. Well, to cut a long story short, she was living in London and had a daughter of her own. You have met her daughter. Evelyn is a lovely girl and so kind to me, and she knows nothing of my past or present misdemeanours.

Now we come to Norma Bradley, the fucking nosy cow. It was partly your fault for stirring up the hornet's nest that should have been left to slumber. That stupid story you were circulating, and the email you sent her, prompted Nosy Norma to mine her memory and to strike upon something she saw while she was living it up in Norfolk with her sexy soldier. She had been on a shopping spree in the quaint city of Norwich the very same day as I had been there and, for fuck's sake, she saw me walking in some street for a fleeting few seconds, thought nothing of it at the time and got on with her wonderful, but tragically short, encounter with her American husband.

Fast forward to the present day. Nosy Norma reads your little tale, works out what really happened, recalls the date she saw me in Norwich, discovers the date that the fucker Miller and his lovely little family were killed, puts two and two together and, Bob's your uncle, sees an opportunity for a smidgeon of blackmail.

She just didn't know what she was dealing with and I just couldn't resist resurrecting the locked room suicide murder!!

Bye, bye Nosy Norma!!

Chapter Twenty

A Chat with a Killer 1 (continued)

'I didn't send Norma Bradley an email,' I say.

'She said you did,' she responds.

I cannot think why Norma should have told her this, but I leave it.

'You cannot prove any of this,' she says.

I shake my head and feel a dread that has evaded me since I met Olivia Bartholomew.

'Why would you kill the children?' I ask.

She smirks again and brushes her knees with her hands. 'They were his blood. He ruined my family; he took my blood; I had the right to do the same to his.'

I feel like strangling her. I feel like walking out and speaking to Piers Vaughan, but I know I have little evidence.

'I could tell the police. There might well be some DNA left at Norma Bradley's house,' I say, more in hope than expectation.

She chuckles. 'There probably is some of my DNA at Nosy Norma's, but I used to visit her on occasions, very easy to explain away, I'm afraid.'

'Your DNA could have been at the Miller house,' I say with little conviction.

She continues to chuckle. 'That's a stretch, Mr Brookes. Just go away and leave me alone or I might well call the police. I am sure they would love to know that you have been harassing a fragile old woman.'

I make to stand up and then sit back down.

'Win Humphrey claims she saw your granddaughter visit Norma Bradley on the day she died,' I tell her. 'It was around about the right time to make it look very suspicious.'

She smirks, but I sense a flash of concern or panic penetrate her eyes.

'Win Humphrey is as blind as a bat,' she whispers menacingly. 'And, of course, it is utter nonsense. Evelyn had absolutely no reason to visit the stupid woman and did no such thing, as you fucking well know.'

I nod my head slowly and swallow deeply.

'When Evie, Evelyn, brushed past me as I left, I accidentally stole away a few of the hairs that had embedded themselves on the shoulder of her delightful jumper,' I tell her with a smirk.

A flash of her anger invades the room and she bares her teeth. 'You fucking leave my granddaughter out of this, or you will be very, very sorry, you snivelling fat unprincipled shit.'

'Oh dear, I do seem to have hit a raw nerve, don't I?' I nervously respond.

'You leave her alone,' she says loudly and firmly, 'for your own fucking good.'

I smile, and, with an arthritic grunt, stand up. 'You either confess, or the hairs will find themselves in the possession of our friendly boys in blue,' I tell her with a calmness that belies my sudden fear of her. 'It is your choice, Miss Edwards.'

She grimaces and throws my mobile towards the sitting room door. 'Fuck off out of my house and do not come back,' she almost whispers.

'I will give you five days,' I tell her as I bend down to collect my mobile phone and walk out of the room. 'I think that should give you plenty of time to put your affairs in order.'

'Fuck off,' I hear her shout as I open the front door, and my hands shake as I slowly close it.

'Everything all right?' I hear Evie say as she enters the front gate with an engaging smile.

I thrust my hands in my coat pockets and smile back. 'Everything's fine, love,' I tell her.

'Oh, great,' she replies with a broader smile and shy giggle. 'Hope to see you soon, Mr Brookes.'

I do hope that Carillon Edwards has no idea that I would never harm her childlike and likable granddaughter.

But, hey ho, who knows?

Chapter Twenty-One

A Chat About a Killer, 2

From: Jonas Brookes
Subject: I am pretty sure I know who killed John Miller
Date and time: 29th September 08:55
To: Simon Humphrey

Dear Rev. Humphrey

I am ready to offer some feedback on the cryptic puzzle you presented to me earlier in the year.

Since we are once again (I do wish our government would make up its mind! Although incompetence does seem to prevail in the higher echelons!) incarcerated in our homes, I think FaceTime, Skype, or whatever is the latest technological craze, may be appropriate.

What do you say?

When will you be free?

Kind regards
Jonas Brookes

From: Simon Humphrey
Subject: A few questions for the bereaved sister
Date and time: 29th September 09:13
To: Jonas Brookes

Ex-Detective Sergeant Brookes

Considering the urgency of the situation and the current restrictive circumstances (Although for those in my profession, pandemics tend to be rather busy occasions!), I could make it tomorrow at three o'clock, if that is okay with you.

Skype is best for me if, once again, that is okay with you.

Simon

From: Jonas Brookes
Subject: A few questions for the bereaved sister
Date and time: 29th September 09:31
To: Simon Humphrey

Dear Rev. Humphrey

Skype it is then and tomorrow is fine with me.

I will also be asking John Phoenix to join us but am not sure if he will oblige. I do hope that is to your satisfaction.

Kind regards
Jonas Brookes

From: Simon Humphrey
Subject: A few questions for the bereaved sister
Date and time: 29th September 09:33
To: Jonas Brookes

Ex-Detective Sergeant Brookes

I am perfectly happy for Mr Phoenix to join us if he finds it is what he wishes to do.

Simon

From: John Phoenix
Subject: Our little get together on line today
Date and time: 30th September 14:32
To: Jonas Brookes

Sorry, Jonas, but I will be unable to attend the planned consultation at three o'clock today. The wife was meant to go shopping with the daughter, but daughter's daughter was taken ill at school and so the little consumer trip has been cancelled.

Please do let me know your conclusions as soon as practically possible (By post?).

Do please offer my apologies to the man of God.

John

From: Jonas Brookes
Subject: Our little get-together online today
Date and time: 30th September 14:35
To: John Phoenix

Dear John,

What a pity.

I will write to you once I have spoken to the Rev.

Kind regards
Jonas

Chapter Twenty-Two

Reverend Humphrey and a Kind of Dénouement

It takes us a good fifteen minutes to get the Skype, or whatever, call working and then, on screen, I see a small child waddle in front of the far-too-close face of the Rev. and begin to scream its head off.

The Rev. smiles an apology, grabs the sobbing bundle and disappears from my laptop screen.

Five minutes later and with a flushed face and embarrassed grin, the Rev. reappears.

'She thought we were going to speak to her grandma,' his enormous seeming face explains dubiously.

'Kids,' I reply.

'Can't hear you, Mr Brookes,' he shouts back.

I have accidently pressed the mute button and then take a further two minutes to discover where it is and to remedy the fault (well, my fault, as many things seem to be nowadays).

'You have some news for me,' he says once we are finally up and running.

'Yes,' I reply.

'Firstly, just to let you know, Mr Phoenix is unable to beam into us today. He said it was inconvenient,' I tell him.

'Such a pity. I would have liked to have finally met him,' he replies with a certain lack of sincerity, 'but do please tell me what you have found out, Mr Brookes.'

So, I do.

I start by telling him what I told Alan Corbett-Hemmingway, well, to be fair, a somewhat abbreviated tale that included everything he needed to know and nothing more.

The Rev. seems a little shocked.

'So that solves the mystery of where John ran off to prior to toddling off to Norfolk,' he mumbles.

'It does,' I reply.

'Does Miss Edwards know about this?' he asks. 'It would surely be some kind of relief, to say the least, to know that her father didn't try to kill Lord Marshall-Atwood nor kill himself.'

'She's known about it for a long time,' I tell him.

He appears shocked and blinks rapidly. 'What? What do you mean?' he asks.

And the screen goes blank.

His large face returns about two minutes later and I hear him say, 'Thanks darling,' as he unmutes.

'Sorry about that, Mr Brookes,' he says with a grin, 'no idea what I must have touched.'

'There was me thinking you young ones knew how to use all these mysterious contraptions,' I reply with the smile of a Cheshire cat.

He seems amused, but then his face drops. 'You said that Miss Edwards knew that her father was murdered.'

I nod my head slowly and tell him the tale.

'So, there you have it,' I say, as the Rev. holds his head in his hands.

There is a long ecclesiastical silence during which I presume he is assessing what to say and ultimately what to do with the information I have given him.

'Fuck, fuck,' is finally his response.

To be honest, it is the very response I would have made in such circumstances, but I am a little shocked at hearing it from a man of the cloth.

'I presume you have confronted her?' he asks dubiously, his face as white as Nigel Farage's fantasy Britain.

'I have and she has not denied it to me but has made it clear that she would vigorously contest it if I were to go to the police,' I reply. 'I need to know what you think we should do.'

He exhales loudly and the connection crackles, flutters and seems to attempt to flee to another dimension.

'It's all very, very sad,' he groans. 'Do you have enough proof to help the police to convict her?'

I shrug. 'Probably not on the John Miller family massacre, but there may be a way of finding some DNA, although I doubt the police would have the appetite or resources after all these years. Probably the same with Lord Marshall-Atwood, although I have no intention of pursuing his murder. He got what he deserved as far as I am concerned.'

'Got what he deserved,' the Rev. muses sceptically and with a prudish hint of disapproval.

'You could say that,' I reply, although I sense the Rev. doesn't agree. He doesn't strike me as an eye-for-an-eye God follower, more a forgiver, I guess!

'But what about Norma Bradley?' he asks, shock still emanating from his voice.

I clear my throat and resist coughing up some phlegm, and instead take a distasteful and loud swallow.

'I will speak to the young copper in charge, Piers whatever. It is possible that she could have left some DNA or something, and Win Humphrey could be persuaded to clarify her possible sighting, but who knows? To be honest, I doubt it.'

The Rev. appears deep in thought and I hear the child crying in the background, accompanied by a woman shouting.

'Will you tell John Miller's sister?' I ask him.

He slowly shakes his head. 'It's difficult, Jonas, I really do not want to tell her he was involved in the murder of Mr Edwards, but she does need some kind of closure before she leaves us to finally join our Lord.'

'Simon, for God's sake can you help me here,' I hear a woman's voice shout. 'You told me you would be no longer than an hour, if you remember.'

I ignore the Rev.'s wife taking his boss' name in vain. 'I think you had better go,' I say.

'You may well be right,' he replies. 'Thank you, Jonas, for all your invaluable help.'

And the line cuts out with a flicker of static.

Chapter Twenty-Three

John Phoenix

'John, there's a letter for you,' the wife almost screams with excitement. 'It appears to be from somewhere in Hampshire, East something or other; the rest of it is smudged.'

I take a deep intake of air, stifle my own elation and promptly concoct a lie. 'Probably my seed catalogue, dear, and about bloody time too, if I might say so.'

'I'll leave it on the hall table,' she huffs. She knows I am lying and stomps up the stairs and slams our bedroom door with an uncharacteristic gusto.

I leave it for a few moments and then, defying my years, lope into the hallway, grab the envelope, bound to my study and eagerly slice open the envelope with my trusty brass letter opener.

Chapter Twenty-Four

A Chat with a Killer, 2

Lockdown has been lifted again and he is sitting in my partly frayed armchair, twitching, falsely smiling, fiddling with a loose fragment on the arm of the chair, tapping his feet, breathing deeply and blinking rapidly.

'Tea?' I ask. 'Or coffee, or something a little stronger?'

He shakes his head, sniffs loudly and stares at my not too clean ceiling and I admonish myself for such neglect. 'I only drink water from a clean glass and it must be properly cold.'

I stand up with a groan, partly faked (but less so as the years take their toll), because that is what I do, shuffle to the kitchen, pour some 'cold' water in a 'clean' glass, shuffle back, hand the glass to him and then, with a further manufactured groan, sit slowly back down.

He glares at the glass, sniffs the water, takes a tentative sip and winces.

'It's not poisoned,' I pronounce with a nervous chuckle.

He blinks rapidly, deeply studies the water while appearing to be considering my comment with an intensity beyond its worth.

He says nothing and places the glass upon the coaster on the coffee table to his right.

'Lord Marshall-Atwood killed the Edwards guy,' he tells me while looking out of the patio doors. 'The water is disgusting.'

I spot a robin glancing at him and he kind of smirks at it in response to its interest.

'I know,' I reply to both comments.

'What? What are you going to do about it?' he asks while continuing to stare at the unusually brightly red-breasted bird.

'What would *you* do?' I ask him.

He sniffs loudly, glares murderously at the glass of water and demonstratively crosses his legs.

He smirks. 'I would leave it alone, a bit like you will very, very sensibly do with me,' he says disturbingly matter-of-factly.

'Really,' I reply with a calmness that belies a seething anger.

'Really,' he says.

And I guess he is probably quite right.

Chapter Twenty-Five

Finally, a Meeting with Alan Corbett-Hemingway

The house is almost a castle. It reminds me of somewhere I would find Jacob Rees-Mogg skulking in the library.

I blink back a feeling that I have travelled back in time as the door is opened by a fully kitted out butler of indeterminate age.

'How can I help you, sir?' a deep public school accent enquires with a slight bow and manufactured smile.

I sniff and blink back the thought that I have entered a dream, and return the fake smile.

'I'm here to see Alan Corbett-Hemmingway,' I tell him with a surprising dose of subservience and an unintended imitation of his accent.

The smile remains on his face as it is joined by a look of surprise.

'And what would you want with young Alan's time?' he cryptically and inappropriately nosily asks.

I am tempted to tell him it is none of his fucking business, but instead grin and tell him I have an appointment with the forementioned young Alan.

He nods an acknowledgement. 'Please wait inside,' he responds, holding open the door and gesturing for me to enter, 'and I will enquire whether young Alan is prepared to make your acquaintance at this juncture.'

I step into the hallway. The butler closes the door and trots off with a surprising agility.

'How nice to finally meet you in the flesh,' young Alan says in an Etonian accent as I, stunned, take a seat in front of him.

Young Alan is young. Eleven or twelve years old, I would hazard a guess. He sits behind a large mahogany desk within a very large library. There are papers strewn across the desk and a closed laptop in front of my host.

He notices me looking at the laptop. 'Writing an essay, old boy, for school.'

I nod and wait for him to continue.

'You appear to be surprised,' he tells me.

He wears a three-piece suit, a checked tie, a bowler hat and round thick-lensed spectacles. He is everything I detest about the United Kingdom and I struggle to mask my instant dislike of him.

'Not at all,' I lie.

'You didn't expect me to be so young, did you, Mr Brookes?' he semi-mocks, 'Or is Jonas acceptable to you?'

'Jonas, if you are Alan,' I respond with a hint of irritation and incredulity.

He smirks, needlessly adjusts his spectacles and stares in deep thought at the desk top.

'Alan, although a touch informal, is fine with me, Jonas,' he says. 'I was impressed by your work with the manuscript. You have certainly earned all that money you partly embezzled from me and, of course, I wanted to thank you in person for such an overwhelmingly impressive achievement.'

I am not sure how to respond. I am happy to take the praise (although a little over the top), feel the need to defend such defamatory remarks concerning my expenses, and am more than pleased to acknowledge his thanks.

'Did you write it?' I instead ask him. 'The manuscript.'

He laughs out loud but fails to answer.

'You did, didn't you?' I persist.

He grins, sniffs and holds out his hands in mock surrender.

'I admire Miss Edwards,' he replies.

I am taken aback for a second or two. 'You do?' I say.

He smirks.

'Why did you get me involved with this?' I ask him.

He shrugs. 'A bit of fun, old boy. Life can get so tedious when one has everything one needs.'

He glances at the screen to his laptop.

'She took justifiable revenge,' he continues. 'An admirable trait.'

'She killed two innocent young children, two innocent women and two not-so-innocent men,' I reply with a surprising calm.

He smirks again. 'Did she, Jonas?'

I do not reply.

'My politics teacher always says you need to be sure of your facts when making assumptions,' he says with a smothered smile. 'That's why I am struggling with this damned essay. I need to be absolutely sure it is completely correct to avoid a classroom and out-of-classroom humiliation.'

He seems older than he appears and a little distant at times.

'I'm very sure,' I reply with a hint of uncertainty wriggling in the back of my mind.

He continues smiling. 'I can see that, Jonas, and good for you, I say.'

It is a cryptic reply and I wonder if he is hinting at the innocence of Mrs Miller or Mrs Bradley. Maybe Mrs Miller was aware of her husband's past misdemeanours, or Mrs Bradley was a secret serial killer.

I doubt it.

'What's the essay about?' I ask.

He glances back down at his laptop screen, squeezes his eyes up as if struggling to see, and pouts as if in deep thought.

'Why do you think the little people of dear old not-so-democratic Blighty tolerate capitalism, Jonas?' he asks with the intensity of Andrew Neil or an in-good-form Jeremy Paxman.

I am taken aback for a moment and decide not to answer his question. 'Why did you include the strange old lady, Miss Hemmingway, in the manuscript?' I ask instead.

'She existed and she provided some vital information,' he replies as if thinking about something else. He appeared distracted for a moment and for the life of me I cannot remember what the distraction reminds me of.

'And why the death of the Poacher, or John Miller, as I now know he was?' I ask.

He grins but doesn't answer.

'Do you think it is right that natural wealth can be turned into private property, and the right of a person or persons to own it corresponds to the numbers in their bank account?' he instead asks.

I am momentarily blindsided by the change of subject and do not respond before he continues.

'And why do you think that the majority of people think that the so-called "invisible hand of the market" can one day solve all our problems, although it has clearly failed to do so to date, and that the unhindered acquisition of enormous wealth by a few could lead to something other than economic and political disaster?' he continues with a seriousness that belies his apparent age and my initial impression of his politics.

'Is this what your essay is about?' I ask. 'Not the sort of thing I was taught in my good old ordinary working people's comprehensive school, full of bored kids expecting no more in life than barely scraping a living in a dead-end job. Although I am talking about a long time ago to be fair.'

He smirks, touches his hat as if thinking of removing it and then straightens his spectacles.

'It's not changed much, Jonas,' he replies. 'And why do you think that these same people, the majority of our fellow citizens, rich and poor, well mostly poor, believe that taxes sufficient to break the cycle of accumulation and redistribute this wealth are unthinkable, or that permitting a handful of offshore billionaires to own the media, set the political agenda and tell us where our best interests lie is somehow alright, or that democracy can proceed in the almost complete absence of civic knowledge and useful impartial information?' he persists with a blinkless stare and an obvious mockery.

'What amazes me is that no terror or torture is required to persuade people to fall into line with such beliefs,' I respond. 'Somehow, our great capitalist system has created an entire class of politicians, officials, media commentators, cultural leaders, academics and intellectuals who support them and help persuade us little people of their worth and that there is no credible alternative.'

He appears a little surprised at my response. 'Reading accounts of twentieth-century terror, it sometimes seems to me that there was more dissent among intellectuals confronting totalitarian regimes like the USSR or Nazi Germany, than there is in our societies of so-called freedom, wealth and choice,' he says.

'It is not total capitulation. There are a few dissenters in the West,' I respond.

He smiles. 'You are like-minded, Jonas, or Mr Brookes?' he says with an almost imperceptible flutter of his eyelashes.

I shrug. 'Just playing along,' I tell him. 'I'm a *Daily Mail* reader myself.'

He smirks and shakes his head. 'The dissenters are not, on the whole, imprisoned or executed (although there are a few exceptions of course). The system is so powerful and manipulative that it doesn't need to crush them. They are simply ignored and marginalised. The great capitalist venture and its enforcers are on the whole entirely unruffled by their objections and, if necessary, laws can be enacted to stop them and to "protect our way of life" against the evil socialists.'

I am not sure how I have been dragged into such a conversation with this young man and I am even less sure that he believes any of this.

'So, what's going on?' he continues, 'How has this wonderful system of "riches for all" (but not really of course) created a near consensus around its ridiculous ideas? How has it ensured not only that people of power and influence defend them, but that almost everyone else nods along to them?'

I am feeling a little hot and a touch anxious. 'No idea,' I manage to respond. 'Really not something I have spent a great deal of time thinking about.'

He stares at me intently, slowly shakes his head but just continues, 'I don't have a complete or satisfactory answer, Jonas, or Mr Brookes. But what about some guesses, hey, old boy? You are good at guesses.'

I am hot, beginning to sweat, feel a little short of breath and feel tongue-tied.

'Let me start, old boy,' he almost mocks in his prepubescent upper class accent, 'How about that petty ambition we all have (better job, bigger house, smoother car, latest designer clothes, latest Apple device) which is as potent an enforcer of consensus as state terror.'

I cannot move and feel a worrying tightness in my chest.

'How about that the billionaire press has become more powerful than human courage, and that spectacle, banter and an obsession with trivia and celebrity are more effective at defusing dissent than coercion and fear,' he continues as if oblivious to my now growing and obvious discomfort.

I am sweating profusely and clearly struggling to breathe.

'Or that our current organisational structures, which look as if they offer choice and freedom, actually do nothing of the kind. On the contrary, though it might have been accidentally achieved, we have arrived at an almost perfectly calibrated system of social control. What do you think, old boy?'

He looks at me and begins to lightly laugh, while I gasp desperately for air.

'Olivia became boring,' he then inexplicably pronounces. 'I really needed a new challenge and little old posh boy Alan seemed the ideal remedy to my growing accidie. So, as I have done before, I fed on the delicious soul and I jumped bodies. I sometimes destroy the body when I gorge on a soul, Jonas, or Mr Brookes, but also occasionally take the body for new, much needed jolly experiences.'

I believe I am dying, but the nightmare of the past visit from Olivia Bartholomew flashes before me, and for some reason this gives me an inkling of hope of survival.

'You disappoint me that you didn't spot why the Poacher had to die and, of course, the way that he died,' he says with a distinct hint of fucking annoying mockery. 'Olivia's suicide note indicated the yellow room and of course the way she died mirrored the fictional death of John, Dusty or Jack Miller. If you put two and two together to reason that I wrote the manuscript, a superior detective should have concluded that there was a link between the death of the Poacher and that of dear Olivia, and therefore little Alan must, with this knowledge, be dear departed Olivia. Just think back to your meeting with Olivia. It may or may not help you trawl through the clues.'

I am unable to respond and deep dive my memory for any indication that I was to know that whoever Alan is jumps between bodies. Maybe my skills as a detective are diminishing or maybe not, but then if Alan was once Olivia, it does make some kind of sense. I think!

I cough deeply and gasp desperately for some air as my body fries. It feels as if I have been transported into a vacuum in the heart of Venus.

He shuffles some papers on his desk and then appears to remember something.

'There were, of course, clues that told you his Lordship killed Sir Terrance Edwards and that the Poacher was Mr Miller, but I will leave you to find these if you have not done so already. Oh, and just to confirm your suspicions, the Taylor guy trained his dog to jump up on somebody wearing purple, so it is likely that the dog pushed Mrs Taylor over the balcony,' he smirks and winks. 'But, of course, you cannot prove it and I would seriously advise you not to pursue it if you know what I mean. But then we may well be wrong. Our work and conclusions on this may end up with a cross and a tick or two, old boy.'

I am unable to respond and he just grins at me.

'You seriously do not look well, Jonas, or is it Mr Brookes?' he taunts through a dry ice-like haze of oxygen deficiency. 'Let me call dear old Jeeves, or whatever the old codger of a sycophantic butler's name might be. Although, I'm not sure he will be of great assistance in your hopeful recovery, but I am sure I will be able to unobtrusively assist.'

He rings a bell and within a few seconds the butler chap bursts through the door with an unerring calm.

He glances at me, seems not to notice my distress and addresses his master's son.

'How can I help you, young Alan, sir?' he says with a menacing smile as I black out.

Chapter Twenty-Six

A Surprising Letter from Alan Corbett-Hemingway

Dear Jonas, or Mr Brookes, if you prefer,

Thank you so much for visiting me. It was such a pleasure and I do so hope that you are now feeling well again. I cannot imagine what may have ailed you, but you did seem to make a rapid and, hopefully, full recovery. It could well have been something you ate.

Anyway, it was certainly a delight to meet and debate with you again. You were, as always, a great surprise and a curiosity beyond most.

Anyway, before I return to the wonderful and educating hallowed grounds of good old Eton, let us forthwith get to the reason I am sending you this little surprise correspondence.

Do let us begin, shall we?

Let us solve a little mystery that may, or may not, be troubling, or nagging at you.

Okay.
Time travel. Is it possible? Is it sensible?
If you could do it, where would you go?
Future? Past? How far forward or back?
Why would you do it?
So many questions and so much time to choose from!
I would go forward, but I have an inkling you would go back just a tick.

How about a little fun; true, maybe, story?

Fact or fiction; is there ultimately a difference?

Anyway, it is the year 2055 and a terrorist group, so-called environmentalists (It's far too late for such indulgences, I'm afraid; the world is going to hell in a handcart and I couldn't be more pleased!), are planning to blow up a nuclear reactor (power station), for some ideological non-reason.

Our slightly authoritarian leaders (Or Government of National Security to you and I, or to be totally accurate, the only way to keep the Conservatives in power!) have a cleverish network of spies, informers, favour seekers, sycophants, whatever you might christen them, one of which has identified one of the terrible terrorist power station destruction plotters.

The plan is simple; capture the plotter, extract the relevant information (target, date, fellow conspirators and Bob's your uncle, all is returned to normal, as it is) and round up the terrorist scum, stop the outrage and, for publicity purposes and deterrence, hang, draw and quarter them to the patriotic blasting of the National Anthem and the over-enthusiastic waving of the cherished and irreplaceable Union Jack.

Sounds simple!

Well, it should be, but things go terribly wrong for our protectors.

The extraction squad, fully trained and supposedly elite, fuck it up and kill the target by mistake.

'What a fucking disaster' is our great leader's response!

The consequences are simple, the extraction squad should pay with their lives.

But, hang on a minute, the leader of the squalid group of extractors is spared and instead bundled into the back of a military van and driven to a black establishment in the middle of nowhere; a place that doesn't exist, never has done and never will do; it's a conspiracy theory after all.

So, the disgraced leader of the extractors, we will call him Agent X for now, thinks he is being driven away to be brutally tortured and killed, but is mildly surprised to find himself bundled into a kind of laboratory that is white beyond dreams. He is met by the supreme leader of the extractors (Let us call him Boris, for want of another name!) and an effeminate lab-coated scientist of most unusual persuasion.

Anyway, to ignore an ensuing long drawn-out explanation, Agent X has the choice of dying or dying!

He can join his fellow failures in being strung up in Parliament Square (Not now in London; it's under water!) or to travel just a tiny bit back in time (Yes, the scientist, although politically deluded, is very smart!).

Let's explain a touch more, shall we?

The clever scientist, let us name him Max, has discovered there is an afterlife (do not scoff please, but it could well be true) and so the dead evil plotter can still be questioned.

How the fuck can that be done, Agent X may have enquired.

Max has devised a machine that kills somebody for a short period of time, which will allow Agent X to extract the required information from the plotter before returning to this mortal world to impart such useful information.

Simple, you may think?

Well, not quite!

There is a tiny but significant hitch (It is not yet world-leading!) which Max is working on, but there is no time to remedy it on this urgent occasion.

What is the hitch you might ask?

Well, to put it simply and in layman's terms, the return to this mortal land, for some yet-to-be-determined reason, takes you back in time.

The only other previous attempt at this amazing experiment had taken the subject back to the 1950s when he returned to life; not far but clearly too far for much use.

Okay, you may well be catching on, but let me continue with the sorry tale.

Agent X, when dead, will have an indeterminate (but protracted) amount of time to extract the required information before he is hurtled into the not-too-distant past.

Now, once the required information has been extracted, how in high heavens does it get conveyed to Boris and his merry band of protectors?

'Why not as an advertisement in *The Times* newspaper', Boris asks Max and Agent X.

'Jolly good idea', Max may have responded. But I have a sneaky feeling that this may not have worked, and an improvised Plan B became necessary (please refer back to Miss Hemmingway's comment).

So, after a little bit of medical preparation, Agent X is wheeled into a scanner-like contraption (I am of course guessing here, or am I?) and killed by some kind of medical poison of indeterminate nature and sent to heaven on his world-saving mission.

We are now in 1963 and Agent X finds himself in the back garden of an eccentric old lady whose ramblings will fortunately, for him, be swept aside as madness.

Agent X, disoriented, finds his way out of the screaming woman's garden and by hook and by crook embeds himself in an alien world, buys an advert in the aforementioned newspaper and the message is sent and not read by Boris and his happy crew, but fortunately Plan B does work and the banner of the Houses of Parliament is picked up by his masters.

Unfortunately, a week or so later in our jolly little world of 2055, the brand-new (supposedly safe beyond imagination) nuclear power station at Sizewell catastrophically implodes.

How on earth could this have happened when Agent X had identified and informed them of the target, and Boris and his mates had put in the requisite protection?

Well, dear Jonas, or Mr Brookes, you may well have deduced that Agent X may not have been all he was portrayed to be. You see, Agent X was what could be called a double agent, our loyal extractor of terrorists was no more than one of the so-called, terrorists himself.

Yes, and as you would have done in such circumstances, he went along with Boris's plan but, of course, told them, via the advertisement and banner, the wrong target and grassed up a few loyal servants of the supreme leader as an added bonus.

Boom and all that!

Do take care of yourself and hopefully we shall cross paths in the near future.

One never knows what the future might hold (Well, Agent X apart, anyway!).

Yours faithfully,

Alan Corbett-Hemingway, September 2023.

PS. If you believe my little ditty has a gram (Or should it be ounce? Or barleycorn, now we have escaped the all-invasive European Union's dreadful rules and regulations!) of truth to it, you may well be right in possibly assuming the implausibly ancient and environmentally obsessed Hugo Coles is Agent X. (Miss Hemmingway does tell you this in the manuscript I provided you with!).

PPS. Now to follow on from the PS. If you continue to follow such reasoning, I need to confirm or inform you that Mr Taylor did not kill his wife. The likely culprit was, once again, the elderly Hugo Coles. I believe he needed to make sure that Mr Taylor's daughter, Matilda, pursued her ambitions to fight for this doomed planet's environment and guessed (Knew?!) that Mrs Taylor was an impediment (Threat?) to this future fight for the planet.

This is very much a guess (Or is it?), but I believe that Matilda may become an accomplice of Agent X in the not-too-distant future, a degree in environmentalism obtained first, of course.

Anyway, Hugo Coles, knowing Mr Taylor and Matilda were not home, visited Mrs Taylor and at some point, took the opportunity to push her off the balcony, climbed onto the balcony next door, from the Taylor balcony, went downstairs, left by the back door, locking it behind him (Yes, he does have a key) and left by the back garden. He was unlikely to have been seen, since if anyone was in the vicinity at that time, they would most likely be looking down at the body on the ground and Mrs Maxwell had left the house as she heard Mrs Taylor's thumping departure. Do you remember that Mrs Maxwell insisted she heard two thumps when Mrs Taylor fell? This can likely be accounted for by my explanation (Hugo's jump onto her balcony) and would also likely explain the broken plant pot on Mrs Maxwell's balcony; Carrie the missing cat (she likely crept out when our Hugo left by the back door; cats are so stealthy and deadly); and Hugo looking distinctly flustered when he miraculously appeared just after the unfortunate incident occurred.

How could an old man, who used a wheelchair most of the time, do such a thing? You may well ask. Well, if he is Agent X, anything is possible, I would guess that his infirmity is no more than a ruse! But then, it is just a guess after all.

PPPS. Gaston Leroux of course.

PPPPS. You are incorrect on one other count and may regret being so in the near future!!

Chapter Twenty-Seven

Jonas Brookes has a Welcome and Surprise Visitor

It is six days since my encounter with Carillon Edwards. Young plod Piers has just confirmed that there has been nothing new to report on the Norma Bradley death, or suicide, as Piers is likely confidently still falsely describing it.

I have not told him anything. I am still unsure about how much he should know or whether he will believe me anyway.

There is some shit on the television, people dressed up as outrageous cartoon creatures and singing out of tune while, for some unfathomable reason, a crowd of gullible punters are screaming with delight and four, unknown to me, so-called celebrities are making mildly amusing, to some, comments on the absurd proceedings playing out before them.

I conclude that I do not belong in this weird capitalist creation of a society, and as time elapses, I feel more and more like Robert Heinlein's *Stranger in a Strange Land*.

There is a knock on the door and I accidentally tap my mobile phone to the floor, 'Fuck,' I grimace, and hope the perpetrator of the offending intrusion will realise they have the wrong door and piss off pronto.

There is another fucking knock, I shouldn't have disconnected the doorbell; the quaint knock is even more irritating.

'For fuck's sake,' I whisper to nobody.

Somebody dressed as a pink pig is blasting out a terrible version of a terrible and unknown-to-me song apparently called 'Hello' as my knees creakingly lift my ever-increasing bulk from the armchair. There is another knock and I shuffle to the front door in preparation to tell whoever it is that, 'I do not want to buy your fucking rubbish, I do not want a conservatory, my windows are fine and could you very kindly fucking well take me off you mailing list', or something to that effect.

I unlock the door and keep the latch on as I open it a crack, and then glance at whoever is interrupting my boring, unpleasurable evening.

Fuck me backwards, it is Evie the gullible carer, emitting her customary smile and a slight curtsy.

'Hi, Mr Brookes, I hope I am not intruding,' she unsurprisingly childishly giggles.

She is, and I am taken aback for a moment, but then, in an attempt to appear human, smile back and awkwardly remove the latch.

'Come in, love,' I say, although I am not sure why she should want to visit me and how the hell she got hold of my address.

She trots over my Union Jack doormat and continues to giggle as she walks through the hallway and, with my guidance, enters the sitting room.

'I see you like *The Masked Singer*,' she says with a smidgeon of incredulity and a sly smirk.

'Is that what it is? I wasn't really watching it. Background company, only company I get nowadays,' I reply as I gesture for her to sit on the sofa, grab the remote and switch the mind-numbing crap off.

She ignores my urging and hops onto the armchair I had been sitting on before I had been rudely interrupted.

Feeling a little miffed, I gruntingly plonk myself in the centre of the sofa, feel a few springs strain and steady myself with both hands.

'What can I do for you, love?' I ask with genuine puzzlement.

She looks to the ground and shyly giggles. 'It is rather a delicate matter. You are alone, aren't you, Mr Brookes?'

'I am, love. My dear wife left me some time ago for a much younger and virile version,' I reply with a matching giggle.

'I am sorry to hear that,' she replies, now looking up, large blue eyes staring intently at nothing in particular.

I ignore the unnecessary commiserations and repeat, 'Anyhow, what can I do for you, love?'

She shyly looks at the floor. 'It's about my grandma,' she quietly tells me.

Oh, fuck, I think. Surely the evil old witch hasn't told her granddaughter about it all.

'And Mrs Bradley,' she continues.

Oh, fuck, I repeat to myself. The old woman really hasn't persuaded this sweet young girl to plead her case, has she?

I compose myself.

'Grandma didn't kill Mrs Bradley,' she says with a surprising naïve conviction and a diminishing smile.

I remain silent.

She giggles. 'I am rather thirsty after such a long journey. Why don't I make a nice cup of tea for the two of us?'

I am somewhat taken aback. 'No, no, let me,' I reply somewhat unconvincingly, since the prospect of a not unattractive young woman waiting upon me seems like an adventure not to be shunned.

She smiles and gets to her feet. 'I'm used to making tea for Grandma, so it really is no problem, Mr Brookes. Where's the kitchen?'

I tell her and sit back to think about what I should say to her.

'I'll make it very special for you,' she calls as she leaves the room. 'Grandma says I am the best tea maker in the whole wide world.'

I suddenly wish I had had a daughter like her; perhaps I would have been happier, or perhaps not.

'I'm not really a carer, you know.' She tells me what I already know.

'I know,' I reply.

She giggles and blushes a touch. 'Grandma wants to keep me a secret so I put on the pretence when I visit her,' she explains. 'I'm really a self-employed copy-editor and part-time ghost writer.'

I take a gulp of the tea and try to work out what the funny taste is. I suspect the milk may be off again!

'And you make a living from that?' I ask sceptically.

She shakes her head and sips her tea. 'Mum and Dad give me a generous allowance; they are loaded,' she says. 'Drink up, your tea will get cold.'

'Never had a penny from my parents; even left their money to charity when they died,' I tell her. 'My Father was a mean old sod and hated me.'

She appears sympathetic but changes the subject. 'You don't really think my grandma would kill somebody, do you?'

I take a further sip of my tea and consider how I can break the truth to her without destroying her apparent hero worshipping of Miss Edwards.

'Grandma wouldn't hurt a fly. She has been so, so kind to me,' she pleads.

'Did she send you to see me?' I ask.

She looks shocked and vigorously shakes her head. 'No, no, no way. She has no idea that I am here, Mr Brookes.'

'But you are here,' I say.

She shyly looks to the floor and seems to consider how to reply.

'I went to university in Winchester you know,' she tells me.

'So, you know the area,' I respond.

She slowly nods her head and smirks. 'In some ways, it's quite good to be back, but in others I cannot wait to leave. Going back can encourage many more bad memories than the good ones.'

'You may well be right, love, but I find it hard to remember any good memories wherever I go,' I tell her not totally truthfully.

She looks sad for me and places her cup and saucer on the embarrassingly old-fashioned coffee table that I had wished my wife had taken with her.

'My grandma has cancer,' she tells me with a sniffle. 'She is very close to dying.'

I find it difficult to feel any pity. 'We all are,' I respond, 'just some closer than others.'

She looks shocked and frowns at me. 'That's not very kind,' she snaps and then smirks.

I do not feel ashamed but do feel a little tired.

I hope she leaves soon.

She seems to study me closely and then grins. 'I had a boyfriend in my first year here at university,' she says. 'He died.'

It is so matter of fact that I am taken aback for a moment.

I feel a little dizzy, place my cup and saucer on the side of the chair and sit back.

'He was okay to start with but then went a little crazy; said he saw the ghost of an old woman,' she continues. 'She was apparently the dead wife of his landlord. Total nutter if you ask me.'

I try to reply but cannot get a word out as the room twirls in front of me.

'I killed him you know,' she giggles, 'made it look like he hanged himself, but I really needed to get him out of my life,' she pauses and smirks. 'He was a total, total weirdo.'

I cannot move and the room is a wispy fog.

'The ghost didn't exist of course, a little practical joke, of sorts!' she says with a wink of her left eye.

The room is revolving and I can barely focus on her.

'Are you alright?' she says, leaning forward and looking me intently in the eyes. 'You really do not look very well, Mr Brookes. Oh, dear whatever should I do?'

I cannot move. I cannot respond to her and need to take deep breaths in an effort to stay conscious.

She stands up, still staring at me. 'I told you Grandma did not kill Mrs Bradley, you know,' she says with a disturbing calmness, 'and I was telling the truth.' She giggles and then broadly smiles. 'You see, I should know because I finished off the interfering old bitch. I really was not having her besmirch my grandma's name just before she became very ill and died. I was not having it. No way.'

She shouts her last comment and picks up her handbag.

'My grandma told me how she executed the evil old man who murdered her daddy and it only felt fitting to duplicate the deed to protect her from the horrible Bradley woman,' she calmly tells me with a giggle.

I can barely stay conscious and it is like looking through a thick fog to see her. She is almost a shadow in the far distance, but I do, with horror, somehow see what she removes from her handbag.

'And then you, you silly old man, come along and start interfering in things you should have left alone. That was very, very, very stupid,' she scolds me with a childlike inflection, 'very silly indeed, old man.'

I just blink through the fog enveloping me and strain to move my leaden limbs.

'Grandma gave me the recipe for the tea,' she continues, and with a broad grin, 'and wasn't it so, so delicious?'

I want to strangle her and hope I am dreaming.

'I believe you are right-handed,' she says as she suddenly and slowly walks towards me, 'so I will need to shoot you through the left temple. That's right, isn't it?' she asks with a chilling laugh as she holds tightly to the pistol she has slowly taken from the handbag.

'I do hope we do not mess up your lovely, lovely armchair and most expensive, if tasteless, rug with our jolly little jape,' are the last childlike giggled words I hear before I finally lose consciousness and a subterranean darkness arrives and 'Welcome to hell' echoes through my head.

Chapter Twenty-Eight

Some Final Correspondence

From: Alan Corbett-Hemmingway
Subject: A few hints
Date and time: 25th December 09:13
To: Our all-suffering and appreciated reader

Dear reader,

I do hope you were able to spot all the clues to solving the riddles (mostly acrostic) within the text.

If you did, you certainly have my admiration, but if not, maybe I should guide you in the right direction?

Let's begin with the entertaining 'party' at the beginning of our journey, shall we?

We are given a clue about where the acrostic will lie (after the drawing of a dog, I scrawl a cross and a tick (Acrostic?) on each of their foreheads), so we learn that the acrostic clue can reside after the mention of a dog. Of course, we learn later that no such message was on the foreheads of the victims.

Let's go to the Joel Taylor narration, shall we?

We learn that a carillon consists of at least one bell.

Joel Taylor's conversation on the train about simulations has an acrostic clue after his mention of Peter (the dog) that tells us 'Evie shot Norma' (the letter at the beginning of each sentence).

Joel Taylor's second conversation on the train about the multiverse, and after the mention of Peter, tells us Miss Edwards killed the Poacher (once again, the letter at the beginning of each sentence).

In the penultimate paragraph of Joel Taylor's narration, and after Peter is told to lie down, the radio voice garbles, 'How useful going out does it do in time', which of course tells us 'Hugo did it'.

Let us now go to, 'A most odd, mysterious and dog's dinner of a manuscript'.

The title, with a mention of a dog, gives us a clue that there is an acrostic puzzle thereafter. Just look at the headings within the manuscript, the first letter of each heading, and you will see that it tells us, 'Lord did it'. We are given a hint to this by the narrator at the end of the narration with, '"It's a cross and tick, I think," the fool Bell responded. It certainly is, I thought, as my eyes closed to the world and I dreamt of chapter titles for my forthcoming book.'

When we first meet the Poacher, we have the mention of his dog and then an acrostic that tells us he is Miller (Making It Look Like Everything Really).

At the end of the section, 'Down to business the next morning', and after the mention of the Poacher's dog, we are told 'it must be just murder.' (Not a suicide nor an attempted murder.)

In the section, 'Discovering some forensic details (well, sort of)' we have the sentence after mention of a dog, 'I winced and wanted to let out really detailed details in determination in truth, but kept quiet, we are told the 'Lord did it.'

At the end of 'Two days later', Abel is heard saying, 'Look out, right down, dug it down in time', which' of course tells us that, 'Lord did it'.

Well, there are likely more, but I will leave these, in your own time, for your discovery.

Toodle-pip.

Printed in Great Britain
by Amazon